DARK CHASE
DEAD RUN

Seth Sjostrom

*wolfprint*Media

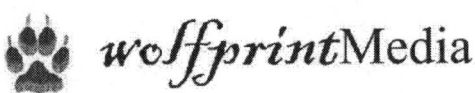

wolfprint, LLC
Camas, WA, 98607

For information, contact wolfprintMedia, LLC.

Trade Paperback
ISBN-13: 978-1-7350236-9-4

1. Ryder Chase (Fictitious character)-Fiction. 2. Paranormal-FBI-Supernatural-Thriller- Fiction. 3. Dark Chase Series-Fiction 4. Dark Chase Dead Run-Title.

First wolfprintMedia edition 2021.

wolfprintMedia is a trademark of wolfprint, LLC.

For information regarding bulk purchases, please contact wolfprintMedia, LLC at wolfprint@hotmail.com.

United States of America

DARK CHASE

DEAD RUN

Acknowledgments

Hayden and Nick, for keeping the hunt alive.

Kathi for your inspiration.

Linda for your enthusiastic support and reader's lens.

Tom for suggesting nothing is impossible and even if you don't quite reach what your chasing, make sure the chase is fun.

DARK CHASE

DEAD RUN

For Hayden

DARK CHASE

DEAD RUN

DARK CHASE
DEAD RUN

ONE

Sarah Whitman's heart was racing and pounding wildly as if trying to claw its way out of her chest. Crouching behind a dumpster, she strained her ears. Erratic footsteps crunched along the gravel that covered the ground. She knew it was that same gravel that alerted them to her presence in the first place.

She scanned the area, searching desperately for her friends, but the tall, overgrown grass made it difficult to see anything from her crouched position. Her mind flashed to Eric. The last image of him made her stomach twist.

As they approached the old insane asylum, they thought they were going to have a good scare spooking each other in the old building. Long reputed for being one of the most haunted sites in the country, they never expected to find what they did. Even before they could step foot inside, the doors burst open and those things…Sarah grimaced at the scene etched in her memory…people…sort of.

Reaching the main entrance, they were surprised by a half dozen figures. Snarling and spitting, they attacked Sarah and her friends. Punching and clawing, the beings leapt on them. Sarah was able to wriggle away. When she looked over her shoulder, she saw Eric. Flailing under three of the frenzied horrifying figures, they slashed and chewed on every portion of his exposed skin. As she turned to run away from her pursuer, Eric was screaming, covered in blood, his flesh being torn away.

Suddenly the footsteps stopped. She could hear her pursuer's wheezy breathing. In and out it rasped. The sound sent chills down her spine. Sarah held her own breath for fear it would alert her assailant to the dumpster she used for concealment. The crunching of footsteps resumed, heading back towards the entrance where Eric's screams finally stopped. Sarah feared she understood the reason why.

Collecting herself, she surveyed the fence line, trying to find the spot in the chain link they had cut to get into the asylum. It surprised them to find the property double fenced, much of it looking new. They assumed it was to keep trespassers like themselves out. Now maybe she understood why.

No longer hearing footsteps, she gathered herself. Taking in a large breath, Sarah launched herself in the direction of the tear in the fence. Her legs wobbled as she ran. Tears streamed down her face. Her focus narrowed to the thin cut in the massive wall of chain link. As fast as she could, she raced away from the awful place. She prayed she could be home, safe with her family.

Behind her, she could hear footsteps heading in her direction. She didn't dare look back, instead remained focused on her goal. Every footstep seemed painfully slow. As much as she willed her legs to move faster, they maintained their gait. The footfalls came closer, she could hear heavy breathing. Step after step, she hurtled towards the fence through the tall overgrowth.

Somewhere in the grass and weeds, a fallen branch grabbed at her feet, snagging her shoe, sending her crashing to the ground. So close to her goal, the tears streamed down her face. Crawling in desperation, she clawed at the ground and kicked with her feet.

The footsteps behind her did not slow, and the imminence of them taking her over was clear. She didn't stop. Hand over hand, she crawled, slipping through the first layer of fencing. Nearly clear, hands bit down on her ankle. In an instant, teeth clamped down on her, tearing at her heel, ripping flesh. Suddenly a scream erupted behind her and a shadowy figure lunged to her side.

"Sarah, run!" her friend Michael, obviously already having breached the security fencing, saw her and came to her aid.

Pain searing through her ankle, Sarah pushed herself up, hobbling on her solid foot toward the outer fence. Michael kicked himself free of a hasty attack and ran after her. Sarah had just slipped through the outer fence, turning to help Michael, she watched in horror as a being leaped into the air and wrestled him to the ground. A second figure joined in, rendering Michael helpless.

For the second time, her friend urged her, "Run Sarah! Get out of here!"

With tears overtaking her cheeks, she hesitated for a moment. Realizing she had no choice, she complied. Dragging her left leg, she pushed herself away from the Northern State Asylum, relieved to be enveloped in the dark of night.

TWO

Special Agent Devon Jeffers choked, "What?" He looked around the room at his fellow agents, Danica Sohn, his seasoned partner, and James Dunlap, the rookie of the team. Across from them sat Professor Ryder Chase, his tech specialist Wally Smyth and Don Tannen, his medic. The three had been on loan to the Bureau from a previous case. At the head of the table was FBI Bureau Chief Charles Witt, who was reading Jeffers' reaction intently.

Unlike Jeffers, who was beside himself, the rest of the room seemed genuinely intrigued in the Chief's proposal to work together again. Smyth even began busily scribbling notes.

"It appears a town in Washington has become overrun with reports of zombies," Chief Witt blurted, his voice losing some volume on the word "zombies".

Jeffers' face screwed into a painful expression, "*Zombies*, sir? You're joking."

"Given what you have been through, I think you are the perfect pairing to tackle this case," his boss replied.

"Oh my gosh, you're serious!" Jeffers steamed.

"Of course, when am I not?" Witt questioned.

"Getting harder to tell, sir," Jeffers scoffed. "I mean, you did just assign us a case about zombies."

"Well, yes, if Dr. Chase's team agrees," Witt nodded, shrinking from his words a bit himself behind the copy of the case file.

"With all respect, Chief Witt, I've done my time with crazy paranormal stuff. How about Simpson and Crane? Those two new agents that just came out of the Academy?" Jeffers pleaded.

Witt shook his head, "You're on the docket. Dr. Chase, your team in?"

Ryder Chase looked at Wally and Tannen, both who were grinning at him eagerly. "We're glad to help Chief Witt."

Dunlap gave a celebratory fist pump in the air while Danica Sohn simply smiled.

Jeffers' sigh turned into a groan, "My career is over!"

Witt patted his senior agent on the shoulders, "I'm counting on you Special Agent Jeffers." Landing a pile of dossiers in front of the lead agent, he smiled and began exiting the room. "You leave tomorrow."

Jeffers collapsed in his chair, refusing to open the file.

Sohn, the second in command, snatched a copy of the dossier and began reading through it.

"Interesting," Sohn read aloud, "Several high school students were attacked, several died during the incident. One girl managed to get away. She had wounds all over her body and wandered into town in despondent. When local authorities questioned her, she babbled about her attackers being "wild people". Her trauma was so severe, she is now undergoing residential psychiatric treatment in Seattle."

"Wild people? What does that mean?" Agent Dunlap asked.

"The zombies Chief Witt referred to," Professor Chase rubbed his chin. "Interesting."

"I'll assume the girl needed psychiatric treatment *before* the incident," Jeffers scoffed. "She and her friends were probably tripping on some illicit drug, might have even carved each other up."

Agent Sohn shook her head, "Toxicology report on the girl came back clean."

"What did the autopsies show?" Don Tannen asked. "May I?"

Sohn handed the report over to the medic. Tannen, a former Army medic, now worked as an EMT and taught emergency management courses at the University. As he read down the chart of the first victim, he shook his head and whistled softly.

"Wow. This is crazy stuff. The victim looks to be probably a junior, maybe a senior. Athletic build...otherwise healthy. Again, clean tox... huh. Cause of death- loss of blood, severe trauma to the neck, limbs and torso. Wounds appear to result from bites," Tannen scanned the first autopsy.

"Washington has lots of wildlife. Were they in Seattle or...?" Jeffers mused.

"Sedro-Woolley," Tannen replied.

Ryder Chase and Wally Smyth exchanges glances with each other.

"So, what is that? A suburb?" the lead agent pushed.

"Sedro-Woolley is a small town a couple hours north of Seattle. It is the gateway to the North Cascades," Chase replied.

"See. The Cascades, wild animals," Jeffers shrugged.

"According to the medical examiner, the bites appeared to be human!" Tannen exclaimed.

Jeffers snatched the file from the EMT and began reading the report for himself.

"The report mention exactly where the incident took place?" Chase asked.

"Yeah," Tannen said. Leaning close to the file Jeffers was holding, he began to speak, but Chase cut him off.

"Northern State Hospital," Chase spat.

Tannen's eyes widened. "Yeah, how did you..."

Wally and Chase pumped their fists at one another.

"Northern State is a former mental institution. It was famous for groundbreaking research throughout the early 1900s, which of course, back then meant lobotomies, shock therapy and other crude techniques," Chase replied.

"And it is one of the most haunted places in the Pacific Northwest!" Wally exclaimed.

Jeffers tossed the file on the table and groaned. "I hate my job."

"A haunted asylum, awesome!" Agent Dunlap grinned.

Tannen had grown quiet. Resuming his reading, he flipped through the pages of the dossier. "They recovered two bodies. One, which the surviving witness had seen being slaughtered by several of the 'wild humans', was not found."

"It disappeared?" Agent Sohn raised an eyebrow.

"Or got up and joined the horde!" Wally spat, wide-eyed.

Jeffers shook his head in disbelief. Dr. Chase and his team had proven themselves useful in their last case. Staring at the zeal painted across Wally Smyth's face at the prospect of actual zombies prowling the Washington countryside, he didn't see how they would manage this one.

"How sure is the coroner about the bites being human?" Chase asked, almost sensing Jeffers' consternation.

"Pretty sure," Tannen replied. "It was odd, so they referenced it several times in the report. It would be best to talk to them in person."

"Zombies….," Jeffers just shook his head.

"Unlikely. The dead actually coming back to life…I don't see it. Most likely feral humans, if the coroner's report is accurate," Chase corrected.

Jeffers stared at the professor. He seemed to fighting for words. "Feral humans. We are talking Washington State. Probably a bunch of hopped up gypsies. Hippies on some bad weed," the lead agent muttered. Nodding to himself, pleased to rationalize the situation in terms he could handle.

"Sure, something like that," Chase appeased the agent.

"Well, we have 3,000 miles to break this case down. Let's get packed and meet back up at the airport," Sohn suggested, scooping up the files Witt had left on the table.

THREE

Special Agent Jeffers waited impatiently alongside the baggage carousel. He had packed everything he needed in carry-on luggage, and that included several boxes of extra ammunition. He admitted it may not have been worth the argument with the TSA officer at Reagan International, but his recitation of regulations for an agent with his clearance was confirmed and he was allowed on the flight.

Dr. Chase and his crew pulled case after case of gear from the carousel. Even then, they had to wait for the oversized cargo to be delivered in the adjacent bay. By the time they had secured their vehicles and started on their way, they had been at Sea-Tac airport just south of Seattle for over an hour.

With the FBI team's SUV in the lead, the paranormal investigators followed in a rented van. Chase took the wheel while Wally and Tannen reviewed the notes on Sedro-Woolley and Northern State Asylum.

The radio the FBI team gave them crackled to life. Agent Sohn spoke through the receiver, "So, what are we heading into here?"

Wally grinned at the request. He was hoping the agents would ask. "Northern State Hospital was built in 1912, the state's mental health institutions were maxing out and they needed a new place to house patients. Northern State was known for two things – running experiments on the cusp of technology for the time and for being a working farm, kind of early occupational therapy," Wally explained into the radio.

"What was groundbreaking technology for 1912?" Sohn asked.

"Lobotomies, early trials of electroshock therapy, surgical exploration of the brain," Wally replied.

"I see. What sort of patients were they looking at?"

"Well, that was a bit of an issue for the times. You would have your schizophrenics, your criminally insane, and yet on the other spectrum, you would have some patients that we would see today as simple ADHD. Men were even known to have had their "hormonal" wives committed," Wally explained.

After a few moments of silence and a few clicks of highway mile markers, the radio crackled again, "That sounds…potentially terrible, for a lot of those that were there."

Wally straightened up in the passenger seat as he flipped through his notes, "Yeah, it definitely wasn't a vacation spot, that's for sure. The hospital had its share of tragedy, patients had killed one another, diseases ravaged at times, suicides… I guess up to fifteen-hundred unclaimed bodies are buried on the property, another couple hundred in ashes that have been left behind. Marker-less graves litter the grounds. Kind of sad, really."

Agent Dunlap snatched the radio from Sohn, "That is a lot of potential walking dead!"

Special Agent Jeffers growled from the driver's seat, "There are *no* zombies!"

"If there were…." Wally started, "That would be a lot!"

Dunlap instinctively checked the clip in his handgun at the prospect.

"The place officially shut down as a psychiatric hospital in 1976. A few buildings have had government and private tenants from time to time, but most of the facility just sits abandoned," Wally completed his report.

"Sounds lovely. I'm so happy our team has been aligned with yours for these...type of assignments," Agent Sohn retorted.

The small caravan pulled off of Interstate Five and headed east toward the North Cascades. Jagged white-capped peaks scattered for as far as the eye could see. From Sohn's vantage in the passenger seat of the SUV, she could hardly imagine such a beautiful area hiding dark secrets under the canopy of the tall evergreens.

FOUR

Not far from the interstate, the welcoming signs of Sedro-Woolley signaled their entrance to a charming little town. Weaving their way to the Sedro-Woolley Police Station, the SUV and van parked out front.

Special Agent Jeffers looked around the streets, a hint of suspicion cast upon his face. He preferred his investigations to launch quietly, without a lot of fanfare. He begrudgingly knew that wasn't always the case.

Entering the sleepy little police station, the lead agent was pleased to not detect any signs of expectant locals or worse – a town meeting assembled to welcome their arrival like their last case.

A man behind the front desk looked up. "You here to see Chief Roberts?"

"We are. I'm Special Agent Jeffers, this is Agent Sohn and Agent Dunlap," Jeffers announced.

The man wrinkled his lips and looked past the agents to Dr. Chase's team. "They with you?"

Jeffers bit his lip and sighed. Emphasizing the term *doctor*, he tried to lend credibility to the cohort assigned to him. "This is *Dr.* Ryder Chase. He and his team have been assigned to...," the agent cleared his throat, "Assist our investigation."

"I see. I don't know that our case warrants such a response, but I suppose the families of the victims will be glad to know you are taking their losses seriously," the man replied. Standing up, he held out his hand, "I'm Chief of Police Shane Roberts. Pleased to meet you all."

Pausing for a moment, he studied the entourage and then summoned, "Come on. I'll let you know what we know and see what you think."

An officer wheeled out of a tiny kitchenette, stuffing the last bites of a donut into his mouth. Chief Roberts asked him, "Could you fetch the files on the incident at Northern and mind the store? I'm going to talk to these folks for a bit and then run them out there."

The deputy nodded, his mouth too full to respond, and shuffled off to the bank of filing cabinets in the back of the office.

Leading the investigation team into the department's small briefing room, the Chief slid out a chair and motioned for the crew to sit opposite of him. The deputy walked in and handed the Chief a stack of files. "Thank you, Davis."

Fanning the files out in front of him, the Chief addressed the team. "Sad night. This is a small community. We all knew these kids. Respectable, good grades…the usual high school aged delinquent stuff- partying, goofing off kind of stuff. You know kids, they get bored."

The Chief sighed and rubbed his hands across his face, "Everyone knows not to mess around at the old asylum. The kids all know better. I suppose I can't blame them. All those stupid stories, I guess if I was that age, I would probably have poked around in there myself as a gag. In fact, pretty sure I did."

"What stories, exactly?" Ryder Chase asked the Chief.

Chief Roberts stared at him for a moment, studied the rest of the group and finally spoke, much in the same tone Jeffers often does, "Ghost stories. All sorts of urban legends about the place, I mean, it is an old, abandoned asylum. Pretty much what you might expect."

"You don't believe there is any merit to the stories?" Dr. Chase pressed.

The Chief looked confused for a moment, "It being haunted? Of course not! It's creepy, sure, but things that go bump in the night? Vagrants, kids poking around and all kinds of wild animals – those are the only things bumping around in that old place."

"Of course," Chase nodded.

"Now, what happened here, I don't know what to think. Three kids dead, another scarred for life and in an institution herself right now," the Chief flipped open the case files, revealing more photos of the scene and additional photos of the victims, gruesome and bloody. "No weapons, just uh…claw marks and teeth impression."

"*Three* kids killed? I had only seen the autopsy reports on two of them," Agent Sohn asked.

Again, the Chief looked perplexed, fighting for the proper words to present to the FBI team. "One of the bodies was never recovered."

Jeffers frowned, "Not recovered? Why not?"

"It…it just wasn't there. We searched, poor Sarah. She was so adamant she saw him lying there dead," the Chief reported.

"Maybe she was wrong, sounds like a pretty stressful experience," Tannen offered.

"Perhaps. There was evidence a body *had* been there. DNA run on blood from the spot confirmed what she told us, but no body," the Chief answered, pained by revisiting the scene in his head.

"Animal attack, hate to say it but, maybe…" Agent Jeffers fought for a pleasant way to suggest the boy had been carried away and eaten by a natural predator.

"Possible, but no prints. We expected to find some, but the search came up empty," Chief Roberts shook his head.

Wally cleared his throat and offered, "Got up and walked away?"

The room fell silent, stunned at the suggestion.

Jeffers broke in, "No, maybe he's right. Not in stupid undead sort of way. Maybe he wasn't dead. Perhaps, he tried to find his way for help and never made it."

"I don't know," the police chief admitted. "There was a tremendous amount of blood. No obvious signs of someone struggling to crawl their way to safety. So much blood…"

"That's okay, Chief. We have the reports, if you don't mind, we'd like to have digital copies of everything you have on the case," Agent Sohn relieved the police chief of having to go deeper into the obviously painful recollections of the case.

"Of course. I'll have Davis do that right away," Chief Roberts stood up. "Might as well show you guys out there, introduce you to Mick. That's about all that I've got for you."

"Uh, Chief, just one more question," Tannen asked, "The Medical Examiner's report, it suggests the teeth were more consistent with humans and not animals. What do you make of that?"

The Chief stopped in his tracks. With a very sober expression, he replied, "I don't know how anyone could have made heads or tails as bad as those bodies were torn up. Fact is, this is a beautiful place, but we have very real, very dangerous animals that we live with. Especially out there by the old hospital. That said, when I read the report, my deputies and I combed that place looking for some crazy vagrant or something. Didn't find anything."

Roberts let the severity of his words sink in. "Now, let's get you those files."

FIVE

With the police chief in the lead, the investigation team snaked through the small town of Sedro-Woolley to its furthest edge, pushing further into the foothills of the North Cascades range.

Pulling into the long drive, Dr. Chase was taken by the property. It was as beautiful as it was immense. Sprawling grounds with lush lawns flowed through a park-like setting until a large building dominated the view. The main hospital stretched wide and tall, visually, a lower ridge of the meandering Cascades.

Tannen craned his neck from the backseat of the van so he could take the entire building in, "Man, this place must have been something else back in the day."

"Gonna be a helluva challenge to investigate," Wally added.

Concrete walls and windows made up most of the facade. A tall, peaked pediment with large arched windows dominated the design of what was once a magnificent building flanked by the ever-majestic mountains of the North Cascades.

"If I didn't know this was an abandoned insane asylum with suspected zombies running around, I'd say this would make a nice vacation retreat," Chase admitted.

"You can *still* say that," Wally grinned. "Just when they ring the dinner bell, know they are calling you to *be* the dinner, not join them."

"Dude, you just gave me a great idea for a fitness camp! Think about it. People running their tails off. Shed weight or get eaten," Tannen chimed in.

Wally slapped the dash, laughing hysterically. "That's brilliant! They are guaranteed to walk away lighter one way or another!"

"Alright you two. Jeffers and his team don't need any ammunition to *not* take us seriously, " Chase warned as he pulled the van under a covered awning that extended out into the driveway. He and his team climbed out of their vehicle and joined the FBI agents.

"Well, it sure looks like your kind of place," Jeffers grumbled to the professor and his team.

Chase followed the lead agent's gaze, drinking in the site. "It *is* impressive," he admitted.

"Folks, I was hoping to introduce you to Mick myself, but I just received a call that I need to respond to," the Chief informed the team. "He should be expecting you. I imagine he'll be more or less helpful to you."

The Chief left the team to explore the grounds with their own eyes, waiting for the caretaker to meet them.

Jeffers leaned against the SUV, sighing out his impatience.

Ryder Chase couldn't resist moving closer to the hospital. His team and Agent Dunlap followed closely behind while Agent Sohn grabbed the case file and flipped to the crime scene photos, looking for ones to compare to the site.

"We've been to some creepy places, this place is way up there," Tannen whistled, peering through dust caked windows.

"You aren't kidding," Wally nodded.

Chase paced along the front of the hospital, taking in the massive building. In his mind, he could picture and hear the chaos of the institution when it was in full swing. "There's got to be so much energy and angst locked up in there," he muttered to no one in particular.

"Seems pretty quiet. Really think there are sick people or 'walkers' roaming around here?" Agent Dunlap asked the paranormal team.

"Could have come from the woods, might have come from within the building," Chase mused. "By walkers, I assume you mean zombies? Not exactly a scientific reality. Zombie-like, maybe. Some excitatory hallucinogen, mental illness, maybe cult activity..."

Tannen piped up, "Or still the most obvious theory-some kind of animal attack."

Agent Dunlap frowned, "What about the medical examiner's citing about human-like bite marks?"

"There are a number of anomalies that could account for that. Tooth damage to the animal, could even be a reason for abnormal behavior. Deterioration to the wounds prior to examination. Tough to say," Tannen shrugged.

"I guess that makes sense," Dunlap shrugged.

"Where's the maintenance guy?" Chase asked, eager to get a pass through the property before light failed.

"Maybe he got eaten!" Wally grinned. His peers failed to see the humor in his quip.

Tannen wasn't listening, anyway. He was peering through one of the dusty windows, squinting against the reflection of the late summer sun. Leaning in, he buffed the glass with his fist. Dunlap caught the medic's focus and peered over his shoulder to investigate. Through the grime and glare, he couldn't be sure. He swore he could make out a silhouette on the other side. As Tannen leaned in, Dunlap followed.

Wanting to confirm they were seeing the same thing, the agent started to ask, "Do you see..."

Dunlap's query was cut off as the figure loomed forward, pounding powerful fists against the window. Tannen and the agent lurched back, Dunlap instinctively drawing his weapon, barely stifling an explicative, "Oh sh....!"

Tannen's heart was pounding in his chest, relieved to see the agent with his firearm at the ready. The window shook violently, increasing in ferocity until it suddenly flung up.

Hands flashed out at the investigators, who couldn't help but to each jump back another step.

"Whoa, Whoa!" shouted a voice that was obviously attached to the hands.

Dunlap holstered his weapon immediately and let out a breath.

"I was just trying to let you know I am coming out to greet you. Gall darn window was stuck," a grisly late-middle aged man spat at them. In mixed disgust and humor, he added, " What did you think was going to come through the window at you?"

Both Tannen and the junior agent cast sheepish glances at the ground in response.

"Well, never mind. I'll come around and meet you out front," the caretaker grumbled.

As Tannen and Agent Dunlap rejoined the group under the weathered main entrance awning, Dr. Chase quipped, "Making friends?"

Dunlap shot a look at Tannen and then Chase, "Saw that, did you?"

The investigation team snickered, with the exception of Jeffers, who looked very disgruntled with his junior agent. "Unholstering your weapon? If you can't handle the stories and control your reactions, maybe you should not be on this case."

"I've got it, sir," Dunlap promised.

The sound of several latches and locks being undone was followed by a loud, metallic screech as the heavy front door swung open to reveal a tall man in a thick flannel shirt and blue jeans. Unwieldy white hair protruded from under a well-worn ball cap.

"So, you're them, huh?" the man eyed the group, scrutinizing each member until he fulfilled some sort of mental log. Turning to Tannen and Agent Dunlap. "I've already met these two."

"Special Agent Jeffers," the lead FBI agent held out his hand. "This is Agent Sohn and *Junior* Agent Dunlap. With us is Dr. Ryder Chase, his medic Don Tannen, and... what is it you do?"

Wally frowned, extending his hand, "Wally Smyth, Tech Specialist."

The caretaker took in the information and replied slowly, "Mick. I guess I'm supposed to show you around this place."

Chase was taken aback by the nonchalance of the man given what had occurred on the grounds.

As if he sensed the questioning hesitation from the professor, Mick quickly added, "Tragedy, what happened to those kids."

"Were you the one that found them?" Agent Sohn asked.

Mick nodded, "I was. Warned the chief something like this would happen."

Sohn looked stunned, "You thought something like this would happen?"

The caretaker stopped and faced the FBI agent, "What exactly do you *think* happened here?"

"We're not sure, but we are going to find out," Sohn snapped.

Mick continued leading the group, "Mountain lion attack. What else could it have been?"

"Why did you say you knew this would happen?" Agent Sohn pressed.

"We've had our fill of looky-loos. Kids sneaking in here, chasing some damn fool urban legend. Someone was bound to get hurt, eventually. Figured somehow inside the hospital, not out here by a random animal attack," Mick replied.

Wally couldn't resist himself, "You don't believe the place is haunted?"

"Of course not," the caretaker looked perturbed. "I don't believe in such things. It is an old building. It creaks and groans, she's filled with long hallways lined with doorways. It seems like things go bump in the night, but the only thing that is there is your own damn fool mind."

Arriving at a tall chain-link fence, Mick turned to face the group. "This is it. Right through there."

Through a thin tear in the fence, an area of matted weeds depicted the grisly scene that had unfolded. The more manicured lawn on the interior had worn to bare dirt at the break, suggesting the area had seen some traffic.

The FBI team scoured the ground around the area. When Jeffers was satisfied that he had studied the spot directly in front of the fence sufficiently, he dropped to a knee and squeezed through the opening. Carefully separating the weeds, he began making a grid radiating out from the opening.

"Where, exactly did you find the victims?" Jeffers asked, looking up from his search.

Mick pointed thought the fence, "One right by the opening about a foot and a half from your left leg. One right about where your junior agent is standing."

Instinctively, Dunlap jumped back from the spot.

"What about the other one?" Jeffers asked. "Where did you find the third victim?"

The caretaker paused and looked at the agent with a look of disdain. "I never did see a third. You gotta understand, the kids that come through here, they've been drinking, doing who knows what is being passed around schools these days. No telling what they might think they have seen. Cougar might look like a puppy dog or a crazed demon to them. No telling."

"Get mountain lions out here often?" Wally asked.

"Sure," Mick shrugged. "Not as often as bear or coyotes. The animals don't usually mess with people unless they're being messed with. Occasionally you get a sick animal, a lot more dangerous then."

"Why here?" Agent Dunlap asked.

The caretaker held his hands out, framing the tree covered foothills. "We're the last thing that separates their world from town."

Jeffers looked pleased. Facing the investigation team, he tilted his head knowingly, "Case for Fish and Wildlife, not the FBI."

Mick bristled at the statement.

Catching the reaction, Chase asked, "What did Fish and Wildlife say?"

Turning away, he admitted slowly, "They said it wasn't an animal."

"That's consistent with the coroner's report," Tannen pointed out.

"What else could it be?" Mick snapped. "Those kids were a mess. Tore up real good."

"How about a cult, or some delusional transient?" Chase asked.

Mick shook his head, "I don't know. There have been all sorts of strange people encountered out here. Most I run out myself, the rest, Chief Roberts had the pleasure. If that is the case, we're talking some real sick bastards."

"Know of any cults around here?" Wally asked.

"I don't know nothing about that stuff," Mick shrugged. "People leave all kinds of strange markings in the hospital."

Chase's eyes brightened. "May we see inside?"

The caretaker paused for just a moment, "If you can get to the bottom of this and maybe prove this is just another ordinary building, maybe people will leave us alone. Come on in."

The investigators followed the surly caretaker to the main entrance of the hospital.

"How long have you worked here?" Agent Sohn asked.

Without breaking pace, Mick replied, "About seven years before it closed down as a hospital."

"Wow, so you have seen this place in action," Wally said.

"Sure did. Was crazy busy back in the day...pardon the phrase," Mick took off his hat and wiped his brow. "A lot of good people and families came here for hope. A lot of bad people too."

"What kind of patients were here?" Tannen piped in.

The groundskeeper fumbled with the keys latched to his belt loop. "All kinds. From misdiagnosed kids that struggled with a little ADHD to homicidal sociopaths," he said, opening the door for the investigators. "They didn't mix the two together, of course. Here, I'll show you around and maybe that'll give you an idea of how things worked."

Pushing in through the heavy main doors, Mick led the investigation team into Northern State Asylum.

SIX

The main doors screamed in agony as they opened under the strain from decades of toil. The team was met with a mix of smells – dust, stagnation, history. For a moment, as they gathered in the main foyer, the silence of the massive building overtook them.

Beyond the reach of the fading daylight, darkness loomed past the foyer.

"This," Mick declared to his guests, pausing for dramatic effect, "Is the main entrance. Patients would be brought in here either by their families or the authorities. The two rooms flanking the doors were administration and reception. The next sets were both intake rooms. Sometimes those would be the last moments families would see of one another."

"Sounds awful," Agent Sohn gasped, hardly realizing she was commenting.

"It was, for some. For many others, they came in, were treated and went on to live wonderful lives. It only takes a few tragic ones to make them all seem bad. They weren't all…necessarily. Certainly not by the time I came on board."

Professor Chase danced anxiously by the double doors that led into the black interior of the former mental hospital. Wally and Agent Dunlap joined him, trying to get a peek of what was beyond.

Tannen and Agent Sohn were more interested in the intake and admin rooms. "Are there still any records stored here?"

Mick shrugged, "There probably were, until HIPAA came out. They were all removed and sent somewhere for storage."

Danica Sohn couldn't resist shouldering the door of the admin office and played her light back and forth. Aside from a few pieces of left behind furniture and a sundry of spider webs, the room had been cleaned out.

Chase was eagerly peering through the interior doors.

"I see the professor is ready to move on," the caretaker noticed and motioned the crew towards the doors to the main halls. "Alright, alright. Come along."

Once more fishing his keys out of his pocket, Mick inserted them into the hallway doors.

"You lock and unlock the doors every time you go through?" Agent Jeffers asked.

Mick swung towards his guest, "They were originally installed to ensure the patients didn't get out, rigged to automatically lock. Minor inconvenience now, but didn't seem worth investing in dozens of locks around the facility."

The interior doors opened with less of a complaint than the front door. The halls were barely lit as only a handful of fluorescent lights that swung in their ballasts from the ceiling struggled to function, casting intermittent light in either direction.

Agent Dunlap shook off a chill as he took in the first floor of the old hospital. "This place just beckons every horror movie I have ever watched," he admitted meekly.

"Then you are going to love our first stop," Mick grinned.

Having reached the end of the first massive corridor, they swung down towards the back of the building. Reaching an especially darkened corner, the caretaker placed his hand on a large metal door.

Pushing into the room, the team found them leaving a dark hallway for an even darker room. Switching on his flashlight, the caretaker lit an old switch on the wall. Giving it a push, several seconds ticked by before the light overhead began sparking to life.

The room was cast in strobing flashes of light as the old fixtures fought to take hold. Each flash highlighted a sundry of medical beds and equipment, projecting creepy shadows on the wall with each burst. Finally, incandescent lamps bathed the room in an uneven, yellowish glow.

"I think I may have preferred the dark," Dunlap said as the crew took in the room.

The caretaker grinned. "This is one of three procedure rooms. These rooms would be used to care for traditional medial issues, first aid…that sort of thing. Doctors also used them for certain therapeutic trials."

"Trials?" Tannen asked.

"Lobotomies, stents, chemical injections and infusions," caretaker replied.

"ECT?" Chase asked.

"Shock therapy? Onsite, for sure. But not in these rooms. There were specific rooms designated for that further down the hall. Each one has one of those dual panel windows where you can see in from an observation room, but where the therapy took place it was like a big mirror."

Dan intently studied the equipment around the room. Much of the items left behind were typical of any modern medical exam room – stethoscope and otoscopes, blood pressure cuffs and jars of gauze and wooden tongue-depressors. But mixed in among the traditional items, were odd and sinister looking calipers, clamps and drill bits.

Most disturbing to Don were the drains in the floor positioned under each exam table. Each stained from years of use, collecting whatever contents spilled from the tables above. His stomach turned a bit with the thought and shook off a shudder.

"Each table has straps," Dr. Chase noted.

The caretaker nodded, "Yes, with the varied states of the patients, it was as much for their sakes as the staff's ensuring they did not react physically while undergoing whatever procedure they were receiving."

"What a horrifying thought," Agent Sohn, said, a chill overtaking her.

"This was a serious place, to be sure," Mick nodded. "It gets a little worse. Come with me."

Ominously, the caretaker led them out of the procedure room and to a central point in the hallway. The panel over the door served as both a warning and a beacon of intrigue. The word "morgue" was just legible through the years of dust and rust on the placard.

"Along with the usual causes of death, this hospital had lived through outbreaks of disease as well. These not only had a devastating effect on the patients that were here, this became a facility for the non-mentally and physically ill suffering from disease as hospitals breached their capacity." The caretaker turned the handle and pushed his shoulder into the heavy door. Leaning into it, he motioned for the others to slip through. As he let go, the door promptly swung back closed with a clang. The light came on much faster and more efficiently than the one in the medical room had.

Walking past two exam tables and a row of stainless-steel doors built into one wall, he paused outside of a large walk-in cooler. "When things were at their worst, during an outbreak of tuberculosis, body bags lined the floors of the room. The cooler overflowed leaving the staff with a very large hygienic as well morale issue. So, they came up with *this*."

The caretaker opened a large square door next to the cooler and cast his light into the void space he had revealed. To the crew of investigators, it looked as though it led to an abyss.

"This unfortunate answer to their problem is what some called the 'death chute'. As the deceased began piling up, the mortuary would send the hearse around back, down the hill beyond the hospital to receive the bodies through this chute. It was far more sanitary and less harmful for the already fragile psyches of the patients staying here, never mind the staff."

"Oh my gosh!" Agent Sohn covered her mouth with her fingertips.

"That's terrible," Tannen agreed.

Dr. Chase looked thoughtful, "Sad situation, emotionally the least damaging solution."

Wally winced, "I already see your wheels turning and can only imagine what you have planned for our investigation in here."

"We will spend time here, for sure. But at least I won't send you down the chute," Chase replied.

"He said nothing about not sending *you* down the chute, Dan," Wally grinned.

The EMT whirled his head around and away from the dark tunnel to face his fellow investigators.

"It is true, you would be an easier fit, but no. No one will be taking a ride down the death chute tonight," Chase assured.

"Sometimes, I hate you two," Dan said, begrudging even the thought of such an unpleasant idea.

"I have a couple of other key areas to show you and we can conclude our tour," Mick said.

Leading them back out of the morgue and down the hall, the caretaker pushed his way into a stairwell. As they ascended past the second and third floors, he paused at each and had the investigators peer down the hallways of dorms and patient rooms. Climbing as far as the steps would lead, he unlocked the door at the top and stepped into the attic.

"Spanning nearly the entire hospital, this attic was useful for storage. As you can see, there are still hundreds of items abandoned here."

While much of the attic was empty, the walls were lined with boxes, mattresses and gurneys. At the far end of the attic, a smaller section was enclosed into a separate room. That location was even more full of discarded hospital furniture and equipment.

Shining his beam on the rafters high above, "You see those char marks? A patient had snuck up here and started a fire."

"I can still smell the char," Agent Sohn said.

"Unbelievable," Dr. Chase mumbled as he stared at the wooden beams that fended off flames so many years ago. "It smells like it might have been weeks ago, not years."

"Decades, in fact. The staff put the fire out before there was major damage to the building, but the nurse who found the patient died herself, unfortunately."

"Wow, this building really has lived through a lot," Agent Dunlap said. "The stories this place could tell…"

"*That*, is what we are here to find out," Chased replied.

"Well, I have one more place to take you. This is the spot that seems to get the most attention and bring the most stories," the caretaker said. Motioning for his guests to follow, "Come on!"

Moving out of the attic and back down the steps to the main floor, the caretaker turned yet another key into a door within the stairwell itself. "This seems to be everyone's least favorite spot," he declared as he pushed through the door. A blast of cool, stale air met the team.

"A morgue, a 'death chute', medical experiment rooms and burned attic from a failed suicide, and *this* is everyone's least favorite place. I can't wait," Tannen groaned.

"Down we go," Wally grinned, following the caretaker.

Descending rough concrete steps, they marched into the belly of the hospital. As the doors swung open, the caretaker revealed a pitch black as dark as the team had ever witnessed.

"These tunnels," the caretaker shared, "Link most of the building. These pipes supply the building with hot water from the boilers, and that maze of conduit has served multiple updates and expansions to the building's infrastructure."

"So, what sort of claims come from down here?" Dr. Chase asked.

"While perhaps not the most traumatic, this area is certainly the subject of the most frequent claims. Shadows, banging, footsteps, whispers and smells have all been reported," the caretaker told his audience who were scanning the extensive system of tunnels that ran the length of the building above it.

"Is the boiler still working?" Chase asked.

"Oh yes, it is still functional."

Turning to Wally, Dr. Chase instructed his fellow investigator, "Make a note, that the reported noises could be from the boiler system."

"My thought exactly," the caretaker said. "These systems are cranky. Expanding and constricting metal from competing hot and cold water displacement, I'm not really surprised at all that people hear noises down here."

"Hallways are notorious for playing with people's perceptions," Wally added. "Noise and shadows bounce through like a creepy concert hall."

"They sure do," the caretaker nodded. "Last stop on the grand tour, the end of the line and of note, the end of the death chute, as well."

Standing in front of a giant door like that which would be attached to an airplane hangar, Mick rapped on the metal. "The hearse would drive right back here. This is how many of the supplies would enter the facility as well, along with some maintenance efforts."

"If people know that, wouldn't that alone make them susceptible to let their mind run a bit wild?" Agent Jeffers, who had been notably silent during the tour, spoke up.

"Absolutely," Chase nodded, "Put the creepy vibe of the tunnel and acoustics paired with the knowledge of so much death and sadness through here, it would be natural for minds to wander."

"A movie crew rented the place once. They wanted to film in these tunnels. The first day filming, reports from the cast and crew started rolling in. Shadows, noises, electrical issues…. by the third day, they packed up and left.

They paid me for a three-week rental, but the producer couldn't keep the crew here."

"Can't say I blame them," Tannen replied.

"I feel a breeze, any chance animals or vagrants live in here?" Jeffers asked.

The caretaker shone his light at the corners of where the old doors met with the side of the tunnel. A patchwork of metal scraps and wood answered the response. "Definitely possible. Storms and age play havoc with this old place. I do what I can to keep it mended and safe, but you can't count out a critter or otherwise finding their way in here."

Turning to Dunlap, the Lead Agent ordered, "Make sure to set up a perimeter during their investigation."

"Got you covered," Wally perked up, "We have a perimeter alarm that will do the trick."

"Very well. That combined with regular patrols, after a thorough search, I think we can ensure the professor and his crew will be reasonably safe," Jeffers said.

Tannen winced at the words "reasonably" safe.

"Mick, thank you. This has been a very informative tour," Dr. Chase said.

"This place is truly amazing," Tannen said.

"It has a sad and at times hopeful history," the caretaker replied. "For purposes of your investigation, the place is yours. If you need me, I'll have my cell on."

Special Agent Jeffers looked as though he were about to burst, and finally let it out in a breathless burst, "Ok. Amazing place, sure. Lots of history and certainly up the professor's alley. How does any of that fit into solving the attack on the kids?"

"If we investigate, in the same manner, or similar perhaps, as the group of kids did, we might be able to better determine how they were attacked and by what," Dr. Chase said.

"If it is an animal, maybe it only comes out at night," Agent Sohn suggested.

"If it was a vagrant, maybe they will return," the caretaker added.

Jeffers studied the crew, his dour expression softening ever so slightly.

"While our methods might seem a bit unorthodox to you, Special Agent Jeffers, you have seen yourself how thorough we are," Chase added.

Finally, the FBI agent nodded, "Very well. Whatever it is, it is clearly dangerous. I want you all with an armed agent at all times of the investigation. Feral animal or indigent human…"

"Or zombie, err, zombie-like figure," Wally cut in.

Jeffers scowled and ignored Chase's lead investigator. "Whatever it is, it is my job to keep you safe."

Chase nodded, "We are glad your team is here."

The team thanked the caretaker once more for the tour and resolved to return as soon as possible with their equipment. Chase couldn't resist one last long look at the old hospital. Northern State Hospital in Sedro-Woolley was one of the more notorious paranormal sites in the country. The old bones and creepy halls lived up to their reputation. With a deep breath, he climbed into the SUV. The site had long been on his list. He never expected lives of teenagers would be on the line when he got the opportunity.

SEVEN

The next morning, the team gathered early in the town of Sedro-Woolley. Caravanning from the local coffee shop, they pulled up to the county morgue. Finding the entrance locked, Agent Jeffers rapped loudly against the steel door.

After a minute ticked by, he impatiently rapped louder, with more insistent knocks. Finally, the sound of a deadbolt turning greeted the investigation team.

"Sorry, sorry. Don't get to many guests coming by here," a slightly disheveled man in a lab coat said. Pushing up a pair of glasses that slid down his nose, he studied the group for what seemed a long time in silence.

Jeffers sighed and pulled out his badge, "I'm Special Agent Jeffers with the FBI. Chief Roberts should have told you we were coming by."

"Oh, yes. Of course. It is nine A.M., isn't it," the man acknowledged. Pausing with a curious look on his face, he squinted at the group. "My, there's quite a few of you. ID's, please."

The team looked at one another reaching for their pockets.

The Medical Examiner studied Agent Sohn and Agent Dunlap's badges, nodding at each. The paranormal team produced their driver's IDs, hoping that would meet the man's needs. Motioning the FBI agents in, he barred the door abruptly preventing Chase and his team access. With a stern look, he snapped, "I'm sorry, regulations. Official personnel only."

For once, Jeffers' face boiled over into a gleeful grin. He turned to the paranormal team and shrugged, "Sorry guys, regulations."

Stepping further into the morgue, ready to move on without Chase's team, Jeffers was stopped in his tracks when Agent Sohn spoke.

"They are official consultants sanctioned by the FBI Director for this assignment," Sohn informed the coroner.

In a complete change of affect, the Medical Examiner released his grip on the doorjamb and welcomed Chase and crew, "Well then, come on in!" Waving the entire crew in, he smiled at each. Giving the parking lot behind them a suspicious sweep with his eyes, he closed the metal door and refastened the deadbolt.

"I am Doctor Lazenby, welcome."

The team shared glances at the abrupt one-eighty in the man's tone.

"Can I get you guys some tea, coffee, scones?" the coroner asked as they passed by his office.

Wally jumped at the offer, requesting a scone. The medical examiner darted into the office and grabbed a scone with his fingers and placed it on a napkin. Returning to the hall, he gave Wally the scone, and they continued down the hallway.

Suddenly, Dr. Lazenby froze in place and clapped his hands together, "Ooh, I have this amazing raspberry compote, it would go great with the…"

Jeffers looked cross and snapped, "He's fine with the cookie."

Lazenby looked puzzled for a moment, and then brightened, "Scones are more of a pastry, I believe you are thinking of a biscotti."

Wally nodded, mumbling through a mouthful of biscuit, "Yeah, I bet you're thinking biscotti."

Special Agent Jeffers expression only darkened, "Can we just get on with it?"

"Wow, he's even more stiff than my usual customers," Lazenby grumbled under his breath as he complied and led his guests further down the hall.

Danica Sohn fought to stifle a laugh.

"Very well, in here," the coroner motioned, pushing through a set of swinging stainless steel doors.

"Are you actually going to show us the body?" Sohn asked warily.

The Medical Examiner looked momentarily perplexed, "No, why? Oh, the exam room. Yes, of course. I am a visual presenter. Being in the room where I examined the body helps me remember the details of my examination. Ok. Here is the report." Laying the contents of the file out on the exam table, he sifted the swiveling overheard exam light to focus on the papers.

The team once more shared glances with one another as the coroner began his tale.

"The victim was in bad shape. Dirt, pebbles, moss under the fingernails. Signs they had struggled. Been dragged through the rubble, scrapes, and cuts on the forearms support that. Bruises covered the body. The deepest along the back of the torso and back of the legs. Much of the bruising matched the pattern of knees, knuckles and from hands gripping, almost wringing the skin and soft tissue," the medical examiner recounted. His eyes shut for most of his description, his hands flowing over the exam table approximating the body part he was discussing.

"Excuse me, you said hands?" Jeffers asked.

"Yes."

"That wasn't in the police chief's report," the lead agent pointed out.

"No. No, it wasn't. Just a theory, one that I looked further into after I filed the initial report. I revised the report in the event a detail surfaced that my observation might support. Especially in light of the…the…"

"Bite marks?" Tannen asked, scanning deeper down the report.

"Yes, bite marks. On the calves, neck, throat, back of the arms. Deep, vicious bites. They dug in and tore at the victim. Common for an animal attack, which further confuses the issue and made me uncertain of the hand marks. But the tooth marks were clearly human. Small canines, small bite radius, flat molars. Most animals have teeth made for specific uses – most predators have sharp, scissor like teeth, including their molars. Great for slashing and tearing away flesh, less about chewing. Omnivores have teeth made to do both, tearing at meat, yet soft molars for negotiating plants and grains. The only omnivore that might be considered a threat here are bear. If a bear attacked this particular victim, it would have been a baby. There were no claw marks consistent with a bear attack. The mandibular sizing was all wrong too."

"Any other omnivores?" Agent Dunlap asked.

"Raccoons. Too small. Size and strength, not proportionate. The only one animal I would be concerned about running into the woods at night would be…people," Dr. Lazenby said, adjusting his glasses on his nose as he looked at his guests.

"People," Wally repeated. He absent-mindedly wiped crumbs from the scone off his shirt. Chase shot him a disapproving glance, especially as the coroner used his bare hands to give his investigator the pastry.

"Any chance you were able to extract an impression or something that can be used for a match?" Sohn asked.

"Maybe. Some partials, nothing complete. Unlike bite marks from most human encounters, these weren't clamp and release bites, these were tearing bites. The marks would have been in the parts of the skin that, uh, didn't make it with the rest of the body."

"Eww," Wally twisted his face. Seeing a crumb fall on the table, he picked it up. Chase smacked the morsel out of his hands before it could reach his lips.

"Have you seen anything like this before?" Dr. Chase asked, shooting his tech a disapproving scowl.

Dr. Lazenby looked thoughtful. After a long pause, he shook his head, "Nope. Never."

The entire team nodded absently in acknowledgement with this revelation.

Abruptly breaking the silence, the medical examiner closed the file folder on the exam table, "Well, alrighty then." Nodding uncomfortably, he scanned the audience.

"I guess, we are done here," Jeffers announced.

"Yes, thank you, Dr. Lazenby. You have been most helpful," Agent Sohn acknowledged.

"Good, good. Please let me know if there is anything else that I may do for you," the man said. His face brightening, "Scone for the road?"

Wally started to raise his hand before a stern look from Jeffers cut him off and he lowered his hand, dejected.

"I think we are good. If you think of anything else, please give…Agent Sohn a call," Jeffers said.

Shooting her lead agent a glance, Sohn reached into her pocket and produced a card for the coroner.

Lazenby studied the card with both hands for a moment, mumbling to himself, "Danica Sohn...Danica Sohn..." Stuffing the card in his wallet, he elicited another group shared glance.

Unlatching the door, he held it open, "Ok, bye bye now. Good luck with the investigation."

The team exited the morgue and the door was promptly slammed shut behind them. For several long moments, no one spoke. Their eyes bounced to one another's before Agent Dunlap finally spoke, "Okay, that was weird."

"Yep," Tannen agreed, rocking back on his heels.

Jeffers took a long look at the team, his delay in speech in large part to refocus their minds away from the oddity of the Medical Examiner.

"Alright, I'd like to have Agent Sohn log the coroner's report. The rest of us gather whatever supplies are needed for the investigation and head out to the asylum this evening. Set up prior to sundown," Jeffers directed to a chorus of nods.

EIGHT

Pulling up to Northern State Hospital was no less awe-striking the second time. As evening began casting shadows on the asylum's facade, it only loomed more ominous. Though civilization was a short drive away, the hospital grounds, flanked by the towering silhouette of the Northern Cascades, left the team feeling incredibly isolated.

Jumping out of their vehicles, Chase's team instantly began toting equipment into the building while the FBI agents divvied up their initial roles. Agent Jeffers set off to sweep the grounds while he instructed Agent Dunlap to search the interior of the hospital. Agent Danica Sohn was to stand guard with the professor's team.

Special Agent Jeffers reveled in his assignment. Despite the case and the relics of abandoned buildings scattered throughout the grounds, the overall setting was remarkably beautiful and peaceful. The setting sun played through evening clouds casting an array of colors in the sky, even splashing pink on a glacier high atop a distant mountain.

Walking away from the hospital and further out into the massive grounds, the farm that had served as therapeutic for the patients of the asylum became evident. Large barns that once sheltered dairy cows and a large grain silo stood as remnants of its days in operation.

The abandoned buildings in the middle of what felt like nowhere certainly had a spooky vibe to them, Jeffers was forced to admit to himself. As he stood in the doorway of one of the barns, he laughed at the hysteria noted in the case files of claims of these building themselves being haunted. Unless they were haunted by the spirits of dairy cows, he found the logic faulty. "People want to be scared. Find an old building and manifest your own demons," Jeffers mumbled to himself.

Pressing on, Jeffers followed trails that were well worn connectors to various parts of the property. As he patrolled deeper into the grounds and further away from the main building, the flora of trees, bushes and tall grass closed in around the path. He paused as sounds of rustling triggered his natural response to freeze and identify potential threats.

As he fell silent, so did the noises around him. Resuming his pace, the noises seemed to join him, raising their chorus on both sides of the trail. Instinctively, he brushed his firearm as he paused once more to listen. Chuckling, he resigned to the idea that this is how tales of ghosts and other supernatural creatures are conjured, the naturally explainable sounds and shadows of snakes, birds and rodents, the wind tingling the protective human instincts to fear what they cannot readily identify.

Pressing on, he found himself in an area of overgrowth that threatened to overtake the trail. Considering turning and heading back, signs of recent trespass caused him to remain vigilant in his reconnoiter. A series of footprints embossed the dirt trail while the foliage along the path was twisted, bent and broken.

As Jeffers strode forward, the agent froze. A heavy footfall and crack of a branch resounded beyond his sight at the bend in the trail. Reaching for his pistol, he drew it from the holster. Cautiously angling around the curve in a wide ninety-degree arch, he brought the trail ahead into view through the sites of his gun.

With a sigh, he dropped his aim and holstered his weapon as he watched an equally alarmed buck look up from his evening meal of low hanging Douglas fir boughs. It seemed to study the FBI agent for only a moment before adeptly leaping back into the cover of the deep brush.

Beyond the interrupted buck, Jeffers spied a building partially obscured by thick blackberry vines that had nearly overtaken the front of the building. Nestled deep into the brush, Jeffers pulled a flashlight out of his pocket and switched it on to investigate the building. The concrete block walls of the structure were well intact and solid. Poking through the doorless entry, he was instantly struck with the amount of graffiti that scrawled nearly every surface of the interior of the building.

Studying the vandalism, he noticed many of the writings and depictions were cultist in nature. Satanic and Wicken messages and symbols defaced much of the old building. More disturbing, a decapitated rabbit lay at the threshold of the doorway. He questioned whether it was left by an animal or one of the human visitors to the building.

Swinging his flashlight around, he focused on a massive furnace that took up nearly a third of the structure. He wondered why it would exist so far away from the other buildings. Dr. Chase's recount of the farm's history and the massive death toll in the wake of historic epidemics gave him particular pause. With thousands of corpses over the years, especially with bodies never claimed by loved ones, an onsite crematorium wasn't that much of a stretch. This building, away from the others and its giant incinerator, would serve that purpose well.

Taking a few photos of the building, the Special Agent walked away satisfied that while unsavory guests frequently visited it, they weren't here this particular evening.

Agent Dunlap pushed through the heavy doors separating the front lobby from the interior of the old asylum. Taking a reverse path from the route the caretaker had taken them on, he meticulously surveyed every corridor, ducked into every doorway and room.

The further the FBI agent explored into the bowels of the building, the more unsettled he became. He couldn't deny the inherent eeriness of an old building with such a rich and at times, dark history.

Dunlap's experience combing the hospital on his own was enhanced by the flickering, pale lights that struggled to illuminate even the spaces closest to them. The remaining areas were patches of dense darkness that enveloped him in each interval.

Leaning his shoulder against the heavy door of the morgue, it groaned loudly, sending a raspy complaint into the air. It wasn't the noise that gave the agent a chill; it was the moment of silence that his entrance shattered, providing potential cover for anything, or anyone, lurking.

Flashing his light around the room abundantly clad in stainless steel, he found it otherwise unoccupied. As Dunlap yanked on the handle of the door, the hair on his neck stood to attention and a chill shot down his spine. With a forceful grip, he failed to pull the door open. Having taken care to not allow it to latch as he entered, he could only reason that someone was on the other side preventing his exit.

Quickly drawing his service weapon, he called in to the jam of the door, "Federal Agent. I am drawing my weapon!"

In an instant, the door was freed and Dunlap flung it open the rest of the way, ready to confront whoever was in the hallway. Shining his light into the inky blackness, he panned it down the corridor and quickly swung it down the opposite way.

Frowning, he holstered his gun and continued scanning the halls. Shrugging, he mumbled to himself, "So that's how the night's going to be. I've got to be the one…in these halls…alone."

Collecting himself, he breathed deep, knowing he had to complete the task. Giving the morgue and the halls outside a hard look, he continued to comb the building.

Dan Tannen and Wally Smyth followed in Agent Dunlap's wake. As sections of the hospital were cleared, they toted surveillance equipment into the belly of the building. Setting up cameras and sensors in strategic locations to monitor any traffic through the old asylum, as well as to study areas of interest relayed in the stories that had been catalogued regarding activity in the building.

Most importantly, they targeted areas where someone may have accessed the building and the adjacent grounds where the kids were attacked.

"Let's save enough cameras to blanket the exterior. The most likely source of the attack was the woods," Tannen suggested.

Wally looked up from the camera he was adjusting, "Maybe. I mean, come on. There are so many stories here."

"Stories of ghosts, not zombies. That's kind of a new wrinkle," Tannen said. "Don't get me wrong, this place has always been high on my ghost hunt wish list. I'm thrilled to have the opportunity. Finding out what happened to those kids, I think they crossed paths with some people that might have found a good use for this place back in its hay day."

"Just a bunch of whackos, huh?"

"Most likely," Tannen shrugged.

"Might be right," Wally admitted. "Never heard of a ghost taking bites out of people."

Wiping dust from an office chair that hadn't welcomed a visitor in years, Agent Sohn grinned at Professor Chase, "This place is a little slice of heaven for you guys, isn't it?"

Taking his eyes off the monitors that were being populated one by one with images throughout the building as Wally and Tannen put them into place, Ryder Chase glanced at the agent. "Yeah, I guess you could say that. History, a dark past, a good mystery…spooky as it gets…I suppose it is in our wheelhouse."

"What made you want to crawl around old dusty buildings and try to talk to people that we're all pretty sure aren't really there?"

"It's that pretty sure, but not *actually* sure part that drives us. There aren't a lot of mysteries left on earth to explore. The supernatural is still a wide-open frontier," Chase answered.

Agent Sohn studied Ryder Chase. "What if it is still a wide-open frontier of a mystery because it doesn't really exist?"

Chase chuckled, "I guess a lot of us would be disappointed. The other side of it is about people. Those who ask us to investigate. They want to know they and their loved ones are safe. And those that are...allegedly lost somewhere in between life and death, well, maybe they need help too. If we don't try, we'll never know."

"Okay, who doesn't love a good mystery, but how did *you* specifically get interested in this spooky stuff?" Agent Sohn pressed.

"My aunt. My family was visiting her at her old farmhouse in Connecticut. We could tell something was up with her. She wasn't her usual, bubbly self. She looked exhausted. Her smiles were feigned. Finally, over dinner, my father pressed her on what was wrong. She broke down sobbing," Chase shared.

"She was worried my parents would think she was crazy, but she was seeing things and she was scared to death. She said she hadn't slept in days. Whether what she saw was real or not, her fear was very real, and no one knew how to help her. I guess that stuck with me."

Agents Sohn drunk in the story. "So, what happened with your aunt?"

"Things kept happening. She would seek a dark figure alongside her bed. The floorboards would creak. Cabinets would be open when she swore she shut them," Chase added.

"The poor woman. Did she live there by herself?"

Chase nodded, "Since my uncle passed. It wasn't long after that when the experiences started. She ultimately couldn't take it anymore and sold the farmhouse and moved into town."

"I can see where you might have an interest in this stuff," Danica nodded.

"What about you? Did you always want to become an FBI agent?" Chase asked.

Danica grinned, "Actually, I wanted to be a ballerina."

"Seems like a wide departure," the professor noted.

"I was more coordinated for rough and tumble than graceful and petite," Danica shrugged. "It's more than that. I took a Criminal Justice course in undergrad, and I liked it more than any other class I took. The pursuit of justice, righting wrongs. It stuck."

"Noble," Chase acknowledged.

"So, what are we looking for here?" Danica asked, nodded at the monitors.

"Sightlines and angles that represent the claims made by the reports and the caretaker walk-through," Chase explained. "Anything that might give us some clue to what those kids saw the night they were attacked – a vagrant, an animal…whatever we can find."

"Cameras inside and out…we'll see what we get," Danica said as Wally's face loomed large on a screen as he leaned towards the final camera with a big thumbs up.

Soon, the entire crew huddled in the monitor room before separating into teams for the rest of the night.

"Show us what you have," Ryder requested.

Wally beamed excitedly, "This place is huge, so we've got a lot going on. Tannen and I placed cameras in each floor's main hall, angling towards areas of described activity. We doubled up with cameras in all four corners outside to catch anything moving along the perimeter. We placed digital tripwires in the halls, the entrance to the death tunnel and again along the perimeter. In high-claims areas, we placed equipment to record movement, temperature and electromagnetic changes. As teams, we'll, of course, have our handheld cameras, EMF detectors, IR thermometers and the thermal camera."

Pushing back away from the monitors he was systematically tapping with the back of his pen, Wally scanned the team proudly, "Eh?"

Ryder clapped a hand on his shoulder, "Nice work guys. As you said, this is a big place with lots of claims."

"Fellas, why is all of this important to the investigation of the attacks on those kids?" Special Agent Jeffers pressed.

Ryder looked square at the agent, "If the years of claims in this building coincide with the occurrence of what happened to the teenagers, we might find the two are the same."

"Like a ghost?" Jeffers scoffed.

"More likely some clandestine human activity being perceived as a ghost," Chase offered. His explanation seemed to sit well with the agent.

"But possibly a ghost," Wally interjected.

"Or zombies," Tannen added.

"Wendigo?" Wally suggested.

"Sasquatch?" Tannen said. Both he and Wally frowned at each other, "What would make a squatch attack after all these years of keeping at distance?"

Wally snapped his fingers and pointed at Tannen, "Someone finally got some good evidence. Bigfoot mystery solved, couldn't let that happen."

"Yes!" Tannen exclaimed.

Jeffers shook his head, rolling his eyes in misery and groaned, "What did I do to deserve this? I had such a promising career."

"Well, we have the very tangible case of killed and maimed kids to solve, regardless of the cause," Professor Ryder Chase redirected the team.

Agent Sohn stifled a chuckle as Agent Dunlap followed the back and forth between the paranormal researchers with wide eyes, and her lead agent nearly blew a gasket. Offering Ryder a smile for reigning the team in and perhaps saving Jeffers from a personal breakdown.

"You're right, Professor. Our own safety in this investigation is paramount. Two-man teams all night. One team mans the cameras while one patrols the grounds, the other searches the interior. When in doubt, hold for back up. There is something genuine and dangerous out here somewhere," Agent Jeffers instructed.

"Alright, let's go dark," Chase declared.

The already dim building plunged further into darkness as the team shut the building's lights off for the night. The handful of lights the caretaker routinely left running remained on to recreate the conditions of the night of the attack. The dim, oft flickering illumination did little to improve the aesthetics and lent themselves to casting shadows and too frequent noises from kamikaze bugs flying headlong into them.

Dan Tannen and Agent Sohn took the first run through the interior of the building. "Not going to lie, this place is even creepier at night. There is so little light that penetrates this building, especially once you push through the interior doors," Tannen described as he combed his flashlight along the halls.

"Don't look at me, I'm not going to disagree with you," Danica responded. "It doesn't feel scary to me, but it has serious creep factor."

"This place is enormous. A lot of good and a lot of bad things happened here," Tannen mused, playing his flashlight into an open patient room.

As they neared the morgue at the end of the back hallway, the investigators paused at the big stainless-steel door. As if on cue, the dim light that hung in that corner of the hallway flickered and went completely out. Tannen sighed and nodded, "Yep, that's about right."

With her flashlight in hand, Sohn didn't flinch. She marveled slightly at the reaction of the paranormal investigator. "You don't take to this stuff like the other two do," she observed.

"I kind of got into it by accident. I stuck with it because of Ryder and Wally. They're like family to me," Tannen said. The hall light slowly grew back to life, at least as much life as it offered in the bleak hallway. Tannen stared at it and just nodded, prodding the pair forward in their sweep.

"So, what happened?" Agent Sohn asked.

"I was on the scene of a terrible a rollover car accident. One of the passengers, a young child had been playing with their seatbelt during the ride, got thrown clear. With no one responsive, we didn't even know they were there. I swear in the chaos, someone urged me to climb down the embankment, a good twenty yards away from the vehicle. There was the child. Unconscious," Tannen reported.

"Oh my gosh, was the child okay?"

Tannen nodded, "I was able to provide CPR, they came around. I hate to think if I didn't get there in time."

"And…who led you to the child?" Sohn pressed, sensing a payoff.

"No one knows," Tannen shrugged. "The entire crew was busy trying an extraction on the driver who didn't make it. No one else was there. I was curious, so I took one of Dr. Chase's classes at the university. We talked, and he offered for me to join him on an investigation. We've been doing it together since."

"It seems like no one gets into your line of research without being drawn by some incident," Sohn said.

"It riles up the curiosity, sure. There are some that just have interest, but personal experiences do bring a lot into the field," Tannen explained as they ascended the first flight of stairs.

Carefully inspecting each room, they were amazed by the amount of furniture and equipment that had just been abandoned when the hospital closed.

"It's like a giant museum, full of memories," Sohn observed.

"Many of them horribly unpleasant," Tannen added.

Agent Sohn turned into a room, tight with furniture and boxes stacked. Suddenly she spun, shining her flashlight erratically around her.

"What? What is it?" Tannen asked, joining her frantic flashlight play, though not knowing what he was looking for.

Shaking herself, Danica rubbed the back of her neck vigorously. "I felt like someone was right there, like I could feel their breath on my neck…hear their breathing!" she gasped.

Hearing her describe the event as she wriggled off a chill, Tannen tried to peer through the thick obstruction of boxes and shelving. "I can't see anything," the EMT said. Moving the flashlight along the ceiling and back to the shelves, he suggested, "Cobweb?"

Danica looked doubtful and shrugged, "Maybe."

"I can't even squeeze through there," Tannen said as they pushed as far into the room as they could.

"Well, it's gone now. You're probably right, spider web," Agent Sohn said, instinctively brushing would-be spiders off her shoulders and shaking out her hair.

The thought of rogue spiders was suddenly disturbing her more than ghosts and homicidal killers. "Let's move on," she suggested, nudging Tannen towards the door to the hallway. She cast a final look over her shoulder as she happily left the room behind.

Wally and Agent Dunlap settled in behind the bank of monitors set up in the command room. Wally held out an open bag of corn chips, "Want some?"

With a shrug, Dunlap accepted a handful of chips and shoved them in his mouth. "Like a stake out. Always have good snacks at the ready," the agent thanked Wally. "Only Special Agent Jeffers has some serious rules about what is allowed. Corn chips are on the list. Tuna…pork rinds…anything too crunchy…anything that might melt or is too liquidy…"

Wally laughed, "Yeah, that sounds like Agent Stuffy."

Dunlap shrugged, "He's a brilliant agent. Just best you do things his way."

They each studied a subset of monitors. They watched Agent Sohn and Tannen leave one hallway and enter another as they pushed through the stairwell.

"What's your take on all this?" Dunlap asked.

"Hard to say," Wally shrugged. "The reports of this hospital and really the entire grounds are rich with paranormal activity. It has often been seriously scary stuff, but never violent. My guess is something from the woods that is drawn to this building for whatever reason."

"Something from the woods?" Dunlap frowned.

"Cryptid, animal, satanic worshipping human opening doors they have no business opening," Wally said.

"Doors?"

Wally looked uncharacteristically serious, "The paranormal field is fascinating, but you can push it too far. There is so much unknown from a spiritual plane, religious boundaries and strange earthly things we have yet to learn. Demons are rich in many cultures and religions. It is never a good thing to put yourself into that realm. As a team of paranormal researchers, that is our line that we never cross."

"Really? Like possessions and that kind of stuff?" Dunlap leaned forward.

"Yeah, there are cases that just don't feel right. They feel...evil," Wally said.

"What do you do?"

"Leave it alone, call in a priest or a demonologist. It's only happened a couple of times, but Ryder has been clear, we won't touch it," Wally announced.

"What about this case?" Dunlap asked.

"I don't know. Paranormal reports crossing over to a physical plane of violence and mortal danger. It's not good," Wally replied.

"Speaking of not good...what is that?" Dunlap pointed to the lower corner of one his screens.

Wally peered over, "What, I don't see anything."

"Right there," Dunlap pointed. "I swear, I saw something move."

"Let's play it back," Wally suggested, taking over the controls. Isolating the screen, he slid the data bar back a few minutes in time. Watching, not expecting to see anything, he leaned forward, "Oh, yeah. What *is* that?"

Rewinding once more, both investigators watched. In the very corner of the screen, a shadow grew out of the corner of the monitor, paused and then pulled back.

"Hmm. We caught a shadow from something," Wally announced. Picking up his walkie-talkie, he called out to Agent Sohn and Dan Tannen on their interior patrol.

After explaining what was seen on the monitors, Sohn and Tannen agreed to head to the location and investigate.

Observing from the command center, Wally and Dunlap watched Sohn and Tannen make their way down the hall. After searching the hall and each room, they spent several minutes trying to recreate the shadow.

"Move back and hold," Wally commanded. As the shape on the screen began to look like what they had recorded, Wally had them move again and the shadow disappeared.

Glancing at Dunlap, the agent shrugged, "It wasn't exact, but it was an awful lot like that."

"You guys found nothing?" Wally asked into the Walkie. "Did you hear anything?"

"Negative. We searched each room and the stairwell. Nothing or no one here," Tannen replied. "We were on the floor above, I can tell you, sound doesn't travel from floor to floor. If there was something down here, we might not have heard it either."

"We'll record the time and make sure we review the footage in detail tomorrow," Wally suggested.

"Okay. We'll continue our sweep," Tannen said, nodding into the lens of the camera placed on that floor.

Professor Ryder Chase and Special Devon Jeffers walked the perimeter of the building. They would appear on the cameras viewed by Wally and Dunlap, easily identifiable as they made their loop.

Jeffers stared at the building as they walked. "It's an old building. There's got to be some ways in…a worn latch, broken window…something."

"That would have been my hunch too, but we found nothing on our walkthrough today. Remember the caretaker with the window he opened, he struggled. Each door, the exterior and interior lobby doors are both heavy, stiff and very noisy to open," Chase countered.

"Then it has to be something from the woods," Jeffers reasoned. The Special Agent was quick to identify the most logical routes in an investigation.

"There is no *definitive* connection with the interior of the asylum from the victim report. The event was all around the hospital, not necessarily from within. She said when they reached the main entrance, they were met by their attackers. She didn't say they were spilling out from the entrance. She said *at* the entrance," Chase said.

"The primary door locks had been repaired. Likely to keep out trespassers like those kids," Jeffers nodded. "So, we need to concentrate on the grounds. Animal from the woods."

Chase shook his head, "Not according to the report, I know in the chaos of the evening there is always the chance for misidentification, but the victim was very clear, they encountered *people*."

"The crematory! That has to be the connection. If not wild animals, which are right out there somewhere, mind you," Jeffers panned his flashlight towards the forest backing up to the hospital grounds. "The most likely scenario are nut job devil worshippers."

Chase couldn't argue the possibility and followed the FBI agent as the pair peeled away from the main hospital building and headed towards the far side of the property. "The high grass and blackberries make this like going down a hallway," the professor observed.

"Both good and bad for our purposes. Harder to get through and if a person or animal did, they would leave a trail of disturbed brush," Jeffers scanned the dense foliage with his flashlight.

"It also limits visibility for what's around the next corner," Chase added, straining his eyes to see as far as they could.

Reaching an intersection, the flora thinned out and the crematorium rose out of the brush. Its large chimney dominating the distinctive building. As the men approached, Chase suddenly froze, Jeffers instinctively following suit. The agent's eyes scanned to see what halted the professor.

"I just saw a flash out of that window," Chase whispered.

Jeffers stared at the window, "I thought I saw a glint of something in my peripheral. I don't see anything now. Let's see if there are kids messing around in there. Maybe you picked up their flashlight."

Darting forward, Jeffers launched himself in the direction of the crematorium. Chase raced behind him.

"Stay here, watch this side," Jeffers hissed as he plunged down the narrow path the led behind the building to the open main door.

Playing his flashlight around the exterior of the small building, Jeffers pushed into the derelict structure. The small building didn't require much of a scan to reveal it was empty. Ensuring he didn't miss a hiding space, he used the flashlight along the floor to look for prints and make sure he didn't trip over any of the debris.

Turning the corner that emptied back out on the trail, he snapped back. His heart raced. To his surprise, a face was staring back at him.

"Did you find anything?" Chase hissed.

Jeffers grew instantly cross, "What are you doing? I told you to stay on the trail by the smaller entrance."

"I'm sorry if I startled you…," Chase began.

"You didn't startle me!" Jeffers snapped, his eyebrows forming a scowl. "I was determining if you were a threat I needed to shoot."

Chase acknowledged, "Right. I heard you exit the building, you didn't chase anything out my way, I wanted to make sure no one doubled back around the building away from the view from the path and to listen for anyone or anything breaking through the brush."

"Oh," Jeffers nodded. "Good plan. Just need to be more careful, that's all. When my other agents and I expect your team to be somewhere, we really need you to be there. For your safety."

"Understood, Agent Jeffers," Chase said.

"I'm not seeing any evidence anyone has been here since our afternoon walkthrough and nothing that would have made that flash," Jeffers said. His eyes widened, fearing he had just admitted that the incident might have been paranormal.

Back out on the main path, Chase spun to again face the building. Staring at the window, he played his flashlight, which instantly lit up the exterior surface of the building, not anything from the inside.

"Would you go back in and shine your flashlight around?" Chase asked.

Jeffers nodded and retreated into the crematorium. Playing the flashlight around the building, inside and at the window, he called out, "Anything?"

"Go back to where you were a second a go," Chase asked. "A little further…there!"

"Is that it?" Jeffers asked.

"No," Chase admitted dejectedly. "It's similar, but it is not what I saw. It's like the angle is wrong."

"There is a bit of metal bracket in here. When I hit it, it must be just shiny enough to reflect back some light!" Jeffers called. Returning to Chase, they both studied the building.

Chase's eyes moved from the building to the skies above. The generally overcast evening afforded only brief wisps of stars and moonlight to aid them. Biting his lip, he mused, "Your flashlight was really close to what I saw. I don't know. Maybe the moonlight in just the right angle briefly breaking through the clouds..."

Jeffers nodded, "Moonlight. A plausible explanation. I like it. Let's head back. Check in with the team."

Taking one last glance back at the crematorium, he thought about the three hundred urns of unclaimed ashes that had been left behind. It was three hundred possible souls looking for closure. Or perhaps, it was just a simple trick of the moonlight.

NINE

After a long night of investigations, the team did their best to catch a few hours of sleep before convening the next morning. Gathering in the breakfast room of the hotel minutes before the cut-off time to plates with strangely textured eggs, bagels and yogurt, they broke down the evening's investigation.

"Nice work last night, guys," Chase declared. "We had a lot of ground to cover inside and outside of the asylum. I think we managed it well. Now that we've had some sleep, what are your thoughts from last night?"

"No doubt the place is spooky. We did pick up some...anomalies," Tanned suggested.

"The light in the hallway, we caught that on camera, we could see your reactions," Wally said.

"The shadow!" Agent Dunlap nearly leaped out of his seat.

The team's heads swiveled to the junior agent.

"We picked up a shadow on camera. We sent Agent Sohn and Dan in to debunk it. We'll analyze it further today," Wally admitted.

"I caught a brief flash of light in the crematorium, but I can't say it wasn't a rogue reflection of light from the moon peeking out," Chase added.

"And footsteps, I mean, every floor. You'd go to investigate, and they'd be gone," Tannen said.

"I would swear that once, we heard the pace pick up, like they were running away from us," Agent Sohn, flashing a look at Jeffers who had remained quiet.

"We'll see if the evidence substantiates anything," the lead agent muttered. "An old building, cooling off at night, you're going to have creaks and pops and bangs as the more than a century old wood constricts."

Chase nodded, "He's right. What we didn't detect was anything or anyone that could have been responsible for the death of those teenagers."

"Or definitive haunting," Wally added. "At least not until evidence review."

"When you two finish with breakfast, why don't you run through last night's evidence. I'd like to head out with the FBI team and do a day investigation," Chase suggested.

"Works for me boss," Wally said. Picking up his breakfast plate, he nudged Tannen. "Might as well get started. Lots to review and I can eat and analyze."

Tannen followed suit, picking up his yogurt, "Keep your phone on. Might be good to have you available for debunking real time with our review."

"Good idea," Chase nodded. Looking at the FBI team, "Shall we?"

Each visit to Northern State Hospital developed a different and evolving vibe for Ryder Chase. Looking out the window, the hospital flanked by the impressive natural landscape took on an aspect of beauty on this daytime visit.

The professor could see how, once upon a time, the hospital made for a tranquil respite for the troubled and the afflicted. People grappling with their mental health demons, typically thrust upon them beyond their own doing. A natural chemical in their brain, missing or too abundant by no fault of their own other than genetics. In a time when mental health was so poorly understood, all they wanted to be was a healthy version of themselves.

Psychiatrists, psychologists, medical doctors and nurses would do what they could to help them. To discover new techniques to offer to the world in hopes for cures to mental illness. Within the magnificent buildings dwarfed by the dramatic natural scenery itself, well intended, at times, very horrible things occurred.

The thought shook Ryder Chase from his daze as Special Agent Jeffers brought the SUV to a stop.

"Dunlap, give me a full fence line sweep. Take photographs with coordinates of any anomalies," Jeffers ordered junior agent.

"Uhm, the property is over one thousand acres, sir," Dunlap sputtered.

"Then you should probably get moving," Jeffers cocked his head.

"Right," Agent Dunlap nodded and made a beeline for the closest section of fence line.

"I have my own real investigative work to do, Agent Sohn, you're on babysitting duty," Jeffers directed. "You're by his side the entire time. I'm not going to let someone go down on this investigation."

Chase struggled to conceal his smile at the concept of the alluring FBI agent was ordered by his side. "Thank...thank you, Special Agent Jeffers. I feel much better with Danica, I mean Agent Sohn, I mean one of your team keeping us safe," Chase stammered.

The professor's struggle to respond appropriately gave Jeffers momentary pause. He eyed Chase questioningly with a raised, concerned brow.

"That is why we are assigned to work together, keep your team safe as we work together to solve this case," Danica Sohn cut in.

Jeffers studied them both for a moment before nodding, "Right. Okay. Stay in radio contact."

"What's first on our list, professor?" Agent Sohn asked.

As Chase collected himself, his phone chimed that he received a text. Giving it a quick read, he replied, "It sounds like Wally and Tannen would like us to check out the area with the shadow caught on the security cameras last night."

"Let's go. I know the spot," Agent Sohn said, taking the lead.

Chase shot a glance at Jeffers, who was already heading off toward his own mission. Seeing Danica Sohn halfway between himself and the foyer to the hospital, he scurried to catch up.

Agent Sohn cast a grin over her shoulder, "You coming?"

"I'm coming!" Chase called as he hurried to join her at the front door.

Pushing the key into the lock, the FBI agent flicked her wrist and pushed the heavy door open. "It's only marginally better in the daytime, isn't it?"

"The atmosphere is every bit as charming," Chase admitted tongue in cheek. "You guys were on the second floor?"

"We were," Agent Sohn nodded.

As they unlocked and pushed through the interior doors, the lights throughout the hospital flickered. Both Dr. Chase and Agent Sohn froze as they watched what was going to happen. Chase stared at the old amber light fixture as though it might afford some answer. After a few moments of fluctuation, they stabilized.

Ryder Chase had a thought and texted Wally only to receive a response, "Already ahead of you from last night's investigation."

"Let's see this shadow," Chase urged as they moved towards the closest stairwell.

Agent Sohn led them to the spot that Wally and Agent Dunlap saw the shadow on the monitor. "According to the boys, it was right…here."

The agent waved around the area that the shadow appeared from the doorway.

Dr. Chase knelt and inspected the area. He studied where the shadow would have been produced and what light sources would have been available in the area. He looked down the hallway where the camera blinked, its lens fixed on the corridor.

Dialing Wally on his phone, Chase waited for the answer. "Wally, can you tap into the camera where you saw the shadow?"

"Of course," Wally replied. "Alright, I've got it cued."

Chase walked into the room and took a tentative stride out of the door, "Did it look anything like this?"

"Let me see, I'll pull up both footages on parallel screens," Wally replied. "Uhm, yeah, actually."

"Is there anything higher on the screen?" Chase asked.

After a pause, Wally replied, "Yeah, kind of. It is not well defined, but the shadow pops up just above the door handle, not as pronounced, but it is there."

"Like this?" Chase peered around the corner towards the camera.

"Uh, almost exactly like that…," Wally replied.

"As if someone is peering down the corridor," Chase suggested.

"Precisely as if," Wally confirmed.

Chase looked at Agent Sohn, "Something or someone...was here last night!"

Agent Sohn looked incredulous, "How...what could have been here? Dan and I were up here, what, forty-five seconds since from the time Wally and Dunlap saw it on camera? We found nothing in this room and if anyone ran out, it would have been caught on camera. There is no way out!"

Dr. Chase studied the FBI agent and then the room. Wearing a serious expression, "I have no answer for that."

Agent Sohn looked aghast, "Please don't make me put unexplained, disappearing apparition in my official FBI report."

"I don't know what to tell you," Chase admitted. "We can't say it's a ghost. An unidentified shadow, yes. Ghost... who knows?"

"Thanks, that helps!" Agent Sohn scoffed.

Ryder Chase shrugged, "Welcome to paranormal forensics."

"How about the light outside the morgue?" Sohn suggested.

"Sounds good," Chase agreed. "Lead the way."

The FBI agent once more moved down the hall with Chase in tow. As they descended the stairs, they both froze. Somewhere deep within the center of the building, the sound of a heavy door being slammed shut followed by a muffled yelp rang through the building.

Agent Sohn was instantly on her radio, "Special Agent Jeffers, what is your twenty?"

"I'm at the crematorium," Jeffers replied.

"Dunlap?"

"Joyfully pushing through blackberries along the northern edge of the fence line," Dunlap reported.

Agent Sohn and Professor Chase exchanged glances, "First floor or basement?" Danica asked.

"Sounded further away, though strangely loud. Basement," Chase determined.

"Let's go, stay behind me," Sohn ordered.

Chase reluctantly complied. Despite the agent's far superior physical attributes and training, the idea of hiding behind her refused to sit well with him.

Reaching the heavy basement door, they paused as the lights throughout the building dimmed, grew brighter and dimmed once again. Pushing through, Agent Sohn descended the steps, her weapon drawn, clamped to her flashlight.

As dark as the old hospital was, the basement was impenetrably black. Without the aid of their flashlights, there was no perceivable light for their eyes to pick up.

Moving through the partitioned space, the pair searched every door and darkened corner.

Navigating the multitude of stored items, Chase suddenly put a hand on the agent's shoulder. Keeping her weapon pointing in front of her, Agent Sohn looked over her shoulder.

"That gurney," Chase hissed.

The agent frowned and followed his sightline. She recognized what he was referencing. The cart had made lines in the years of dust built up on the basement floor. The gurney had recently been moved several feet.

As they swept the area, a large patch of dust seemed to be disturbed, but no definable footprints- human, or otherwise, could be found. Looking at one another, they shared a mutual shrug and continued their sweep. Finding nothing, they paused in the dark subterranean space and listened, but their ears did not reward them with any additional noises.

Satisfied there was no one in the building and they had combed every possible inch of the basement, they retreated to the upper floors to continue their investigation.

Reaching the first floor, Sohn asked, "Lights outside the morgue?"

To her surprise, Chase shook his head, "No. After witnessing the fluctuations in power, it is too easy to dismiss. The old utilities in this building are erratic. Timing is unusual and power drains are certainly signature clues, but unless you had a specific experience while it was happening, old wiring has to be the de facto explanation."

Agent Sohn's eyes went wide, "The room where I got the chill. We chalked it up to spiderwebs at the time, but it felt like breath. *Warm* breath."

Chase cocked his head at the description, "Warm. Now that is a new variable. Show me."

Danica nodded, and they made their way to the patient room piled high with storage items. Even as she entered, she shuddered as a chill ran down her spine.

"You okay?" Chase asked.

Annoyed with herself, Agent Sohn waved him off, "I'm fine."

Chase took in the scene. The room was chaotic with items crammed in. Aisles that once snaked through were blocked with additional boxes. Scanning the ceiling and taller boxes along the narrow, meandering path, he said, "I don't see any webs now."

"Probably because I pulled them all down last night," the FBI agent grinned.

"Certainly a reasonable explanation," Chase mused.

"What about the warmth? It felt like warm, moist air," Agent Sohn refuted.

"Thermogenic stress response? Walking in here amidst the chaos creates a bit of a funhouse affect, throwing off your senses," Chase suggested.

"I am trained in stressful situations, I don't typically get flushed with hot flashes during an investigation," Sohn replied.

The professor shot her a quizzical look.

Agent Sohn looked cross, "Don't even go there. I am years away from that!"

Chase shrugged sheepishly. Poking around the shelving, he asked, "Where exactly *were* you at the time?"

"Right about where you are standing. I was following Tannen as far as we could into the room."

"Following Tannen, who is hardly taller than you," Chase observed.

"Should have picked up spider webs, not me," Sohn cocked her head.

Peering through the collection of items on the shelf, Chase said, "There is space back there for someone to stand. You would conceivably pass them between these two shelves where they come together. Why someone would be back there, I have no idea."

"We looked and didn't see anyone, but admittedly, we didn't search *behind* everything," Sohn reported.

"Can't rule it out, though not entirely plausible," Chase said.

"If it were an FBI report, I think I'd have to go with spiders, however unimpressive that finding might be," Sohn admitted. As they entered the long hallway with light fighting its way through the dusty windows at the end of the hall, she laughed, "This place definitely has a strange vibe. It's got that going for it."

"Lots of curious things happening," Chase added. "None adding up to the mauling and deaths of teenagers."

"We'll get to the bottom of it," Sohn assured.

Agent Jeffers voice called through the radio, "You guys ready to wrap it up for now? Dunlap is back . I'd like to assess where we are with the investigation back at the hotel."

"We're on our way!" Sohn responded. As she resumed their walk down the long hallway consumed by the dark save for a respite of light spilling in through a window at the entrance to the stairs, her flashlight failed.

Chase watched the agent shake the flashlight and ultimately giving it a good thwack to no avail. "Here, I have a spare," he fished a small tactical light from his pocket.

"Of course, you do. You're the boy scout of the paranormal field," Sohn accepted the light and snapped it on. "Thank you."

As the light swept across her face, Chase stopped her.

"Hold on!" stepping close, Ryder brought his hand to agent Sohn's shoulder, his fingers gently sweeping through her hair, softly grazing her neck.

Danica Sohn's lips parted instinctively as a brief shudder swept over her. She looked at the professor with anticipatory curiosity, wondering what he was up to. She didn't move back, she didn't respond. She waited to see where he was going.

Realizing he was violating her personal space, Chase looked sheepish. Pulling away, he raised his arm, shining his flashlight. On the back of his hand crawled a spider he liberated from the agent.

"You had a hitchhiker. Evidence to support your theory," he whispered.

Sohn closed her eyes just briefly, and smiled, "And here I thought you just had really bad timing for a romantic interlude."

Chase's cheeks flushed fiery red, "I...uh, I mean if..."

"It's okay. I'm kidding," Sohn giggled. "But, uh. You can let go of your little friend there, now."

Chase shook himself and then guided the spider off him and back onto the light fixture he likely sprung from as he hijacked the agent as she walked by. "Right. We should…"

"Yes, we probably should," Sohn nodded, leading them out of the hospital.

TEN

When Danica Sohn and Ryder Chase joined Agents Jeffers and Dunlap, Chase was still shaking off his fluster from the incident with Agent Sohn in the hallway.

Jeffers never one to miss an observation cast a suspicious eye at the professor. "Did you two find anything?"

"An abandoned building does indeed have spiders in it, old wiring is erratic at best and the video evidence regarding the shadow cannot be confirmed or debunked," Agent Sohn replied.

Jeffers scowled at the report, "What does that exactly mean?"

"We caught a shadowy image matching the shape of someone peering out of one of the rooms on the second-floor hallway," Chase confirmed.

Jeffers sighed. His affect didn't belie whether he was looking for solid evidence of a human or refute that there was anything there at all. He cast a glance towards Dunlap.

"I patrolled the entire fence line. Overall, it is fairly new and well-constructed. There are portions, especially along the forest line that have weak points. I took pictures along the way," the junior agent leaned his phone over for the others to see the screen. "Animals have clearly dug under."

"Enough space for a person, if they were so motivated," Sohn noted.

"This spot is right behind the crematorium. And we know about the cut in the fence. Lots of animal evidence at each weak spot. Only the crematorium and the break in the fence show any signs of human trespass, though they are evident. One thing of note, near the tunnel used by the morgue during the pandemic, there were a number of vehicle tracks," Dunlap completed his report.

"We have determined that the attack could be an animal or could be a human and has little to do with ghosts," Jeffers folded his arms. "Maybe interviewing the witnesses further will move this investigation along."

"We haven't proven it isn't ghosts, just yet," Dunlap raised his in correction. "Wally says…"

Jeffers' stony stare stopped the junior agent mid-sentence.

"Right," Dunlap nodded sheepishly. Moving the conversation, he asked, "Were you able to find anything, Special Agent Jeffers?"

Jeffers fished a handful of evidence bags out of his pocket. "A random sample of DNA, finger-prints and other sources of identification. If my hunch plays out and I believe it will, that the whacked-out satanic kooks are at the bottom of it. The connection to the killer might be in one of these bags."

Wally Smyth and Dan Tannen were ready and waiting for the team to arrive. Perched behind a row of monitors and speakers, they launched directly into their evidence review.

"We had several things the team asked us to follow up on, along with the footage from the running cameras and hot mics," Wally announced. "We'll run through the highlights."

Tannen cued up the shadow footage.

"We worked with Agent Sohn and Ryder on the shadow on the second-floor hallway. You can see what we captured last night on the left screen and what we captured today with Ryder's recreation here," Wally pointed at the screens.

"Run it again," Jeffers ordered.

Tannen complied. Following the loop, he played it once more, freezing the screens at similar points. Leaning back, he let the evidence speak for itself.

Jeffers struggled with what he witnessed. Shaking his head, "Like everything else with this case, I can't confirm that the shape coming out of the door is or isn't a person."

"If it was a person, how would they be able to be there without us noticing? Without the camera seeing them walk down the hall?" Agent Sohn asked.

"Or hide so effectively that we couldn't find them," Tannen added, recalling their scan the evening prior.

"If you're not a fan of in-definitive evidence, you're not going to like this one either," Wally warned with a nod to Tannen to run the next clip. "This is the audio recorder synched to Tannen's body camera. You can see him follow Agent Sohn into the patient room. As they wind through the tight space among all the junk, Tannen pushes forward. You hear something right...here."

The monitor shows Agent Sohn spinning and rubbing at the back of her neck before playing the flashlight around the room with Tannen joining by her side. Agent Sohn cocked her head, "Play it again."

Tannen reloaded the scene. Isolating the audio, he put it on loop.

Agent Sohn's eyes widened. "That sounds like a breath! I felt a breath!"

Jeffers' typical look of disdain only grew more pronounced. "Old building, breezes, stuffy room…sure it *sounds* like breathing. Maybe it was Tannen."

"I felt it from behind me. Tannen was further in the room at that point," Agent Sohn said.

"You pan your light immediately behind you," Jeffers pointed out.

"You can't tell from the footage. By the time Tannen comes over with the body cam, there's nothing to see," Wally shrugged.

"Did you search the room?" Jeffers asked.

"We did," Agent Sohn nodded, but then admitted, "Though not thoroughly. There were so many things in the way. I can confirm I didn't see anyone, but I can't confirm that it was impossible for someone to be in there with us."

Jeffers rubbed his face. "Do we have anything anywhere to indicate a human or animal or some combination thereof that would explain the death of those teenagers?"

Wally shook his head, "Nothing that we recorded last night."

"It's part of the scientific process. We start broad, build some basic clues and narrow down towards an answer," Chase promised. "Wally, make sure to add a camera to that room tonight."

Wally grabbed one he set aside on the table and held it up, "Same thought, boss!"

Wally snapped his finger, "There was one thing. I pulled the electrical records for Northern State. There are frequent fluctuations, enough to easily make old wiring flicker erratically. But, there was a sustained spike that began three months ago."

Professor Chase cocked his head in curiosity, "Why would there be a sustained spike on a building that has remained dormant?"

"A question for the next time we see that caretaker, Mick," Jeffers sighed. Panning the team, he announced, "Let's round up the locals and see if we can tease anything out of their interviews. Dunlap, you come with me. We'll work through Chief Roberts. Agent Sohn, why don't you take...Tannen with you. The EMT seems useful in medical discussions."

"What...what do we do?" Wally waved his finger back and forth between his chest and Professor Chase's.

Jeffers frowned, "Anything that keeps you out of the way."

The lead agent spun, bobbing his finger up and down, "On second thought, there is something you two can do. Find the wildlife officer, North Cascades ranger, whoever would have jurisdiction over this area and get their official statement. Not some hand-me-down from a nervous caretaker."

Wally agreed and then shrugged, "I kind of like Mick."

Jeffers cast him a stern glance and nodded towards Dunlap, "Let's go."

ELEVEN

Sedro-Woolley Police Chief Roberts was layering butter on a biscuit across from his plate piled with chicken fried steak.

"Special Agent Jeffers and Agent Dunlap, you're just in time for lunch," Chief Roberts suggested as he panned his hands on a pair of empty seats at the table.

Dunlap's eyes widened but quickly fell as Jeffers dashed his hopes of a delicious diner meal. "Just here to ask a few more questions and see if you can help fill in some holes," Jeffers said, taking a seat across from the local officer. The lead agent nodded for Dunlap to sit next to the Chief.

"What can I help you with?" Roberts asked, slicing into his fried steak.

Jeffers leaned in, "Has there been increased traffic out towards Northern State over the last few months?"

The Police Chief frowned, "No, not that I am aware of. Why do you ask?"

"Agent Dunlap, in his surveillance of the property lines, noticed a number of vehicle tracks down by the tunnel area," Jeffers said.

"That place gets its share of looky-loos but I can't say I'm privy to any increase in such activity," Roberts shook his head.

"The tracks are more consistent with a heavy vehicle with highway treads," Dunlap described. "The same type typically seen on delivery vehicles."

The chief put his biscuit down, "Delivery vehicles...now why would anyone make a deliver out there? Did you see any evidence of deliveries? Boxes, manifests, new items perhaps?"

"Well, no," Jeffers admitted. "That is all part of the mystery. There certainly seems to be traffic to that location, both foot and vehicular, but no evidence of what is going on, or where precisely in the hospital they have been going."

"Quite the confounding conundrum," the officer said.

"Maybe search your records for traffic stops out that way? Local companies that have deliveries with commercial vehicles?" Jeffers suggested.

"Sure, sure. Happy to oblige," Chief Roberts smiled, holding his coveted biscuit high in the air. "You sure you two don't want to stay for a bite? Best food for nearly a hundred miles."

"No, thank you. Just let us know what you find," Jeffers said and rose from his seat.

Chief Roberts grunted through a mouthful of food as the FBI agents headed for the exit. Wiping his mouth with a napkin, he called, "One thing that has come up, I'm not sure how it fits with the investigation, but we have seen an increase in missing persons reports from Seattle area colleges."

"You think more attacks?" Dunlap asked.

"Hard to say," the chief shrugged. "I surely haven't seen anything like what happened up at Northern State or anywhere else. No bodies mauled. Just kids going AWOL from school."

Jeffers thanked him, "Likely no relation, but better to have known all the possibilities."

As they hit the sidewalk, Dunlap cocked his head, "Think there's a connection there?"

"I can't see how. There's no indication those students came up this direction. As the chief said, no bodies discovered never mind matching the ones at the asylum. Probably nothing," Jeffers scoffed.

Dan Tannen and Agent Danica Sohn rapped gently on the frame of the door. It wasn't long before a woman draped in a cardigan, carrying a fistful of tissues arrived at the door and waved them in.

"Thank you, Mrs. Whitman," Agent Sohn said as she followed the woman into her living room.

Sitting in a rough circle on a mix of living room furniture and dining room chairs, several pairs of parents greeted them. Mrs. Whitman sat next to a man who put his arm around her.

"First, let me say, there are no words to express the sorrow for your loss, the pain of worry you all must feel. We are grateful for the time for you to answer questions, I know it must not be easy for any of you," Sohn shared with the group.

Mr. Whitman took over for his wife, who buried her head in the pile of tissues she carried. "That's the Lunds…Michael's family. That is the Joneses, Eric's family and the Stolts, Willy's family."

"Thank you all for being here," Agent Sohn nodded. "I am Agent Danica Sohn. This is Dan Tannen, a medic and consultant for the FBI on this case. Like you, I'm sure, we want to get to the bottom of what happened and ensure it doesn't happen to any other kids."

"We warned them for years to stay away from that place!" Mr. Stolt growled, the other parents nodding in unison.

"Old buildings can be dangerous…" Sohn nodded.

"It's not the building, it's the inhabitants of the building!" Mrs. Lund's eyes grew wide. "Demons!"

"Demons?" Agent Sohn cocked her head.

"Demons," Mrs. Lund nodded. "That place, a century full of pain, is a portal. And those wicked devil worshippers conger beasts that escaped the portal. That is what took our Michael away from us."

"Now, Molly, we've talked about that," Mr. Lund scowled. Turning to Agent Sohn and Tannen, he forced a half-smile. "We don't know they're demons. Ghosts or poltergeists…"

"Enough, you two! It wasn't ghosts or goblins. It was wolves. Ranchers warned about letting them back onto our lands," Mr. Stolt spoke up.

"Wolves don't normally attack people," Tannen refuted.

"Bears then!" Mrs. Stolt spat.

"Have you had a problem with bears attacking people in this region?" Agent Sohn asked.

"Well, no. It was just a matter of time," Mrs. Stolt said.

"Transients, I say! Sarah said it was people. Not wolves, not bears. People," Mrs. Whitman said.

"We get hitchhikers here all time," Mr. Whitman nodded.

"Are you aware of any other cases of anything like this happening in Skagit County, whether at the hospital or not?" Agent Sohn pressed.

The families scanned each other and each shrugged.

"Any other missing people or odd injuries?" Agent Sohn asked.

The parents looked pensive until Mr. Lund snapped his fingers, "I have a friend down in Mount Vernon. His kid went missing. Older boy, college age, I think. At first they thought he was partying in Tijuana or something."

"What about siblings, have any of them provided any insight?" Sohn asked.

"Just that the buzz around school was there are zombies. One even said to have seen one," Mr. Whitman said.

"Zombies," Sohn nodded, unimpressed with the response.

Tannen leaned forward, "Do you know which student saw the zombie?"

Mr. Whitman frowned, "Not off-hand. I'll ask and find out for you if you think it might be helpful."

Mrs. Whitman glanced at her watch, "Visiting hours at the hospital will be over soon. You wanted to see Sarah. This will be your chance."

"Give her our best," Mrs. Lund said as everyone rose to leave, offering a chorus of nods and yeses.

Mrs. Stolt and Mr. Stolt, stopped Agent Sohn and Tannen on their way out. From quivering lips, they impassioned, "You find our Willy!"

Sohn put a hand on Mrs. Stolt's arm, "We will do everything we can."

Sarah Whitman sat motionless on her bed, knees curled to her chest. Staring out of her hospital room window, she did not acknowledge the guests as they walked in. Mrs. Whitman put her arm around her daughter while Mr. Whitman stood idly by, clearly frustrated knowing there was nothing he could do to help his daughter.

"She's been like this since she was admitted," Mr. Whitman explained. "I wouldn't expect much from her, but you're welcome to try."

"Honey, these investigators are here to help you and your friends. They need to ask you a few questions," Mrs. Whitman cooed in her daughter's ear. Shrugging, she turned to Agent Sohn.

"Sarah, my name is Agent Sohn. I am with the FBI. With me is Dan Tannen. He is a medical professional who helps to understand strange things," the agent began. "We have a few questions. Your description of the…attackers. You are sure they were people? Did they come from *inside* the building?"

Sarah remained unmoved, her unblinking eyes fixated on the forest outside of her window.

Tannen tried a different tact, "Sarah. My team and I, we work cases others won't believe. We go where others won't go. We investigate what others won't investigate. I will believe you. My team will get to the bottom of it. We might be able to save Willy."

Moments ticked by and Sarah's breathing barely changed tempo never mind issued any physical or verbal response.

"I'm sorry, I don't know what else we can do. The doctors are looking to move her to psychiatric hospital in Seattle as soon a bed opens up," Mr. Whitman announced.

"Sweetie, we love you. Dad and I are going to walk the investigators out," Mrs. Whitman said softly to her daughter and rose from the bed.

As they turned to leave, Agent Danica Sohn had just taken a step away when Sarah lashed out, grasping Danica by the arm. She stared directly into the agent's eyes, her own twitching as she began to speak.

"Don't go inside!" she rasped.

"The asylum?" Agent Sohn asked.

"Dead. All dead!" Sarah insisted.

"Michael and Eric, I'm sorry," Danica nodded.

"Willy. The got him. They took him. He was all blood," Sarah exclaimed.

"Who? Who took him, Sarah?" Agent Sohn bristled.

"Zombies!" Sarah sobbed.

"Zombies again," Mr. Whitman scoffed.

"From inside the asylum," Agent Sohn pressed.

Sarah's eyes widened, fear clearly drenching the girl, she nodded.

"We'll find them. We'll make sure you are safe," Agent Sohn assured.

Sarah immediately snapped back into her listless pose in front of the window as if a switch had been turned off.

Chase and Wally pulled up outside of the Sedro-Woolley Ranger Station. The gateway to the North Cascades National Park, the station was a place to buy books, maps and note weather conditions and animal sightings throughout the region.

A bubbly woman greeted them as they pushed into the building. Giving the men a once over, she raised an eyebrow, "You're not exactly outfitted for a back-country adventure. What brings you in today?"

Wally started to speak but his words twisted as he was clearly taken by the vivacious young lady.

"We are to visit with Wildlife Officer…Raines?" Chase stated.

"You're here to see Adam," the woman said thoughtfully. Looking up, she stepped away from the men and flashed a wide smile at a man leaving. He cast a quick wave as she watched him exit. "Bye, Sean!"

The woman stood for a moment, staring at the closed door before snapping back into her conversation. "I'm sorry…right. Officer Adam Raines. Follow me."

Wally and Chase exchanged glances, as the woman turned, Chase delivered an elbow to Wally's ribs and cast a disapproving glance. Wally shrugged and grinned sheepishly.

Leading the men to a slightly disheveled office, the woman rapped on the door. "Adam, two men are here to see you."

"Me?" the burly man stood up from his desk.

To Chase, the man was the depiction of Paul Bunyan. Tall, muscular, red hair and beard. His jovial nature and booming voice only added to the persona.

"I am Dr. Ryder Chase from the University of Virginia. This is my associate, Wally Smyth. We are assisting the FBI with an investigation," Chase announced themselves.

The wildlife officer extended a sturdy hand, "Adam Raines. Please, have a seat. You want some coffee or something?"

Chase shook his head despite Wally reaching out to place his order.

Raines looked up, "Thank you, Paige."

The woman lingered for a moment before she was waved off by the wildlife officer.

"FBI, huh? Let me guess, Northern State Hospital," the officer suggested.

Chase nodded, "Yes. We are reviewing all possibilities in the cause of the tragedy."

"If you're in my office, it means one of two things…could an animal possibly have done or is someone in my park causing harm to people," the ranger said.

"That's right," Chase agreed. "The coroner's report is…conflicting."

"Conflicting? How so?" the ranger leaned in.

"The attack was very much in the manner of an animal attack. Scratches, biting, tearing at flesh," Chase said.

"No knife, machete…garden tool involved?"

Chase shook his head, "No."

"Leans towards animal," the wildlife officer said. "As I told Chief Roberts, the wilderness right outside the door of the old hospital has black and brown bear, mountain lions, bobcats, wolves…they all have the ability to levy such an attack but from what I saw, it isn't in any of their nature to attack in that manner."

"What about rabies, distemper or some zoonotic disease?" Wally suggested.

Raines wrinkled his nose, "Possible, but unlikely. Sure, it has some characteristics, but the one witness report and the scene had no signs of animal prints with the size that could carry out such an attack. There was no fur in the fence, no animal saliva on or around the victims' wounds, according to Lazenby."

Chase nodded, "The evidence and the eyewitness reports suggest that the attacks very well may have been human."

"Well, I'm not gonna mince words. We've had our share of criminal activities in the North Cascades over the years. Based on my money, that is where I would concentrate the investigation," the wildlife officer said.

"Any other reports like this throughout the region you cover?" Chase pressed.

Raines shook his head, "Not that my office has received. I can't say without question that somewhere in the over five hundred thousand acres that there hasn't been an incident that we haven't discovered. If it was North Cascades focused, the puzzling thing for me, is why an event so close to town?"

"Something about the asylum that drew people there," Wally suggested.

The federal officer leaned back and studied Wally for a moment. Shrugging, he waved his hand, "Maybe. Maybe."

The team assembled outside of a small shopping center. A coffee shop would serve as their headquarters for recapping their interview sessions. As they headed into the shop, with the sound of a burr grinder growling in the background, they nearly ran into a man deeply focused on the treasure he carried in his arms.

"Oh, hi guys!" Dr. Lazenby looked up. He was still wearing his lab coat streaked with reddish-brown smears. To their horror, the coroner had a matching glob staining the corner of his mouth.

His eyes widened as he detected the splotch and using his tongue, he swept up the reddish bit and nodded.

The team froze and stared at the man.

"Oh, I'm a big fan of BBQ," Lazenby grinned. Holding a box close to his chest, he wiped his hand down the front of his smock, leaving a trail of afternoon snack in its wake. Extending his hand for the others to shake, they politely refused.

Nodding, he smiled knowingly, "I get it. If you're going to grab some, bring enough to share, right?" Digging in the box, he pulled out a large bone.

Again, the team waved him off until to their disgust, Wally stepped up, "Love some!" Grabbing the bone, Wally inspected it as though it were a fine Cuban cigar and proceeded to dig his teeth into.

"There you go," Lazenby admired. "Another B-B-Q aficionado. Excellent."

Wally raised his half gnawed on bone in appreciation.

Lazenby snapped his fingers, "That reminds me. I noticed an anomaly on the bite imprint in one of the victim's bones. Canines mixed with grinding molars in a continuous arch – it was definitely human...or something closer to human than any animal found in the North Cascades, though wild pigs have a surprising similarity and certain species of orangutan..."

Jeffers leaped at the plausible explanation, "Are there wild pigs here?"

Lazenby looked up curiously, "No. Why do you ask?"

The team exchanged incredulous looks, other than Jeffers who was peeved.

The nature of Jeffers question dawned on the coroner, "There have a been rare reports of feral Russian hogs elsewhere in the state. But not in this region."

"If you think of anything else, doctor," Agent Sohn said and encouraged the team into the coffee shop before her lead agent had a coronary event.

"Sure will. Hey, if you're up for lunch tomorrow...," Lazenby started.

Jeffers' affect was grim, "We'll call you."

Wally raised his rib in a goodbye.

As they walked into the coffee shop, breezing by a trash can, the lead agent swatted Wally's wrist, flinging the gnawed bone cleanly into the receptacle. "Wash yourself up," Jeffers glared.

"I'll get your coffee," Chase nodded and encouraged his investigator to comply.

Gathering around the table, the team sipped on their coffee and tea drinks while pouring over notepads.

"The trip to visit the North Cascades Park wildlife officer suggested some serious doubt that any animal, even the predators in this region are to blame for the attacks on the teenagers," Chase declared.

"That and Lazenby's description of the teeth further points away from an animal encounter," Agent Sohn added.

"Sarah as the only eyewitness simply refers to the attackers as zombies or wild people," Tannen reluctantly shared.

"Human/animal analog, we have to think...sasquatch," Wally offered.

"The witness clearly stated 'zombie'," Tannen asserted.

"Which is definitively more humanoid," Agent Dunlap nodded in earnest.

Jeffers twisted in his seat and grimaced, "Are we really having a debate of Bigfoot versus zombie?"

"You're right," Agent Sohn supported. She was tightlipped as she knew she was about to push the lead agent over the edge, "I'd have to lean zombie."

"Enough!" Jeffers exploded. "I'll go zombie-like. What's zombie like? Meth heads. That's what we're dealing with."

"No signs of human activity consistent with a meth addicts," Dunlap countered.

"They're like nomads. They had their fun and they moved on," Jeffers reasoned.

"Maybe," Chase shrugged. "But something is off out there."

"What? We're back to ghosts now? Why exactly have you been using your ghost hunting equipment, anyway?" Jeffers snapped.

"The reported instances that make the building seem haunted might be explainable by some other entity or analog activity," Chase said.

"A living one," Jeffers pressed.

"Formerly living?" Dunlap added. "You know, zombie…"

Jeffers look shut him down.

"Let's focus on what we know and can forensically determine," Chase suggested. "We have another nighttime investigation planned. We have a bit of a narrower lens to look through, which is good. We can revisit a few scenarios from last night to further debunk and investigate a few areas we didn't get to last night."

Jeffers sighed. Rubbing his face, he nodded, "Let's go."

TWELVE

Set up for the night investigation was easy as many pieces of their surveillance puzzle were already in place. Wally took care under Agent Sohn's guidance to add a camera to the patient room filled with storage that she thought to have felt the breath.

Placing another device, the agent cast Wally a curious glance. "This will detect heat signature changes in the room. If something warm-blooded comes in here, we should know. It will send an alert to the command center," the tech advised.

"You boys and your toys," Agent Sohn shook her head as they made their way back to the team.

As night descended, Jeffers placed the teams once again in pairs, "Agent Sohn, you've got the professor and are on the interior sweep. Agent Dunlap, you and Wally have the perimeter. I'll man the monitors with Tannen."

Wally double checked his flashlight and back up flashlight. Looking towards Tannen, he said, "Make sure the perimeter IR alarms are on. We'll note if we cross the beams."

Tannen hit a button on one of the computers in front of him, "Good to go."

"Let's do this," Wally said. Eyeing the junior agent's nine-millimeter agency issued handgun, "That thing good against bears? Just asking."

Jeffers laughed, "A nine? No. I did pick this up from the ranger station, though." The lead agent tossed the paranormal researcher a can of bear spray. "Nozzle out and mind the wind."

Dunlap glanced at the can, "Maybe I should carry that?"

Wally grinned, "Do I get your gun?"

Dunlap glared, "Just make sure you point that in the right direction if you need to use it."

"Where are we off to, professor?" Agent Sohn asked.

"The three areas of hotspots involve the tunnel, the attic and the surgery room. I'd suggest we concentrate our investigation in those three areas," Chase suggested.

"Let's go," Agent Sohn beamed.

The pair had barely entered the dark hallway of the inner security doors when their radios came to life. "Uhm, guys," Tannen's voice called to them. "We have a hit in the patient room Agent Sohn and I were in last night. There is a light disturbance on the monitor."

"Light disturbance? What kind of light disturbance?" Chase asked.

"Not quite a full shadow, but a darkening. I just switched to audio, I can detect rustling and what sounds like…breathing," Tannen announced. "There goes a temperature spike, there is *something* in that room!"

"Agent Sohn you have lead, back up on standby," Jeffers broke into the radio call.

"Copy that, Dr. Chase and I are on our way," Agent Sohn replied, casting Chase a wary tilt of her head.

Moving as quickly as they could without creating excessive noise, they jogged through the halls, up the stairs and leaned against the wall just outside of the patient room. Agent Sohn readied her firearm with her flashlight. With a nod, she rounded the doorway and burst into the room. Chase followed closely, his flashlight making a methodical sweep of the room. His body camera capturing the scene from his perspective.

Both investigators panned the room carefully. "I don't understand it. There was visual, audio and thermogenic evidence of someone or something being in that room," Tannen said over the radio as the search came up empty.

"Any chance they escaped down the hallway while we were en route?" Sohn asked.

"Negative. I had eyes on the hallway. Tannen pulled the room camera and the hall camera up on adjacent screens," Jeffers reported. "The room is empty? Check the boxes?"

Agent Sohn and Chase shrugged at one another and began moving smaller boxes out of the way to reach larger containers that might hide something human sized. Once again coming up empty, they retreated to the command center. "I want to see this evidence for myself," Agent Sohn said.

Leaning over the chairs of Dan Tannen and Agent Jeffers, Agent Sohn and Professor Chase studied the monitors. Running the replay Tannen had time-stamped, a dark mass appeared behind one of the shelves.

"You can see it through the gap between boxes and shelving. A mass, roughly five or six feet high, appears. Stays for a few moments and then suddenly slips away right before you two enter the frame," Tannen says.

"You said you heard breathing?" Sohn asked. Tannen nodded and had her don a pair of headphones. What she heard sent a chill down her spine. Removing the headphones, she looked at the team. "That is what I heard last night. I can feel the breath on my neck," she shuddered.

Jeffers studied the monitors quietly, a frown saturating his face. "We need to tear that room apart," he announced. "I don't want to separate the pairings though."

The lead agent recalled Dunlap and Wally from their perimeter duty.

"Copy that, we're coming towards the front lobby," Dunlap announced. Moments later, their movement tripped the perimeter alarms.

Tannen reset the alarm on the computer as Jeffers sent Agent Sohn to open the front door and let the exterior team in.

Suddenly, the perimeter alarm sounded again. The screen dedicated to the system blinked on the rear of the hospital. Tannen frowned, and Chase and Jeffers spun to look at the screen. "That them again?" Jeffers asked.

"Not unless they can be in two places at once," Tannen said, resetting the monitor and pulling up the nearest camera on one of the main monitors.

"There," Jeffers nearly screamed, "I saw something move from east to west across that camera."

All eyes focused on that screen. Multiple shadows formed and streaked past the camera. "What the...," Jeffers started. "Where does that direction head?"

"From the path that leads to the tunnel to one of the rear doors," Tannen said.

"Professor, you're with me," Jeffers said. As Agent Sohn returned with Dunlap and Wally in tow, he added, "Agent Sohn, come with us. Agent Dunlap, keep these two locked down in the room. You three are our eyes. Let's go!"

Jeffers pushed ahead with Agent Sohn and Professor Chase following close behind. Both FBI agents had their handguns drawn, unsure of what they would face. "Chase, whatever happens, you stay behind us!" the lead agent commanded.

Circling the hospital towards the camera that caught the movement and the side of the asylum where something tripped the alarm, they pressed their backs against the side of the building. The sound of a branch breaking in the distance followed by what sounded like a shriek snapped them into action.

Their lights did their best to cut through the dark of night. The shouts and shrieks stopped, but the footfalls continued until they heard a guttural "Oof!"

Breaching the line of trees closest to the hospital, their lights picked up the first of the intruders. Writhing on the ground, a forearm raised to deflect the lights shining down, the figure kicked its feet, trying desperately to create distance between them.

"Federal Agents, freeze!" Jeffers growled.

Below his feet, the forearm lowered and the face of a frightened boy stared back at the FBI agent. "Oh, thank God!" the boy gasped.

Two additional figures stepped out from nearby trees and into the light. In their hands, video cameras and a device Chase recognized instantly. "They are ghost hunters," he muttered.

Jeffers cast him a quick glance and then returned his attention to the kids in front of him. "This all of you?"

A young woman strode forward and shook her head. She wore a genuinely concerned look across her face, "No. There are six of us. We heard something following us. We got separated. We ran towards the building and the others ran down past the big patch of blackberries."

"Heading towards the crematorium, maybe," Chase suggested.

Jeffers sighed, "You two take these kids to the command center. I'm going to see if I can find the others."

"By yourself?" Chase cocked his head.

"I wouldn't do that!" the boy on the ground warned as he pushed himself to his feet and dusted himself off.

"I'll be fine," Jeffers assured. "Get them locked up safely and then help me in the search. Professor, you stay on Agent Sohn's side."

The lead agent ran down the trail without another word.

"Let's go guys," Agent Sohn prodded, waving the kids towards the hospital.

One reviewed his camera footage as he walked. "Sweet. I think I caught one of them!" he exclaimed.

Chase couldn't resist stopping and leaning into watch the small screen. The face of an unkempt being with wild eyes was just within the corner of the frame. Everything else was a blur. "We'll put that on the screen inside and see what we're dealing with," Chase suggested.

"Uhm, Ryder, can we get these kids to safety before we get too distracted?" Agent Sohn demanded.

Chase shook himself, "Yes, of course!"

"Ryder….," the young woman amateur ghost hunter mused. "Ryder…Chase! You're Dr. Ryder Chase!"

The boy next to her nodded his head, "Cool! We're with a real ghost hunter!"

"*The* ghost hunter!" the other boy exclaimed.

Chase beamed and then let his face fall flat as Agent Sohn shot him a disapproving glance.

Pushing into the building, they prodded the kids into the room serving as the investigation command center.

"We have guests," Dunlap acknowledged the group. "Where's Jeffers?"

"He went to find the other half of the amateur sleuths," Agent Sohn frowned.

"He's got some evidence on his camera I'd like you to analyze," Chase said to Wally who nodded.

"I want you to confiscate all of their cameras and recording equipment," Agent Sohn demanded.

One of the kids frowned as they were excitedly capturing the moment on their video camera. Sweeping the fleet of monitors and giving a thumbs up as he tried to shoot a selfie with Dr. Chase and the FBI agents in the background.

Dunlap reached out and snatched the camera away, turning the recording off.

"Where are you two going?" Tannen asked.

"We are going back out to support Jeffers. You guys hold the fort here and don't let any of these three out of your sight!" Agent Sohn said.

The kids circulated the room admiring the equipment Chase's team brought with them. "This is so cool!" one of them exclaimed, picking up a thermal camera that Wally quickly liberated from him.

"Dr. Ryder Chase and the FBI. So, this *is* the real deal!" the other boy nodded with a big grin.

"You three behave…and don't touch anything. Agent Dunlap, arrest them if they don't comply," Agent Sohn glared. Pulling at Chase's arm, she urged, "Come on!"

As they were once again outside of the hospital, the FBI agent called into her radio, "Jeffers, what's the sitrep?"

A few moments passed before Jeffers' voice cracked through the radio, "I'm combing through the crematorium. Looks clear. Going to push further up the trails."

"If I was on the run and got diverted from the main building, I'd head for the dairy barns," Chase suggested.

"Copy that. I'll head that way. We'll meet up where the trails connect," Agent Jeffers agreed.

Agent Sohn and Professor Chase hustled along the path. The night was only the more eerie now that genuine danger was afoot. Instead of wondering what might be around each bend, they *knew* something was out there with them. The question was, *what* was out there and where.

Reaching the intersection, they found Special Agent Jeffers scanning the paths.

"They both span around this field and end up at the dairy barns," Chase said.

"You two go right, I'll go left," Jeffers nodded and took off down his alternate path.

Chase and Sohn continued towards the barns. They could just see the cupola of one of the barns looming above the tall grass and blackberries. Their path made a direct line to the first of the barns.

Agent Sohn's hand flashed out catching Chase in the chest. Her flashlight lit upon the side of the barn. A streak of blood was smeared along the frame of the large, open doorway. Moving cautiously and methodically, they stepped towards the building, Sohn radioed in to alert Jeffers.

Commanding them to wait, they saw the lead agent's flashlight loom towards them. Seeing the blood, he nodded. The agents moved side by side with Chase close at their flank as they entered the building. A trail of blood and freshly disturbed dirt was evident on the floor of the barn.

Each agent took a side to search as they swept from the middle of the walkway to the individual stalls and debris littering the sides of the barn. They moved deliberately and quietly until Jeffers' voice broke the silence.

"I have something!" Jeffers broke from the group as Agent Sohn kept vigil. Chase monitored their flank. Jeffers was on high alert as he kneeled next to a mass on the ground. Chase could clearly see the trail of blood they followed end in a gathering pool, a smashed video camera lying beside it.

"It's one of the kids," Jeffers said, leaning in to check for a pulse. Shaking his head, he sighed, "He's dead."

They scanned the area for threats or signs of the other two kids. Jeffers called the death into the Sedro-Woolley Police. "The others shouldn't be far. We need to find them!" Jeffers urged.

Moving with earnest, they hastened their search. Moving from one long barn directly into the next, Chase called and circled with his flashlight, "I've got a shoe!"

As he studied the area, a drop of blood splattered on the ground. Swinging his light upwards, he followed the path of another descending drop. Between two boards of a catwalk that encircled the interior of each barn, he spied a wide eye staring back down at him.

"I think I have another one!" Chase said. Without awaiting instruction, he scrambled up the nearby ladder to the catwalk. Maneuvering along the planks, he reached the young man. His legs drenched in blood.

"I've got one," Chase called. "He's still alive!"

The boy shuddered, "They're here! Not ghosts!"

Chase looked at the boy, "Who's here? Who's here?"

The boy slumped unconscious. Checking for his pulse, he found it, though weak. "He's going into shock! I think I can stabilize him, go find the other one!"

Jeffers hesitated leaving the professor and the boy unprotected. Scanning the area, he found the ladder Chase descended as the only viable way up. Delivering a pair of vicious kicks, he freed the ladder from its mooring and sent it crashing to the barn floor in a shower of dust.

"We'll be right back," Jeffers called. With a nod to Agent Sohn, they continued their search.

A scream from a nearby building sent the agents running. Sprinting towards the structure, they glanced up. They saw a girl atop a silo, screaming out of a window at the top. Shining their lights in the window as they ran forward, she whisked from view as she flew backward, pulled from behind. Suddenly, her screams stopped.

Racing into the doorway, they wasted no time leaping towards the lowest rung on the ladder and began climbing to the top of the silo. As they were halfway up, a heavy mass flew through the air past them landing with a sickening thump at the bottom. Jeffers and Sohn stared at each other for just a moment.

Agent Sohn wrapped her sleeves around the sides of the ladder to protect her hands and slid down in a free-fall. Landing in a squat, she quickly drew her weapon and flashlight, panning the area before lunging towards what she feared to be the mass that fell.

Contorted atop a pile of discarded farming equipment, lay the body of a young woman. Her body torn viciously with gashes in her neck, torso, and limbs. It was a foregone step, but Agent Sohn placed her fingers against an artery just to confirm.

Jeffers continued scrambling up the ladder, reaching the top, he saw a figure leer in his direction. The FBI agent fumbled to draw his flashlight, as he found the button and swung the light towards the figure. He saw a flash of clothes and bare feet leap out of the window three stories off the ground.

Climbing onto the derelict platform at the top of the silo, Jeffers peered through the window to see the figure sliding down the side, clawing with its fingers in an attempt to slow its descent. Landing in a harsh heap at the bottom, the figure shook itself, glanced around and disappeared headlong into the nearby blackberries.

Seeing Agent Sohn appear where the figure landed, Jeffers scanned ahead from his taller vantage, but the figure vanished.

"Teenager?" he called down.

Sohn looked up and nodded sullenly, "Dead."

"I'm coming down, let's get back to Dr. Chase!" Jeffers declared.

Chase hovered over the teen as he heard Jeffers call up and the wooden ladder being leaned haphazardly into place. Agent Sohn's face suddenly appeared.

"In and out of consciousness, in a lot of pain," Chase said to the expectant agent.

"Help is on the way," she assured. "We have a trauma kit at base, I can go get it."

"I'll watch the patient, you two go together. I'm not leaving anyone on their own tonight," Jeffers demanded.

"What about you?" Agent Sohn frowned.

"I'm the lead agent. You are all my responsibility, now go," Jeffers scowled replacing Chase's place by the victim's side.

In the distance, the sounds of sirens filled the night as emergency vehicles screamed towards the hospital. In their wake, an armada of local, county and state police.

Chase and Sohn ran up the path towards the hospital and the command center where they could grab medical supplies to bridge the gap while EMS made their way to the scene. As the hospital loomed into view, a shadow lunged towards them, just within Chase's peripheral vision.

Powerful arms tackled him to the ground. Agent Sohn spun in time to see Chase wriggle free. As the agent's flashlight swept across the trail, the figure leaped straight into the blackberries and slipped away.

"Are you okay?" Sohn asked.

Chase nodded, "Yeah, I'm fine!" Scrambling to his feet, "Let's get to the hospital!"

Closing in on the hospital, a wild rustling in the brush alerted them just in time to see several figures racing towards them. Cutting them off from rounding the path towards the hospital's front entrance, they veered towards the rear, searching for a way in.

As footfalls closed in, Agent Sohn ran to a rear doorway. With a kick directly towards the handle, it splintered from its hold. With a yank, she tugged Chase's arm, pulling him inside. Racing down the hallway toward the security doors of the command center, the sound of persistent footsteps rattled terrifying echoes throughout the hallway.

Racing down the corridor, something lashed out at their feet, catching Agent Sohn, spilling her to the floor. With Chase directly on her heels, they both crashed to the ground. Spinning their bodies, they landed on their backs, sliding along the floor. Agent Sohn raised her gun as she slid, firing several shots directly into a sinister black mass that had loomed directly above them.

Despite a grunt, the shadow and the two trailing figures that chased them into the hospital were undaunted, closing in on Sohn and Chase. Suddenly the security doors burst open, with Dunlap standing in the doorway. Next to him, Wally shone a large work light down the hall.

Dashing into the darkened doorways of the nearby patient rooms, the figures disappeared. The sounds of their bodies hurling against the glass and shard raining on the ground below filled the night air. Scampering footfalls echoed into the night.

Agent Sohn and Ryder Chase sat up on the floor, their lights dancing along the hall, alert for additional threats, their hearts racing. After the concussion and gun smoke cleared, the hallway was hauntingly empty.

THIRTEEN

The mosaic of flashing blue and red lights made the night scape of Northern State Hospital only more surreal. The added presence of the medics, local, county and state police did offer a sense of comfort as the investigation team collected themselves.

The priority of rescuing the boy in the dairy barn and ensuring the teen amateur ghost hunters that survived the night, got to safety kept them focused. Those that weren't as fortunate and the health of the team themselves became the next emphasis as the ambulances were loaded and headed for town.

"Are you okay?" Sohn asked Dr. Chase.

"A few bumps and bruises, I'm fine," Chase reported. "You?"

Agent Sohn grinned, "Physically? I'm fine. Mentally, I don't know what to think."

"Horrific scene out there," Chase said softly.

Agent Sohn could just nod as she tried to compartmentalize the images of the mauled teenagers so that she could do her job and bring their assailants to justice, whatever they were.

Jeffers had corralled the responders from the various police departments and assigned four-man teams to lock down the scenes allowing proper forensics to be conducted. The dairy barns and silo had priority while the hospital was secondary.

Police Chief Roberts had a city maintenance worker repair the door that Agent Sohn broke through to eliminate a gaping hole in what appeared in the building's armor. He remained on standby to assess the first-floor windows as the FBI team investigated the hall where Sohn and the professor were chased.

Jeffers beckoned Agent Sohn to lead him to the location that she fired her shots. Chase rose to join them, but Jeffers waved him off. "Oh, no. This is all police work at this point," he stated.

"According to Deputy Director Witt, I am part of the FBI team," Chase countered. "And I am a material witness."

Jeffers hesitated only for a moment, "Fine!" Glancing at Wally and Tannen, and then at Police Chief Roberts, "These guys are on lockdown."

The police chief nodded.

With two fingers, the lead investigator waved for Agent Dunlap to follow. "You two were attacked somewhere along the path from the dairy farm to the hospital," Jeffers said.

Chase nodded, "Figure leaped straight out of the blackberries, tackled me and took off in the brush on the opposite side of the path."

"I swung my flashlight and it took off," Sohn nodded.

"And, what was it?" Jeffers asked as they made their way to the hallway.

Sohn hesitated for a moment, "It was human, but not exactly. I mean, I only caught a glimpse."

Jeffers stopped and looked at Agent Sohn squarely, "What do you mean...not exactly?"

"It *was* a person. It just didn't act human. More animalistic. The way it looked up at me. But like I said, it was a just a glimpse," Agent Sohn reported. "After what I saw in the barn and the silo, nothing would look normal at that point."

"You ran towards the hospital…," Agent Jeffers prodded.

"We ran up the path and then a group of figures came from the shadows. They cut us off from heading to the lobby entrance, so we ran to the nearest entry point in the building's rear. It was difficult to identify the threat. I didn't want to engage unless I had to. Keeping Dr. Chase safe was imperative," Sohn continued. "I breached entry. They continued to follow. Something tripped me in the hallway, right around this doorway. We both fell, I spun, I targeted an imminent threat and fired my weapon twice center mass."

"And then what?" Jeffers pushed.

"Whatever…whoever…was chasing us continued to move in when Dunlap opened the security doors and provided additional support," Agent Sohn reported.

Jeffers cocked his head and frowned, "The threat continued after you shot? You mean the other assailants?"

Agent Sohn hesitated to answer, "*All* of the assailants. I was about to fire again when they jumped into the nearby rooms and exited through the windows."

Jeffers shone his light into each opposing room. Windows were smashed from the inside out. "They just dove through the closed windows," he studied the shattered glass and splintered wood frames.

"That's the way it seems," Sohn nodded.

The FBI agents noticed Dr. Chase detached from the conversation. Bent on the floor of one of the open patient rooms, he moved his flashlight around. Looking up at the investigators, he said, "The dust is disturbed here as though someone was lying prone. Someone reached out and tripped us."

"They were slowing you down so the ones chasing you could catch you," Dunlap observed.

Jeffers turned his head towards Dunlap, "What did you see?"

"Not much, really. I heard the shots and ran to assess the scene. Not knowing the situation, I was locating threats and identifying Agent Sohn and Dr. Chase in danger. Whatever was closing in on them paused for just a second when they saw me. Before I could identify them, they just vanished. As Special Agent Sohn said, they spilled off into opposing rooms and disappeared," Dunlap reported. "I heard the windows crash, and they were gone."

Jeffers considered what he had just heard and walked down the hall, replaying the scenario in his head. Turning to Agent Sohn, he asked, "Where exactly were you when you fired your weapon?"

Danica Sohn walked a few steps, placed herself to the best of her recollection in position and pointed, "Right about here."

Waving his hand at the floor, the lead agent commanded, "In the position you were, if you will, Agent Sohn."

Sohn kneeled to the floor and did her best to emulate the position she was in when she fired her weapon at their pursuers. Holding her hands up, she froze.

Jeffers walked around her. Following the line from her trigger finger, his eyes traveled an imaginary line through the air. Walking several paces, he ran his flashlight along the ceiling. Jeffers looked back to ensure he had captured the right line. He announced, "You must have hit them. Otherwise, I'd find your bullets right about…here."

Agent Sohn looked surprised, "I had a clear shot. But there was no indication I had hit the subject."

Jeffers mused, "I've had cases with meth heads shot multiple times, especially with a nine mill and they just keep coming. One reason I carry a forty."

"I suppose that could be the case," Agent Sohn nodded. Scanning the floor, she scowled, "There should still be blood."

Once more, Dr. Chase seemed to wander off. Jeffers looked up, "Uh, professor. If you will, I'd kind of like to keep the team together."

"Camera," Chase swiveled his head toward the FBI agent. "We had this hallway on surveillance."

Jeffers looked oddly pleased, "Good work, professor. Let's check out that tape."

The team gathered around the command center monitors as Wally brought the footage from the hallway up on one of the larger screens. The infrared camera strained to capture the scene until the chase reached a third of the way into the hallway.

The faces of Agent Sohn and Dr. Chase came into view as they raced down the hall. It was evident that masses were in pursuit but remained unidentifiable shapes until the investigators fell to the ground. The camera picked up three human figures closing in on them.

Agent Sohn's pair of gun blasts brightened the screen to the point the image was a bright cloud. As the lighting adjusted, the figures were steps away from Sohn and Chase's positions on the ground. As light from behind the camera panned the hallway, the figures paused, look towards the source and dove for the doorways nearest them.

"They look human to me," Jeffers muttered.

Tannen scrunched his face, "Something about their faces…it's off."

"Meth," Jeffers acknowledged.

"Maybe," Tannen shrugged.

"Play it back in slow motion and focus the display on this doorway," Chase instructed.

Wally nodded and cycled the video footage to where Agent Sohn and Chase were just visible.

"Stop!" Chase instructed.

Wally froze the playback.

Pointing, Chase circled his finger around the lower section of the doorway. "There's a hand."

"That's what tripped me," Sohn nodded.

"A human hand. Not a ghost, not sasquatch…a human hand," Agent Jeffers stressed.

"Or zombie," Wally pursed his lips. Looking up at the grimacing lead agent, the tech pressed, "Still could be zombie."

"Keep running it," Agent Sohn instructed.

Wally hit the play button advancing the video. As they watched the scene play out again and the figures were as present on camera as they were going to be, the agent had him pause the video.

"What is that one wearing?" she frowned.

The crew squinted and studied the image.

"Looks like a dress," Tannen frowned.

"It looks like a trench coat, to me," Wally suggested.

"Hard to say," Chase admitted. "Definitely flows oddly as the figure moves."

"I'm less interested in what it is wearing versus where it disappeared to," Jeffers said. "We have a major crime scene to investigate and a manhunt to get underway."

The vast campus was locked down. Roads in and out of Northern State were blocked by Skagit County deputies. Washington State Police forensics teams worked under the direction of Special Agent Jeffers.

The entire hospital was swept as were the outbuildings and trails. What meager evidence they could find, traces of blood and tissue, mostly from the hospital window glass fragments, were sent to the FBI's lab in Quantico for analysis. Fingernails and tissue were pulled from the siding of the silo. It appeared as if one of the attackers tried to slow their descent by clawing into the aged wood as they fell to the ground.

The bodies of the deceased teenagers were taken to the medical examiner's office where an FBI expert was being flown in to assist with the autopsies.

As the sun rose, the long night finally overcome by daylight, the biggest mystery remained. Where had the assailants disappeared to and how?

Jeffers gathered his team after providing specific instructions to the state police commander on site to keep all civilians and all reporters away from the scene. Studying the weary investigators, he suggested, "We're all beat. Let's get a few hours of rest and see what we can make of things with fresh eyes."

With complete lack of argument, the team headed to town. Leaving the horrors of the evening and the mysteries of Northern State Hospital behind them.

FOURTEEN

Exhaustion allowed the team to actually capture a few hours of sleep. Physical weariness allowed their perpetually spinning minds to silence themselves enough that they could enter the day with some degree of clarity.

Meeting in the local coffee shop for what would be the first of many injections of caffeine, they caught up on early morning analysis and laid out a plan for the day.

Special Agent Jeffers looked very serious as he addressed the team. Looking specifically at Dr. Chase and his pair of paranormal researchers, he asserted, "I think it would be best if we take the rest of the investigation from here. This is getting really dangerous and frankly, worrying about you and your team puts my agents in danger."

Dr. Chase and his team's jaws fell as they stammered for words. Chase finally spoke for his group, "Special Agent Jeffers, we understand the risk and adding to the peril of your agents is certainly not something we would want to enhance, but there is something going on out there that defies conventional crime."

Agent Jeffers scoffed, "The response of meth heads to some new designer strain of drug, can be unusual, sure, but you have to admit, things have spiraled to downright unsafe."

"We'll remain in the command center and only leave at your direct request and approval," Chase suggested.

"Professor, I...," Jeffers started to protest. Seeing the anticipatory looks not just on Chase and his team, but on his own agent's faces, he relented, "Fine. Strict adherence to the command center."

"Great," Chase acknowledged. "Thank you, Agent Jeffers. Any updates from forensics?"

"Samples have been sent to the FBI crime lab in Quantico. I was just about to meet the M.E. they are sending in from D.C.," Jeffers said. Again, seeing expectant faces staring back at him, he sighed, "Would you like to come with?"

Chase shot up, "I would like to hear what they find."

Stepping out of the coffee shop, the team realized how much news had spread about the previous night's attacks. A dozen news trucks and caravans of onlookers streamed into the normally quiet town.

The scene did not sit well with Special Agent Jeffers. As the team piled into their vehicles, he was on the phone with the state police demanding they keep the chaos at bay of the investigation.

"Uhm, it looks like word of last night is going viral," Wally said as he scanned through his social media accounts.

"Just what we need, this freakshow opening up to an audience," Jeffers grumbled as he pulled in front of the coroner's office.

Knocking on the door, the lead FBI agent waited impatiently. The sound of laughter greeted him as the slits in the blinds covering the door parted and Dr. Lazenby's fingers were joined by his wildly peering eyeball. Suddenly the slats were closed and the door flung open.

Lazenby smiled as he greeted the team, "Come in, come in. I was just about to order some *malasadas*. The Hawaiian joint down the street makes them, they're delicious. Dip them in their homemade raspberry and huckleberry preserve, they are little balls of heaven," the Medical Examiner licked his finger to emphasize the pastry's delectability.

The smock caked with human blood made the team queasy. Other than Wally who brightened on the prospect of the snack, "I'm in!"

Jeffers shot a disapproving look that he knew would be to no avail. An elderly man behind Lazenby caught Jeffers' attention. The man was familiar. As he pushed forward and extended his hand, Jeffers paused eyeing the man's equally tainted lab coat.

Wincing, he realized why the man was so familiar, "Dr. Burbee. You're the M.E. Quantico sent. I'll have to thank Deputy Director Witt."

The man smiled, "He told me directly, if there was anyone you could use on a case such as this, I was the one. Took that as quite the highest compliment."

"As I am sure it was intended," Jeffers gritted his teeth.

The man dropped his unrequited handshake and pushed past the lead agent. "*This*, must be Dr. Ryder Chase and his team. Big fan!"

In lieu of a handshake, Chase offered a friendly wave, keeping his hand close to his chest to not encourage contact.

"That case you did on Saint Augustine Lighthouse…brilliant! As incontrovertible proof of the paranormal as I have ever seen!" Dr. Burbee beamed.

"Unfortunately, as you well know, Dr. Burbee, this case has a rather tragic element to it," Dr. Chase said, his tone dead serious.

The man snapped his fingers, "Right you are, professor. Let's take you in to see our preliminary findings. Dr. Lazenby is as competent a professional as I have ever worked with in a lab."

"I'll be right behind you," Lazenby held his phone up, "On hold for the *Malasadas!*"

"Indeed, good sir! I'll hold your place," Dr. Burbee acknowledged and led the team into the morgue.

The team shot each other looks as the two M.E.s carried such a peculiar affinity with one another.

Dr. Burbee looked over his shoulder, "Quite the unusual case. I have only seen this a dozen or so times in my career."

Agent Sohn was taken aback, "You have seen cases like this a dozen times?"

"Well," the medical examiner frowned, "This is the first time in the United States."

The team collectively shook their heads.

"I have seen cases from Papua, New Guinea, Liberia and the Congo over my decades in practice," Dr. Burbee informed the group. "It does, sadly, make me the foremost expert in the auspices of the FBI on these matters."

Rallying the team around the first exam table, the young man's body recovered from the previous evening's scene laid out on the table. The condition of the teen was worse than the investigators remembered.

"We took flesh samples out. You can see them over there, hanging on the examination rack for digital photos. Here, we see the poor victim was gnawed to the bone. Teeth marks left indentions here, here and here. The indication from the bite marks combined with the outer flesh is a near definitive clue. This was caused by a human or a humanlike entity," Dr. Burbee exclaimed.

As Dr. Lazenby entered the room, Burbee added, "Supporting what our esteemed colleague Dr. Lazenby claimed from the original victims. You have humans or some sort of human analogues killing young people by attacking them. Bludgeoning them, slashing at them with poorly defined claws and ripping apart their flesh, veins and arteries with teeth consistent with the anatomy of a human."

"Well said, well delivered, Dr. Burbee," Lazenby beamed.

"Why, thank you, sir. It is indeed a pleasure to work alongside you," Burbee glowed.

"So, humans did this," Jeffers said flatly.

"Yes!" Burbee and Lazenby declared together.

"Any clues to who the humans might be?" Jeffers asked.

"We may get some hits on dental profiles, but the D.N.A. sent to the lab in Quantico is your best bet for actual identification," Burbee said.

"Is there anything else you can provide right now?" Jeffers asked.

Burbee and Lazenby looked at each other and replied in unison, "*Malasadas* will be here soon!"

As excited as Wally was at the prospect of the fried treats, Jeffers was not nearly as impressed. With a warily raised brow and questioning tone, he said, "Thank you, doctors. Please let us know if you find anything else that will indicate the who or why in this case."

With a simple nod, the lead FBI agent beckoned the team out of the room. Wally hesitated. He looked at the pair of medical examiners and then at the investigation team spilling out of the room. Dejected the Hawaiian pastries would not be in his future, he sullenly followed his team.

As they reached their vehicles, Wally started to ask, "Can we…?"

"No!" Jeffers snapped, knowing the tech was angling for a trip to the Hawaiian café.

The FBI agents cut a path through the swath of reporters, each refusing to make eye contact. The less trained paranormal team exchanged glances and smiles. Wally winked at an especially attractive reporter who leapt at the opportunity to engage until Jeffers hand flew in front of the tech's face. Without changing gait or his visual alignment, the lead agent got the team to their vehicles without incident.

Taking off out of the parking lot, the heavy V-8 engine roaring to life, Jeffers sped to their next location, wanting to get into the building before the reporters could catch up.

The hospital parking lot and entrances were manned by Skagit County deputies. Seeing the investigation team, they were quickly waved through before halting the vehicles behind them. Ushering the team into the small hospital, the front desk directed them to the patient room for the teenager they found alive in the dairy barn.

Approaching the room, Jeffers gently knocked on the door frame. A man and woman who had been sitting at the patient's side jumped up and met them at the door. Jeffers introduced the team.

"You're the ones that saved him!" the woman said, tears welling in her eyes.

"We did what we could, ma'am," Jeffers nodded.

"Thank you," the woman wiped the tears from her face.

"How is your son doing?" Agent Sohn asked.

The father collected himself, "He's stable. The doctors were most concerned about loss of blood and shock, then it was concern about infections and damage to…well, just about everything. They plan to move him tomorrow to a hospital in Seattle if his vitals improve."

Agent Jeffers looked anxious, bobbing his head to peer into the room, "May we speak with him?"

"Marty has been in and out of coherence. He is heavily sedated and sleeping right now," the woman answered through pursed lips.

"Did he say anything about what happened while he was awake?" Agent Sohn asked.

The husband and wife exchanged glances before the husband replied, "He awoke in a start. Almost screaming, breathing heavily, muttering something about monsters."

"Zombies, I think, dear," the mother corrected.

The father nodded, "Probably both at some point. And then, of course, he wanted to know about his friends. I didn't have the heart to tell him about Ben and Roxy. They have all been friends for so long."

"I can't...I can't believe they are gone," the mother sobbed.

The father looked grim, "It could have been Marty. Likely would have if it weren't for you."

Jeffers handed the parents a card with his contact information on it. "If he says anything else, what exactly he saw, how many they were there, any descriptions, it would be most helpful," the lead agent stated.

Agent Sohn leaned in, a hand on the mother's arm, "We wish him a fast recovery."

The parents nodded and the investigation team pushed down the hall. Skagit County Sheriff Watts was waiting for them outside a door where he had a pair of deputies monitoring.

"Figured you might want to have a conversation with them before they are sent home with their parents," the Sheriff said.

"Thank you, Sheriff Watts," Jeffers acknowledged. "Agent Sohn and Dr. Chase, you two come in with me, the rest of you, collect whatever statements the Sheriff's department and Sedro-Woolley police have gathered so far."

With a flick of the handle, Jeffers burst into the room and strode with purpose to the table the three teenagers sat behind. Agent Sohn and Ryder Chase filed in beside him.

Jeffers stared at the three weary teens for a long minute before speaking. "Have any of you applied a trauma kit to anyone? Desperate to stop the bleeding, hunting inside of their bodies with your fingers to ensure arteries aren't severed and tying them together once you do find them? Have you had to decide which limbs you thought might be okay to lose as you consider applying a tourniquet? That is what Dr. Chase and I had to do last night to save your friend Marty."

The lead agent allowed his works to sink in before he continued, "Have you ever had to stuff a lifeless body in a bag, looking to see if you collected all of the relevant pieces?"

The teens eyes were wide.

"We had to do that too, to….," he started.

"Ben and Roxy," Agent Sohn supplied the names from her phone notes.

"Let me know if you still think that trespassing, impeding on a federal investigation and getting involved in things that are so over your heads, I have no idea where to begin to tell you, is okay?" Jeffers scowled.

"No…no, sir," one boy stammered.

Jeffers eyed the other two who shook their heads through teary eyes.

"Good. Now that I am confident you won't do anything that stupid again, we can get down to the facts of what happened last night," Jeffers sat in a chair and leaned against the table. Pointing at the boy to the far left, he urged, "You. What's your name? You go first."

The boy collected himself, "My name is A.J. We heard activity had been heating up at the old hospital and we wanted to check it out for ourselves."

"Did you know that my team was there conducting an official investigation?" Jeffers pressed.

The boy nodded. "It kinda amped up the excitement a little. We just didn't expect…," the boys head fell.

"Expect what?" the lead agent asked.

"Those *things*," A.J. replied.

"Things?"

"I don't know. They were people, they just…they were different," A.J. said.

"Different how?" Dr. Chase leaned in.

"Their eyes, their skin, the way they moved," A.J. said.

"Like zombies!" the boy next to him spat.

Jeffers moved his focus to that boy, "Zombies?"

The boy squinted, "Well, not in the movie kind of way. They weren't all slow and stuff. They were kind of regular speed, just really angry. They ripped through the sticker bushes like they weren't there or they didn't feel any pain."

"Did they say anything?" Agent Sohn asked.

"Not really," the girl said. "They kind of grunted a bit, but really breathed heavy. Like Tommy said, they were kind of like angry animals instead of like people."

Agent Sohn cued on the girl. Glancing at her notes, "You must be Angela. How did you three happen to get away, Angela?"

"We were all together when they came after us. We hit the intersection that connected the main hospital from the crematorium and dairy barns. Half of us went one way while the other half went the other," Angela said, tears welling in her eyes as she thought of her friends.

"We got lucky because the three of us hesitated," A.J. replied. "The movement of Marty, Ben and Roxy must have, I don't know, incited their prey drive or whatever... and they entered chase mode. We slipped in the other direction a second or two later. We were just lucky."

"How did you get out there in the first place?" Dr. Chase asked.

"We parked down by the tunnel entrance below the hospital. The rough terrain makes a few spots in the fence line that are enough for us to slip through," Angela admitted.

Dr. Chase spied one of the boys nervously turning something over and over in his fingers. "Tommy, was that in your camera last night?"

The boy froze and stared at the paranormal researcher.

Jeffers slammed his down on the table, "Hand it over!"

The boy reluctantly opened his palm and the FBI agent took the data card Chase had noticed.

"Is there anything else you guys haven't given up? There are half a dozen laws you broke last night, never mind the lives of your friends lost with one hanging in the balance," Jeffers scowled. "How old are you guys? Sixteen, Seventeen…you'd probably be tried as adults."

The kids all swapped glances with one another. "Just what was posted from our live stream. It's automatically uploaded on to our site, GhostHounds2143," Angela admitted.

"You'll need to give us admin access to extract and then remove the post as it part of an ongoing federal investigation," Agent Sohn said.

"I set it up, I can give it to you," Angela nodded.

Agent Jeffers rubbed his face and sighed, "Is there anything else?"

Once more the teens studied one another. Tommy shook his head, "I don't think so."

"If you think of anything else, reach out to us immediately. Don't let my team and I find something you might have left out," Jeffers warned.

Giving the teens a moment to offer any last-minute clues, the investigators pushed away from the table.

Entering the hallway, Sheriff Watts was leaning against the wall opposite the room used to hold the kids. "Thank you, Sheriff. That's all we need from that. Hold them, release them, book them, whatever you think is right," Jeffers said.

"They seem pretty miserable to me. Just trespassing?" Sheriff Watts asked.

Agent Sohn shot her lead investigator a look and nodded, "Yes. They couldn't have known how serious the situation was."

"They certainly know now," the sheriff countered. "I'll continue to work with Chief Roberts to secure the site out there for you. How long do you think?"

Jeffers paused and turned his head, "Until we find whoever is doing this."

FIFTEEN

After the stress of the previous evening's events, the team was both anxious and trepidatious in their return to Northern State Hospital. The paranormal team assembled in the command center with Agent Sohn and Agent Dunlap while Jeffers paced outside.

The lead agent had been negotiating with his director to send a full detail from Quantico given the gravity of the incidents that had taken place, even with their presence.

Pushing his way into the command center, he stuffed his phone away. Agent Sohn cast a glance over her shoulder.

Jeffers shrugged, "Deputy Director Witt is hesitant to send a full team until we know what we have."

"Did you tell him people were being torn apart by Zombies?" Wally asked. "Seems like a pretty convincing "get a team out there right away" kind of detail."

Special Agent Jeffers frowned, "Strangely, the word 'zombie' did not enter the conversation, at least not by me."

Agent Sohn laughed, "Witt mentioned it though, didn't he?"

"He sent us out here on this case with the idea of 'zombies' but won't send any more agents with that as the proposed case," Jeffers scoffed. "I remember when I *liked* this job. With all due respect, it was right before I met you three," his hand panned the paranormal researchers.

Dr. Chase scrunched his nose, "I had a college president with much the same sentiment once."

"What do you say we get to the bottom of this and quickly, eh?" Jeffers suggested.

Wally looked over his shoulder, "I was just cueing up the footage the kids livestreamed to their site."

Pressing the play button, they watched the six teens gather around the fence line just outside of the Northern State Hospital property and one by one, slip through the fence as it ambled along a rough hillside.

"That's just outside the dirt road that leads to the delivery tunnel," Agent Dunlap pointed out.

Wally sped through the footage of the teens talking and laughing as they made their way up the trail. When they neared the intersection described in the afternoon interviews conducted by the team, he let the video play at its normal speed.

At first, a single shadow appeared just in frame. It didn't seem as though the teens noticed right away. Only as the shadow was joined by two more figures, did the amateur ghost hunters react. The shadows approached from the bushes just to the left of them, sending the kids scattering. Three instantly ran down the path furthest from the shadows. The moment they ran, the shadow figures pounced.

Hazy images of people bounding after them momentarily splashed on the screen. The video suddenly bounced up and down as the feed moved in the opposite direction.

"This must be Angela's camera. Just as Tommy suggested, those three hesitated. The figures appeared to click into chase mode following the first set," Agent Sohn narrated.

They continued to watch the footage as the teens ran past the hospital just before they were discovered by Jeffers and Chase.

"Run that back again," Tannen asked, leaning in towards the monitor.

Wally nodded and looped the footage back. They again watched the trio of terrified teens race past the hospital.

"There, did you see that?" Tannen called out, poking his finger towards a window at the highest point of the building.

Wally moved the footage back and few frames and paused it, "Yeah, right here! There is a silhouette in that window."

"Where is that?" Agent Jeffers asked.

"The attic," Dr. Chase replied. He scanned the team, "All were accounted for at that time, right?"

The team nodded.

"While we were outside and the other three were being chased towards the dairy barns, somebody was in the attic!" Chase announced. His excitement spilling over as he dashed around stuffing equipment into his pockets.

"You want to go up there, I take it," Jeffers mused.

Chase nodded in earnest, "I do."

"Alright," Jeffers sighed. "Agent Sohn will go with you. We'll stay in the command center and observe. We have the perimeter monitors on?"

Wally nodded. "And the cameras and a mix of state, county and local officers minding the known entrances onto the grounds."

Danica Sohn instinctively checked her weapon to ensure a round was in the chamber. With a nod, she and Chase headed out of the command center and through the security doors. The federal agent laughed inside her own head. The eeriness of the poorly lit halls never faded. If anything, the events they went through the night before, only increased the feeling of unease.

"You think there was someone in the attic?" she asked the professor as they navigated the hallway and began ascending the stairs.

"It sure looked like a silhouette to me. And it wasn't static, it seemed to move, like it was tracking the teens out on the back lawn," Chase said.

The words sent a shiver down Agent Sohn's spine. As they prepared to enter the attic, a horrifying thought crossed her mind. "Last night, the bullets didn't seem to have an effect."

Chase paused, "No. No, they didn't."

"I didn't miss," Sohn assured.

"I know," Chase nodded. "Either Jeffers is right and these...people are so hopped up on a stimulating drug that they can press on or..."

"Or what?" Agent Sohn asked.

Chase squinted in the light of the agent's flashlight, "Or we aren't dealing with people. Not normal ones, at least."

"That's comforting as we are about to try and find one," Agent Sohn whispered.

"Facts aren't always comforting," the professor said and pushed his way into the attic. The door creaked on its hinges, announcing their presence.

"Not helpful!" Agent Sohn croaked.

Chase pressed on, taking careful steps, sweeping his flashlight to cover every inch of the attic as he moved. Agent Sohn joined him and together, they split the darkness with the powerful beams of their tactical lights.

"Didn't the caretaker say something about the attic when he walked us through?" Sohn asked.

Chase nodded, "There are claims of people seeing and hearing an apparition believed to be a nurse that died up here."

"Right, and there was a fire," Sohn recalled. "Stop, you can smell it!"

Chase paused and sniffed the air. The charred beams seemed like they could only have recently been extinguished, even though the fire took place decades before. While they surveyed the burnt wood of the attic, a light breeze seemed to brush past them.

Through the light of his flashlight, Chase could see they both had goosebumps. The professor was on high alert. Ensuring his body camera was on, he switched on a digital recorder.

"Do you hear that?" he asked.

"What is that?" Sohn whispered. "It sounds like humming!"

"From down there," Chase nodded. "Come on!"

Step by step, their flashlights leading the way, they moved down the length of the attic. "It's like it's moving," Agent Sohn said.

Chase cocked his head, "It's almost like singing. It's in there now!"

Moving quickly, he flung open a storeroom door. The room was full of boxes, but not of people. "There's no one in here!" Agent Sohn said as she looked beyond each row of boxes.

"We both heard that," Chase hissed.

"We did," Sohn assured.

"Well, it's gone now."

"Yeah, I don't hear it," Sohn agreed.

Giving the room one last pass through with his light, Chase retreated for the main part of the attic. "The window, it must have been that one over there," he pointed.

Making their way through the clutter of items still stored in the attic, they peered through the window and out into the night. Chase suddenly looked puzzled as he tilted the light on his flashlight to shine *at* the window instead of through it. "This pane looks like it was cleared," he nodded towards the section of glass that appeared to have been wiped in a rough, circular motion.

"Let's have Dunlap bring up the evidence kits," Sohn suggested. "Might have prints."

Chase peered out on the lawn, "Before we do, let's have someone look up here. I want to match it with what we saw on the livestream."

The Agent Sohn called the request to Jeffers. After some contemplation of team safety, the lead agent marched outside himself. Walking towards the tree line, just as the teens had the previous evening, he peered up at the attic window. Raising his radio, he relayed, "It looks pretty much just like the video."

"Someone was up here last night!" Agent Sohn confirmed. The wealth of darkness behind her mixed with the realization, sending a renewed chill down her spine.

"I'm...I'm going to go back inside now," Agent Jeffers said as he played his light around the grounds. Even for him, having the heavily wooded area immediately to his flank was unnerving.

Danica Sohn and Ryder Chase waited for Jeffers to return to the command center and Dunlap to bring up the evidence kit. Deciding he had enough of his having his back to the darkness, the professor cleared off a nearby trunk and knocked dust off for the two to sit.

After a grueling week, the agent accepted. As she sat, she shook off a chill.

Chase removed his jacket and slipped it over the agent's shoulders. As she started to protest, he gently pressed it on to her shoulders as if to refuse her impending refusal.

Relenting, Sohn breathed, "Thank you."

For several moments that sat in silence next to each other. The size of the chest put them close to one another. As Chase leaned his hand back, he was startled when his fingers landed on top of hers. He opened his mouth to apologize and pull away, until a single finger laced over his, gently holding him in place as though it had tremendous power.

Turning toward the agent, their eyes met. Danica's eyes glistened the reflected light of the flashlight. The professor breathed deep. His heart raced. He was unsure of what to say, of what to do. The simple gesture of their hands just barely intertwined was overwhelming.

"So, you do this on a regular basis?" Danica asked.

Chase flustered, his face filling with color, "Well, no, I mean investigations, yes. Hands, I mean, women…hunt…no."

Agent Sohn laughed, "I meant investigations, Ryder. If it wasn't for all the nasty stuff, I might well enjoy being here with you. I mean, I *enjoy* being with you, these just aren't the best of circumstances."

Her breath fell almost to a whisper as her lips lingered mere inches from Chase's. The professor swallowed hard as the two leaned closer together.

A sound froze them in place, less than an inch from their mouths connecting. Both of their eyes widened. Swinging their flashlights around, they searched for the owner of the noise just as heavy steps approached from the far end of the attic.

With a correcting breath, they saw another light bobbing their direction. "Guys!" Agent Dunlap called through the dark.

"Over…," Agent Sohn cleared her throat and stood. "We're over here!"

Dunlap's smiling face appeared as their lights met. "Man, am I glad to see you. Combing these halls on my own is about the creepiest thing I have ever done. Here's the kit," the junior agent presented a toolbox.

"We, uh, Professor Chase noticed smudging on the window we saw the figure in. I thought there might be prints," Agent Sohn declared. "Uhm, Agent Dunlap, before you called out, did you happen to giggle by any chance?"

"Giggle? No, why?" Dunlap shook his head as gently blew powder against the glass.

Chase swiveled his head, "You heard that too?"

Sohn nodded, "I did. Almost as if we were being watched."

"Watched? Watched doing what?" Dunlap scoffed as he placed collecting film against the window.

"Uhm, you know, investigating," Sohn flattened her lips.

"Hmm," Dunlap's head bounced. "All done."

"Let's get back to command," Agent Sohn suggested.

Dunlap shrugged as he latched the kit, "No argument from here."

"Professor, are you ready?" Agent Sohn asked, casting Ryder Chase a knowing glance.

The professor had to admit, amidst the strange smells, noises and impending danger, he had just begun to enjoy his time in the attic. Since his reasons for wanting to stay had no relevance to the case, he relented, "Yes, I'm ready."

Returning to the command center, they reported their findings, including the mutually heard sound of humming. Wally snatched the recorder from Chase and began playing it over the computer speakers.

Leaning his ear towards the speaker, Wally announced, "I hear it!"

As they all listened intently, Tannen chimed in, "I hear singing. It's faint, but I hear it."

Wally let the recording play even as they confirmed the sighting with Jeffers and waited for Agent Dunlap.

As the tape began to share Chase's fumbling response to Agent Sohn, he lunged across Wally and hit a key on the keyboard halting the playback. "That's... that's all there was," Chase stammered, realizing he had failed miserably to appear anything close to nonchalant. "What did you guys find on the data card we got during the interview?"

Dunlap frowned, "Didn't you guys say something about a giggle? Maybe that's on the recording. Let's play it through."

"No, no," Chase waved him off. "I don't think...we'll find anything else. Uh, Tannen?"

Dan lingered a moment, eyeing the professor. With a glance to Agent Sohn, who cast just the slightest grin at Chase's discomfort, he jumped in.

"I think we might have something. They didn't capture any compelling video, but you can hear what sounds like hoarse whispers among the...uh, feral...people," the EMT said. With a nod to Wally, the audio clip played as Chase swiped his recorder back.

Though mostly guttural grunts, there were murmurs amidst the commotion that caught the team's attention. "I can't quite...Wally, play it again," Chase requested.

Wally played the section back.

Agent Sohn squinted, "I can't quite make it out, but there are words."

"It sounds like coordinating their efforts in the attack," Agent Dunlap suggested. Snapping his fingers, he added, "I've heard that sound before. I couldn't find it and I couldn't confirm but...the walk through! When I was doing my fence line perimeter walk..."

The agent closed his eyes as he retraced his mental steps. Suddenly his eyes opened, "The tunnel. I heard similar muffled communication near the tunnel. Like these odd hoarse whispers."

The team thought about the agent's experience for a moment. Chase pulled at his lip until he stepped forward. "The attic and steam tunnels, are major passageways that would allow hospital staff to circumnavigate certain patient areas, that's why the death tunnel was used for carting out the less fortunate so the patients didn't have to see them."

Jeffers nodded, "That is why activity is so prevalent in those areas."

"The only other location that is predominant in the lore is the surgical room," Tannen said.

"Which is right next to the morgue," Chase added.

"Which would have access to the tunnel," Jeffers concluded. Taking a glance around the room, he winced, "Smyth, you're with me. The rest of you stay here."

Wally grinned and pushed up from his chair. Gathering an armload of gear, he waited for the FBI agent to lead the way.

SIXTEEN

Special Agent Jeffers held the door for Wally to follow him down the stairs to the subterranean tunnels that ran the length of the hospital and connected with the delivery tunnel. With a raised brow as he observed the array of paranormal equipment the tech was lugging.

"Do you really need all that stuff with you, Smyth?" the agent questioned.

Wally flustered at the inquiry, "Yeah. I've got geo-sensors that will pick up vibrations, an anemometer to detect wind, temperature gun, camera and flashlight."

Jeffers rolled his eyes and continued descending.

Wally stopped and groaned, "We need to go back. We should grab the thermal. Do you mind?"

The FBI agent looked cross, "Yeah, I mind. Let's just get down there and see what we can see."

"Alright, but the thermal might have been the most important," Wally grumbled.

Pushing a heavy metal door open, its rust-laden groan echoing through the halls. "Not going to sneak up on anyone," Jeffers said.

"They aren't going to sneak up on us, either," Wally announced, laying his geo-sensor in the main intersection of the hallway. "Let's see. Ambient temp is sixty-four degrees…little to no breeze."

"Thanks for the weather report. Now can we go find some bad guys? Real, talking, upright bad guys," Jeffers pressed.

With a nod from Wally, they began exploring the tunnels in earnest. Following the long lines of the utilities and boiler pipes, they explored the length of the hospital.

"Man, I do not like it down here. Feels off," Wally complained. He froze as a loud bang resonated through the cement halls.

Jeffers drew his firearm and pivoted in both directions. "It came from this way, come on!"

In a jog, their footfalls echoing as they moved, they hit the intersection of the delivery tunnel.

"The death tunnel!" Wally gasped.

Suddenly a loud clang beckoned from the direction they had just come.

"Come on, this way!" Jeffers called and sprinted in the direction of the sound. Running the length of the tunnel, his search came up empty. Checking the door on the far end of the underground system, it was bolted and padlocked shut.

Wally rechecked all of his instruments. His anemometer registered a breeze. Raising an eyebrow, he scanned the tunnel. A slight movement caught his eye near the ceiling. Walking to the wall, he reached up, hooked one of the boiler pipes with his fingers and let go. The tunnel was suddenly bathed in the resonance of metal on metal.

"There's our clang," Wally frowned. "Breeze picked up, just enough to jostle these pipes and..."

The paranormal researcher was cut off by a warning chime deep down the tunnel. His eyes widened, "The geo-sensor! That can't be set off by anything else than vibration."

Jeffers looked confused.

"Walking. Someone had to walk by!" Wally explained.

Once more, the two men ran down the tunnel towards the alarm. Ending up at the intersection with the delivery tunnel, Wally panted as he placed his hands on his knees. Looking up at the FBI agent, he said, "What? There's usually not so much running in ghost hunting."

The sound of footsteps seemed to scamper further down the tunnel. "I know," Wally panted. "Let's go!"

Jeffers resumed the lead and moved more cautiously down the tunnel. As they moved, the footfalls only seemed to keep pace ahead of them. Moving quicker, they ultimately found themselves at the heavy gate of the delivery door. Shining their lights around the tunnel, they couldn't find any openings that whoever they were pursuing could have disappeared into.

"What was it Tannen said? There should be a connection to the surgery room or the morgue," Jeffers said.

Retracing their steps, they looked for a door or hatch. Above a pile of wood and cement blocks, their flashlights danced around a door in the ceiling.

"That has to be it," Jeffers said, carefully climbing the pile of debris. In doing so, he realized that he could reach the door. With a shove, it flopped open with a healthy bang. The two investigators cast glances towards one another. They had heard that sound before.

Needing both hands to climb up, the FBI agent reluctantly holstered his weapon and set his flashlight on the floor above. Grasping the ledge with both hands, he hoisted himself up. Sitting between the two floors, he played his flashlight around to ensure the room was empty.

Climbing all the way up, he spun around and helped Wally up through the trap door.

Wally looked around. He found himself in the hallway just outside the morgue and next to the surgery room. "This must have been a chute, but it's all fallen apart now."

"Looks that way," Jeffers agreed. "I don't see any sign of anyone else being up here."

"They couldn't be that fast, we should have been right behind it," Wally said.

Jeffers closed the trap door. Poking his head into the morgue, he shined his light, ensuring the room was empty. Leaning into the next closest room, he motioned for Wally to follow.

Light fixtures swung overhead, the agent's flashlight gleamed off of stainless-steel surfaces. At the foot of each table were stirrups once used to lash patients to the tables. Leather straps deteriorated from years passing lie tattered at the center and head of the table.

"This is where they did lobotomies and experiments with the brains of the patients," Wally cooed as they swept the room.

Jeffers crossed the room and kicked open a closet door. Pouncing, he fully expected to discover whoever was running ahead of them. Wally peered over his shoulder at the crude surgical equipment covered in dust.

A metal bang rang through the first floor of the hospital. Wally and Jeffers spun and looked towards the entrance of the surgery room door, the lights above the tables swinging wildly.

"The morgue!" Wally said, urging the agent with the gun forward.

Jeffers sprinted out of the surgery room, banging his thigh on equipment as ran. Flinging the door open, he frowned, "I thought we left that open."

Not waiting for a comment, he burst into the morgue. No one was inside, but one of the cadaver drawers was slid open. The FBI agent looked at Wally, "None of those were open when I looked inside. This room was empty."

Dashing out into the hallway, both men scanned one direction, spun and scanned the other. The hallway was completely empty.

"Damn!" Jeffers scolded himself. "They hid in a drawer!"

"If they did, and they somehow got past us down the hallway, we should have it on tape," Wally said.

Taking a final glance in all directions, the FBI agent nodded, "Let's go find out."

Jeffers burst into the command center like a child eager to open presents on Christmas morning. He was close to identifying whoever it was they were chasing.

Wally plopped into his chair and starting the scanning the video footage. Closing his eyes, he leaned back to his chair and sighed. His hands rubbing his face with vigor, he announced, "Cameras aren't on. I must have accidentally hit a button when we were reviewing the footage from the livestream. If someone, or something, ran down that hallway, we have no evidence of it."

Jeffers was dejected. He sensed that they were close.

"We'll get it," Chase assured. "It's like I said the other day, each investigation, each clue narrows our scope. We get closer and closer."

Jeffers looked serious, "Each day that we don't have this case wrapped up, people's lives are at risk. We had it…him…whatever. I know it!"

"Welcome to hunting the paranormal," Wally scoffed.

"I'm not convinced this is paranormal," Jeffers scowled.

"Well, whatever is going on around here, it sure ain't normal," Wally concluded.

Jeffers shot him a disapproving glare and then softened, "You're right about that."

SEVENTEEN

The team stared quietly at their coffee cups and breakfast plates. Special Agent Jeffers was as surly as ever. His one piece of solace was that the state police shutdown the town of Sedro-Woolley to all outsiders, including the media remanding them twelve miles south to nearby Mount Vernon.

Setting his cup down with such force that a wave of coffee crested the lip and crashed onto the table, elicited a barely audible curse from the lead agent. Surveying the team, he tapped his notes and cast out assignments.

"I can't have incidents occurring in the midst of our investigation. We need to figure out what is going on here," Jeffers stated. Looking at Wally and Tannen, he spat, "You two. Rerun all of the footage captured at the hospital. Inside and out. We're missing something."

Turning his attention to Agent Sohn and Dr. Chase, he instructed, "Agent Sohn, take Dr. Chase and scour the police reports leading up to the first incident and since. Go through our interviews, victims, victim's families and pull every string we haven't pulled or yanked on hard enough."

"What are we going to do, boss?" Agent Dunlap sat up in his chair, ready for his orders.

Jeffers mulled his response. "You and I are going to scour Northern State Hospital. The perpetrators appear and disappear at will, right under our noses. We need to figure out how," Jeffers stated.

Agent Dunlap nodded and leaned back as the others sipped on their coffees.

Jeffers scowled, "Well, go on. They have to-go cups!"

The team only shared brief glimpses before sliding out their chairs and gathering their breakfast items to finish on the run.

Agent Sohn and Professor Chase sat across from Police Chief Roberts and Mick, the caretaker of Northern State Hospital. "I appreciate you two meeting with us. As you know, the case at the asylum has only become more tragic," Agent Sohn announced. Her eyes soaking in the caretaker's reaction.

The caretaker frowned and twitched, "I heard. I'm terribly sorry about that. The whole thing is nuts. It has gone from occasionally creepy to downright terrifying."

"We'll get to the bottom of it," Agent Sohn assured.

"What can I do to help you?" Mick asked.

The agent glanced at Dr. Chase, who leaned forward. With a nod, she encouraged the professor. "Can you give us a bit of more background on the hospital?"

The caretaker looked at Chase, "Well, I told you the nut of it when I walked you around the place. It opened in 1912…"

Chase waved him off, "All of that was great for the foundation for our research, I was speaking more of modern history."

Mick nodded in understanding, "Since the seventies, it has been in the trust of the Department of Enterprise Services. They manage properties, facilities, that sort of thing for the state of Washington. The hospital and most of the grounds is included in the Historic Registry, so the buildings need to stay intact one way or another. These old buildings get lost to dust in time as they are forgotten about or groups like the D.E.S. don't know what to do with them. That's why I was kept on, to take care of the place and keep it standing."

"I see," Chase said. Folding his hands around his crossed knee, he asked, "Is that where Northern State is now, in forgotten status?"

The caretaker shrugged, "I don't rightly know. No one tells me much of the details. I just get calls to open gates, unlock doors, make sure power is running to certain sections. Like for movies. Had a few movies filmed out here."

"Movies?" Agent Sohn leaned forward.

"Yeah. Mostly low budget horror flicks. I watched one of 'em once it came on my streaming service. It was a 'B' film, but it was fun to see the ol' girl on the screen," Mick beamed with pride.

"I bet, I'll have to check them out," Chase said. "Who else have you opened the hospital up for?"

"Well, state and county folks have the occasional notion they can put the space to use for public needs or lease it out for commercial stuff," Mick shrugged. "Even one of the big state universities poked around for a bit, seeing what they can make of the property. Was told to oversee the fence getting put up not long after that."

"It's quite the secure fence, at that," Chase said, his head cocked to a side.

Mick pursed his lips, "I suppose so. Probably opens up the list of prospects, I suppose."

"No takers? Take away the recent events, it is an amazing property," Chase said.

"Too far from the big cities, I guess. Unless they want to fire it up as a mental hospital again," Mick grinned.

"Thank you, Mick. You've been most helpful," Dr. Chase smiled.

"Can you provide us with your contact that sets up the visits with you?" Agent Sohn asked.

"You betcha," Mick scrolled through his phone emails. The caretaker pulled out a pen and sticky note, scribbling the name and email address. Handing it to the FBI agent, he shared, "Here you go."

"Well, I sure hope you folks figure this out soon. I'm not scared of much, but the thought of going out there with...beings chewin' up folks gives me the willies," Mick scrunched his nose.

"We will, Mick. Thanks again," Agent Sohn promised.

The caretaker left and the room fell silent for a few moments. "So, what do you think?" Chief Roberts asked.

"I don't know yet. There is a clue out there I haven't quite put my finger on just yet," Chase admitted.

"We'll see if anything strikes me on the list of official visitors when it comes in," Agent Sohn said.

Agent Dunlap was surprised when Agent Jeffers drove out to the open field near the dairy barns. Cresting one of the nearby hills, a black helicopter swooped down, hovered and set down in the clearing.

"There's our ride," Jeffers said, getting out of the SUV.

"Alright!" Dunlap grinned, following the lead agent to the helicopter.

Once the men were inside, they were handed headphones, the aircraft lifted in the air. The pilot turned to Agent Jeffers in the seat beside him. "It's your show. You point, I fly."

Pointing upwards, Jeffers had the pilot lift high in the air over the entire property.

The lead agent studied the breadth of the grounds before having the pilot circle the entire fence line. Once the circuit was complete, Jeffers had the pilot hover much closer to the ground. He surveyed the main hospital, the outbuildings, and spent a great deal of time at each access point.

From his notes, he directed the pilot to each location that the team or victims had an encounter.

Something he was unaware of specifically was beginning to take shape in his mind. Mapping out the zones on the grounds where video, perimeter alarms, his team or teen trespassers had an incident, he grinned and nodded. "Son of a…," he started. To himself more than anyone, he said, "They strategically are using areas of dense foliage and shade to their advantage. Every move they make is to stay as much in the shadows as possible. Whoever we are dealing with, they are well-trained and very clever."

"What's that, sir?" Dunlap desperately wanted to see what his superior was seeing.

"Look at where the initial points of attack have taken place," Jeffers shared. Leaning against the window so the junior agent behind him could see where he was pointing, "The intersection the kids were attacked…is at the convergence of the high blackberry bushes. At night, the entire location would be completely enveloped in shadow."

Nudging the pilot, they hovered closer to the hospital building, "Each path they took, whether caught on camera or in person, they took a line that moved from that stand of trees and blackberries, to the back side of the building. They are skilled in ambush tactics."

Once more, Jeffers urged the pilot to fly to the area near the dairy barns. "Here, the night of the second attack,

Agent Sohn and I ran along the path, as most people would. We were angling for max visibility. Whoever we are dealing with moved painstakingly through the brush, including the stickers to remain hidden. This is no group of normal people."

"What are you suggesting, boss?" Dunlap questioned.

"We might have stumbled onto a black ops team," Jeffers leaned back, extremely satisfied with his answer.

"You think so?" Dunlap called from the back.

"It is the first thing that has made the slightest bit of sense," Jeffers grinned. He motioned for the pilot to bring them down.

Agent Sohn paced back and forth on the phone. When she thanked the person on the other and hung up, she looked at an expectant Dr. Chase.

Sohn shrugged and smiled, "They're emailing a list. You want to grab a cup of coffee or something while we wait?"

"Yeah, that would be great!" Chase nodded.

Getting out of the car and into the coffee shop was easier without a throng of reporters surrounding them. Receiving their cups, they looked around at the tables, deciding where to sit. The barista called from behind her machine, "You're welcome to stay here, but if you're looking for an exceptional place to enjoy your coffee, just a few miles down State Route Nine is a bridge over the Skagit River. The view east is majestic. Just sayin'!"

Danica Sohn looked over her coffee cup, "What do you think? Majestic view while we drink our coffee and wait for an email?"

"Got to sit somewhere," Chase grinned.

As they parked their rented SUV at a pullout alongside the bridge, they took in the vista. "The barista was right. This is wonderful," Agent Sohn said, putting the vehicle in park. "Come on, let's walk out there."

Professor Chase followed the FBI agent to a little rock outcropping at the base of the bridge. "It's beautiful," he said, standing next to Agent Sohn.

"It is," Sohn murmured as she sipped her coffee and enjoyed the scenery.

The current gurgled below as ospreys played in the light breeze that followed along the Skagit River.

Danica cupped both hands against the walls of the coffee cup, allowing the heat to warm her. As the light breeze penetrated, she gave a slight shiver.

Dr. Chase noticed and began to remove his jacket.

"Uhn-uh," the agent shook her head. "Just stand closer, I'll be fine."

Dr. Chase hesitated for a moment and then complied. He pressed in close so that their mutual body heat would warm the other.

"It would be better if you put your arms around me," Sohn shivered, a slight grin piercing her lips unbeknownst to the professor.

Chase swallowed hard and nervously moved behind the FBI agent. Gently wrapping his arms around her, conspicuously leaving space between them.

Agent Sohn grasped the open edges of his jacket and wrapped them tight around her, forcing him against her. "That's better," she smiled and resumed gazing out at the mountains and twisting river.

Dr. Chase scarcely moved, frozen in place.

Agent Sohn raised an eyebrow, noticing the professor ceased to breathe. With a foreshadowing chuckle, she punched backwards with an elbow, forcing Chase to gasp in a breath. "Relax, professor. Breathing is a natural thing. Unless…you're too aghast by the company."

"No, I like…I like the company," he whispered.

Agent Sohn strained her neck backwards so that she could see him in the corner of her eye. Spinning so that their chests were together, she looked up at him and grinned, "This is a way better moment than an attic with things wanting to maul us."

Reaching up on her tiptoes, she pressed her lips against his, which he readily accepted. "Way," he breathed.

Wally Smyth and Dan Tannen scoured the video clips and audio evidence they had accumulated over the course of the investigation. Much of it, they had already catalogued.

"This is all retread. Some of it is interesting, but its stuff we already knew," Wally wailed as he took a sip of giant convenience store soda.

"I just keep trying to find something that tells us where they come from and how they disappear," Tannen called, his eyes glued to the monitor.

"Underground passages, teleportation, just way better at concealment than we are…who knows. How does Bigfoot always seem to disappear?" Wally groaned.

Tannen turned away from the screen. "How *does* Bigfoot get away?"

Wally shrugged while subconsciously leaning forward, "He hides in the trees. He knows the terrain better than his pursuers. In terms of the Skunk Ape, he goes where others don't or are unwilling to follow."

"Like the briar patches," Tannen suggested.

"No pain, or at least resistant to pain," Wally acknowledged. "Explains why a couple of nine-millimeter gun shots didn't slow them down. But why no blood trails? There should be blood."

"There has been a little, around the stick bushers, but just a trace," Tannen said.

"Bloodless? That would support the zombie theory, maybe," Wally's eyes went wide. "Maybe that's why they attack victims the way they do…replenish their blood supply."

"Like vampires?" Tannen asked.

Wally squirmed excitedly, "Never thought of vampires! Could they be confused with zombies?"

Tannen shrugged, "I don't know. Neither have been known to actually exist."

"Actually, there have been several documented cases, the most recent in Romania…," Wally began as his phone buzzed. "Ryder says to stay put. The medical examiners have something to share and the whole team is on their way."

"Hmm," Tannen nodded as he mulled what medical evidence might come their way.

"You hungry?" Wally asked as he began punching keys on his phone.

The team piled into the room they used as their research center. Wally and Tannen shared their evidence review and theories that didn't sit well with Agent Jeffers. He, in turn, shared his thought on the black ops theory with as much exuberance as he had had the entire case.

Professor mulled the theory, struggling to discount it wholly, other than the whole eating people issue.

A rap at the door broke their conversation. Agent Dunlap turned the handle and Dr. Lazenby burst through followed closely by Dr. Burbee. Each medical examiner's hands were full. Lazenby slid evidence packets out of the way and set his arm load down.

Special Agent Jeffers raised an eyebrow, expecting to see something pertaining to the case. Instead, as the coroner ripped off the foil lid, he revealed rows of Mexican food.

"Enchiladas!" Lazenby beamed. "The pan below has reefers."

The coroner's eyes panned the field of mostly federal agents and clarified, "Refried beans, that is. I mean, the other is legal in Washington now...."

"And Coronas!" Dr. Burbee let his arm load of beers slam on the table next to the trays of food.

The investigation team looked confused at the delivery. Lazenby panned the audience and shrugged, "Can't investigate on an empty stomach, now can you? I mean, one of your team texted to bring 'grub'!"

All eyes fell on Wally, who shrugged.

"The father-in-law of my…third wife," Doctor Burbee added, "Said never to arrive at a party empty-handed. I'm pretty sure he meant beer. Or wine. Or maybe Jager…"

Jeffers gritted his teeth as his lips moved from side to side and glared, "The food is fine. If any of you touch the alcohol, you're off the case."

The team nodded and Wally dropped a Corona back in its slot and dove in to dish up a plate.

"You got the drive?" Lazenby asked as he moved towards one of the computers.

Dr. Burbee pulled a small device from his pocket and raised it in the air, "I remember when we had secretaries to make mimeographs of things and the couriers would take them from one place to the other." His head fell, "I miss secretaries."

"Right," Jeffers interceded. "Back in the twenty-first century, we need evidence. What is it you guys have?"

Dr. Lazenby got excited while Dr. Burbee nodded and popped the top of a Corona while he stared wide-eyed at the screen.

Jeffers shook his head slightly and focused on the monitor. Wally helped the M.E. get the image on the large screen.

"Here you see," Lazenby pointed, "A segment of the boy who died the other day."

"His name was Ben," Jeffers said flatly.

"Yes, victim Ben," Lazenby clarified. Zooming in on the screen he highlighted, "The marks on his legs…and his arm…and his abdomen…and his throat…they are definitively and without question…human."

The team froze and turned their attention from the screen to the coroner. Agent Jeffers shrugged, "Yeah. We assumed as much."

Lazenby held a finger in the air, "The previous results were *presumed* human. These *are* human."

Jeffers raised an eyebrow. His mood was not entirely tolerant of the M.E.'s quirks. "And?"

"These are not only human, but I matched them to the FBI database with the assistance of Dr. Burbee," Dr. Lazenby stated and turned to Dr. Burbee who slammed an empty Corona bottle down. Springing the top of a second beer, he raised the bottle in the air before taking an enormous swig. "The dental impressions match within 99.2% those of a University of Washington student reported missing."

The team collectively pondered the words uttered by the coroner. Even Wally put his fork down and frowned.

"A student attacked one of the teenagers?" he asked, dabbing a bit of enchilada from his chin as he spoke.

Lazenby nodded, "It appears so."

Jeffers frowned and shook his head, "So, what? We're supposed to accept this is some sort of college stunt? Some frat exercise gone wrong?"

"Not exactly," Dr. Burbee finished his second beer and raised a finger in the air. "The student in question is one Marcus Fisher. An Army ROTC scholarship recipient."

The room went still.

Jeffers grinned and snapped his fingers, "That aligns with my theory on their tactical awareness!"

"Perhaps," Burbee nodded. "This one was also being treated for a rather severe case of PTSD."

"Well, there you are. Well-trained military operatives with severe mental issues, potentially hopped up on inferior drugs prescribed by the V.A.," Jeffers got excited. "I could almost hug you two."

Lazenby stepped forward.

"Almost!" Jeffers glared.

Lazenby nodded and stepped back.

"Well, there you have it," Dr. Burbee liberated the top of his third Corona.

Lazenby looked distraught, smacking himself in the forehead. "Nuts! I forgot my suit. We were going to celebrate the big reveal with a group plunge in the hotel hot tub!"

The team scanned the room, more confused than ever.

Burbee tossed Lazenby a beer and burped. He rubbed his sixty-one year old belly and began to loosen his clothing. With a slash of his hand he exclaimed, "We're all adults. We don't need suits, now do we?"

Lazenby caught the beer and looked up. With a quizzical glance, he cast it off, "No, I guess not. To the hot tub!" The coroner raised his beer triumphantly into the air.

To the rest of the investigation team's relief, Jeffers stepped in, "Doctors, thank you for your excellent work. I think we'll take your evidence to the investigation scene and see what we can find. You…do whatever it is you're going to do."

"Cheers!" Lazenby exclaimed, quickly drinking the foam from the lip of the beer that that had fizzed from Dr. Burbee's toss.

The team swapped glances and other than Wally who scooped up another enchilada, they made a hasty exit for the rented vehicles.

Outside of the hotel room, as the team reached for the door handles, Special Agent Jeffers announced, "We have a killer to catch. Let's end this!"

EIGHTEEN

The team parked in front of the hospital with renewed vigor. They were more confident than any other point in the investigation that they could handle what they were up against. They hadn't reconciled why Agent Sohn's bullets didn't down one of the subjects, but enough plausible explanations were bantered about to resolve their concerns.

Ensuring all of the cameras and equipment were on and functioning properly, they proceeded with their investigation. Working in three-man teams, they took turns manning the command center and providing back up while the patrol team prodded the hot spots.

Agent Jeffers demanded that he always be on the team that was pushing into the areas of provocation around the grounds. On his first stint, he took Agent Dunlap and Wally with him. He thought having the tech on hand to install any additionally needed surveillance would be useful.

Together, they plotted where wireless cameras and sensors could be installed based on the attacks. Producing a sheet that he sketched while surveying the property by helicopter, Jeffers had several key locations he wanted monitored.

Wally inventoried the desired equipment while Agent Dunlap served as sort of a bodyguard. When they catalogued their additions, they began installing cameras and perimeter alarms along the trails and outbuildings.

"Here, help me with this, if you would, Agent Dunlap," Wally called to the junior agent as he wrapped a cord around a tree and positioned a camera on the path leading away from the hospital and towards the dairy barns.

Jeffers used his flashlight to highlight his sheet for the next location. With each team member focused on their individual tasks, they didn't notice the figure moving carefully through the shadows towards them. The figure was measured in its approach, poised like a cat waiting for the right moment to strike.

Agents Jeffers and Dunlap started their way to the next location while Wally paused to observe the sight line he had on the camera. Eyeing the device while he checked the view on the command center monitors with Tannen via radio, he was unaware that he had just been separated from the FBI agents.

Taking advantage of splitting one of the prey off from the group, the figure seized on the opportunity and sprung forward.

Satisfied with his placement of the camera, Wally spun. He didn't expect to turn smack into a menacing being, wild eyes reflecting the light of his flashlight as he swung. Before he could react, powerful hands reached out, pulling him to the ground.

Kicking, hitting his attacker in the face, Wally launched himself up and raced down the clearest path he saw, putting him further away from the agents. His pursuer was relentless, closing ground with every step they took.

"Cardio!" Wally gasped as he stumbled, arms flailing over his head as he collapsed on the ground.

Strong hands gripped his leg, fingers began to dig claw-like nails into his thighs. Teeth gnashed as they tried to cut through his trousers and gnaw into his flesh.

Wally wriggled and kicked as he knew his life depended on it. His assailant was resistant to the abuse and only gripped harder, finding its way through the cotton trousers and sinking its teeth into a mouthful of flesh. Oblivious to Wally's punches and kicks, the being sought another chunk of flesh to imbibe.

Screaming wildly, Wally led the FBI agents to his location. Agent Jeffers arrived at the scene, tactical light and firearm married in a single grip, the agent was able to deliver several clean shots.

Agent Dunlap added a pair of well-aimed bullets to the attacker. To their surprise, the being jumped to its feet and darted for the nearest stand of blackberries even while taking several more punishing bullets from the agents.

Dunlap dropped to Wally's aid, quickly assessing the severity of his wounds. Noting he needed medical attention, he incited Jeffers to give up his pursuit. The lead investigator was already several steps into the brush before Dunlap called to him. Reluctantly, Jeffers turned away from the chase and dropped to assist with medical aid. Applying pressure to Wally's most severe wounds, he craned his neck over his shoulder in the direction of his assailant. He could still hear branches crack and break further into the briars.

Dan Tannen rushed to the scene with Dr. Chase and Agent Sohn in tow. Taking over the medic duties, the EMT did his best to stabilize his friend, dressing the most severe wounds with bleed-stop bandages from his trauma kit.

Wally sputtered as they waited for the ambulance to arrive. "X-ray!," he gasped.

Tannen looked confused, "Yeah, probably. The hospital will take care of all that. The ambulance is on its way."

Wally looked frustrated. Beyond the pale tone of his blood starved skin and the overall look of entering shock, he shook his head feverishly. "X-ray!" he repeated.

Chase cocked his head and looked at his friend. "X-ray?"

Wally moved his hands up and down his torso. "Wore…X-ray.

The words failed to resonate any more clearly with the team as their attention turned towards the flashing lights of the ambulance with the blue and red escort of the Sedro-Woolley police.

"It's alright, buddy. Help is here," Tannen assured.

Chase nodded as the ambulance team loaded Wally onto a stretcher, "Go with him. We'll follow."

Tannen walked alongside the team as they loaded Wally into the ambulance and wasted no time accelerating out of the asylum grounds and towards the hospital.

"What the hell happened out there?" Agent Sohn asked.

Jeffers shook his head, more dejected than ever. "We turned away for a second. That's all it took," he started. "Dunlap and I were looking at the next section we wanted covered, turned and something was chasing Wally."

"Something?" Sohn pressed.

"It was a man, just…off," Jeffers grimaced.

"It flowed," Agent Dunlap added.

"Flowed?" Chase frowned.

"Yeah, like it wearing a dress, or a cape or one of those hospital gowns," Dunlap suggested.

"Hospital…," Jeffers mused. "You think Wally meant one of those aprons they use for X-rays and stuff?"

Dr. Chase frowned, "Maybe. They're made of lead. Lead is soft and aprons are less than a millimeter thick. Think that would stop a bullet?"

Jeffers shook his head, "No. I guess it wouldn't. It might slow it down, maybe flatten it a bit if using a hollow point. Might lessen the impact and the lethality of penetration, but it would still hurt like any other bullet and ultimately lead to death like any other bullet."

"Are we skipping over the question of why anyone would be running around with a lead apron in the first place," Agent Sohn asked.

Chase gazed at her, "Why would anyone run around trying to bite people?"

"Good point. None of this makes sense," Sohn bit her lip.

Glancing towards Police Chief Roberts, Jeffers asked, "Can you take the professor to the hospital? I'm sure he'd like to keep tabs on his man."

"What are you going to do?" Chase asked.

"We're going to find a madman," Jeffers growled.

Dr. Chase rode to the hospital in silence. He was worried about Wally and his thoughts were strangled by the case. It was as if a clue wanted to leap out of the shadows, just like the creatures at the asylum, but like those creatures, remained elusive.

Thanking Chief Roberts, Chase climbed out of the police car. He found Tannen just inside the lobby.

"How's he doing?" Chased asked.

Tannen nodded, "He's good. They stopped the major bleeding. There was no major tissue damage outside of the exposed skin. No arteries were severed, he's clear from shock. I asked them to run a blood panel just to be sure. He's good, considering."

"I'm glad to hear. Have you been able to check on him?"

Shaking his head, Tannen acknowledged, "No. The treatment team sedated him so that they could clean the wounds thoroughly and stitch him up. Probably a few hours before he's salient."

"I saw Marty's parents. He's stable enough that he'll be moved to Seattle in the morning. It sounds like Sarah Whitman is moving on as well. There is a neuroscience center at the university hospital that opened up space for her," Tannen said.

"I'm glad those kids are going to get the help that they need," Chase said.

"Yeah. I wish we were able to help the others," Tannen admitted.

"Me too," Chase said. "There's a phrase I heard Jeffers use, 'You can't save them all.' I don't get the impression he cares for that any more than I do."

"He's taking the investigation pretty hard," Tannen observed.

"He is. It's one thing to have a challenging case, it's another to have people get hurt…and die, on your watch. He's the lead investigator, it's his watch, according to him. I think it's all of our watch," Chase countered.

"Me too," Tannen agreed.

The FBI agents combed the trails, the outbuildings, and the hospital grounds before turning their attention to the hospital itself. They followed footfalls and snapped twigs. All that they were able to reveal was a curious family of raccoons and an irate owl.

Agent Jeffers rubbed his face in frustration as they paused to collect themselves in the command center. He scanned the camera feeds, desperate to find something tangible to chase. Nothing moved past the cameras. No alarms were tripped.

Snatching his phone from his pocket, he dialed Deputy Director Witt. After several rings, a sleepy voice answered, "This is Witt."

"Deputy Director, it's Special Agent Jeffers."

"I'm not on west coast time like you, Jeffers. It's the middle of the night here. It better be good," Witt snapped.

"It's not good, sir. It is important, however," Jeffers stated. "You got my report on the trespassers?"

"I did. It's unfortunate, but you sneak into a crime scene and bad things can happen. You have everything in control out there, Agent Jeffers?" Witt asked.

"Honestly, sir. I'm not sure. One of our own, one of Dr. Chase's team was attacked. He's at the hospital now," Jeffers reported. "Agent Dunlap and I were immediately on the scene and shot the suspect."

"Justified. What's the issue?"

"The suspect got away," Jeffers said.

The FBI director stammered, "They what? You're sure you hit them?"

"I don't miss, sir. For all of Agent Dunlap's shortcomings, he doesn't either," Jeffers said.

"What is it I can help you with at this hour, agent?"

"I need another team. It is too dangerous and there is too much ground to cover while needing to keep tabs on the paranormal team all the time," Jeffers said.

"Then dismiss them or quarantine them at the hotel," Witt suggested.

"It's not that they aren't useful, I won't admit it in the same room with them or at a formal review, but they have their points. Even without them, I'd be asking for assistance on this one," Jeffers said.

"The bodies are piling up," Witt admitted. "I'll start putting a response team together tomorrow."

"Thank you, sir," Jeffers said.

"I'm going to go back to bed now, agent," Witt said and hung up his phone.

Jeffers looked at his fellow agents who had never heard the confident lead agent request for help.

NINETEEN

The team gathered around Wally's bed the next morning. The beleaguered investigator being in good spirits was infectious for his weary teammates.

"Thanks for coming to my rescue," he looked up at Agents Jeffers and Dunlap.

"Should not have gotten that far," Jeffers said, his voice flat.

"Whatever we're up against, is cunning. Advantageous," Wally shrugged. "It struck so fast. And persistent. I couldn't get away."

"Well, it got away," Dunlap murmured to Jeffers' disdain.

"We searched the entire grounds. I can't figure out where they come from and where they disappear to," Jeffers admitted.

"Mole people, maybe they go underground," Wally grinned.

"I'm about ready to accept one of your silly paranormal theories," the lead agent said. "On that thoroughly distasteful note, I'll let you rest up. I'm glad you're feeling better."

"Thanks, Jeffers!" Wally acknowledged.

"You look good, considering," Chase nodded.

"Doc says just superficial cuts and abrasions, no serious damage," Wally said. "Didn't feel like it at the time."

Tannen burst into the room, "Just spoke to the physician on duty. Looks like you'll be cleared for release soon."

"That's good news," Agent Sohn chimed in.

"Fit and ready for action," Wally grinned.

"Doc says zero physical activity," Tannen declared.

"I think I'll stick with the command center," Wally admitted.

"After last night, Agent Jeffers is mandating the command center be at the hotel," Agent Sohn replied.

"Will that work?" Agent Dunlap asked.

Wally frowned, "If we have access to a router and wireless signal, it will work. Won't be the best FPS out of the video feeds, but it should be fine."

Chase rubbed his lip, "I agree with Wally staying at the hotel, but I believe Tannen and I would still serve useful onsite."

"I think I need to agree with Jeffers on this, sorry," Sohn winced.

"I'm trained in forensic science and Tannen as a medic would be of value," Chase pressed.

"I'd feel better with you both there," Agent Dunlap admitted. "But for your safety, I think it is time for L.E.O.s to take it over completely."

Chase stepped out and moved quickly down the hallway. Like a laser guided missile, he zeroed in on Special Agent Jeffers.

"Agent Sohn shared my thoughts on keeping your team at the hotel," the FBI agent observed.

"With each incident, we get closer to the truth. I'm as confounded by the case as you," Dr. Chase said. "I'm also as ticked off, because like you, my team's safety is my responsibility."

Jeffers relaxed his usual stiff demeanor, "Look, I get it. I do. This case is not some spirit who can slam a cupboard door or make the lights flicker. People are dead, professor. You have a man down the hall that likely would be dead too, if Agent Dunlap and I weren't on the scene."

"But you *were* on the scene, Agent Jeffers. And working together, you *did* prevent a tragedy. We can tighten up our protocols. Do you know what I did before paranormal psychiatry?" Dr. Chase asked.

"I couldn't even begin to...," Jeffers started.

"I was a forensic scientist. I know how to work a crime scene and follow minute evidence to its ultimate conclusion. Just like we did in North Dakota. We are close. We can do it again. Together," Chase said.

"Fine. Fine. You were...good on the North Dakota case," Jeffers admitted.

"Time is of the essence, Agent Jeffers. You need all hands on deck. We can help you end this," Chase looked hard into the lead agent's eyes.

"Okay. You and Tannen are in, but Wally would be a liability. And you two will be on a leash. I mean it," Jeffers said.

"You got it," Chase agreed.

Jeffers sighed, "Alright. Get your man to the hotel and then we have work to do."

Chase slid into Wally's patient room. All eyes fell on him.

"Well, you're not peeved, so you must have gotten your way," Wally noticed.

Chase nodded, "You are remanded to the hotel. Tannen and I are in with precautions."

Agent Sohn's and Agent Dunlap's mouths fell open, "You got Jeffers to change his mind? That doesn't happen."

Chase shrugged, "What's important, is we need to close this case before anyone else gets hurt."

"After last night, I know what we're up against," Wally stated.

"What's that?" Tannen asked.

"I'd have to confirm," he swallowed hard. "These are most definitely…zombies."

TWENTY

"How're we looking Wally?" Tannen asked into his cellphone.

"Not bad, really. It has a little frame stuttering at times, but I can see you and three of the cameras," Wally said.

"Yeah, it's a shame you can't real time all of them," Tannen said.

"Not up here. If we were in a town with civilized internet, but we have what we have," the team's tech said.

"Sorry you're not out here with us," Tannen said.

"It's not so bad. At least here, I have a plentiful supply of snacks," Wally grinned through the phone. "You guys watch yourselves out there."

Tannen assured his friend that they would and ended the call.

"We ready?" Chase asked.

"We're ready," Tannen nodded.

"Agent Sohn, you're with Dr. Chase. Agent Dunlap, you're with Tannen. If either of you lose sight of your partner, I'll have your badges yanked," Jeffers warned.

"We're not losing another teammate," Sohn replied, her voice even and serious.

"I had the entire property swept by drones and dogs. There is nowhere anyone or anything of consequence is hiding on the property. That means they are coming from outside of the fence line or…," Jeffers started.

"Or somehow, from inside this building," Chase finished.

"The Skagit County Sheriff's department is maintaining drone surveillance and again has all roads in blocked, not that that has made a difference. Point is, they have the grounds, we have the building," Jeffers said. "If they are coming from somewhere we have missed, we'll find them."

Wally's voice broke the discussion via the radio, "Hey guys, I have been reviewing the footage from the camera I had just placed last night. And I'm not gonna lie, it scared the heck out of me."

The tech swallowed before he continued, "You can see me set it up. I started to walk away with Jeffers and Dunlap when I doubled back to check the sightline with Tannen. The moment I turned and broke away from the agents, the figure appears. It stayed in the shadows of the high brush. It isn't evident on tape, but that is likely where it came from. Anyways, here's the thing. It observed. It let the situation develop and the gap between the agents and me grow. And then it pounced."

"This is no dumb predator," Chase observed.

"It uses the environment to its advantage. Once it goes, though. It goes. There was no stopping it until Jeffers and Dunlap started unloading their mags into it," Wally said.

"Great. Crazy people with tactical awareness," Jeffers snapped.

"That's probably why we have such a hard time finding them. They aren't dumb. They aren't mindlessly attacking. Whatever they are…they are mindful until they go into a frenzy, until something snaps them out of it and scares them away," Chase added.

"There are examples like that throughout the animal kingdom," Tannen said.

"We excluded animals and the video and eyewitness we have, these are people," Agent Dunlap interjected.

"Humanish!" Wally exclaimed.

"Whatever, we need to find them and take them down!" Jeffers growled.

Another radio chimed in, "Agent Jeffers, the drone pilot caught activity by the north western wedge of the property along the fence line. I'm going to send a team in to check it out."

"Copy that, Sheriff Watts. Have your men proceed with caution," Jeffers stated.

"Inside or outside?" Chase asked.

"The professor wants to know if the activity is on the inside or outside of the fence line," Jeffers called.

After a delay, the sheriff's voice came back, "Inside."

All eyes fell on Dr. Chase. "If the activity was outside and looking to get in, that tells us whatever has been attacking people here come from outside of the estate."

"And if inside looking out…," Dunlap started.

"Then it's coming from somewhere on the property," Agent Sohn finished.

"That part of the property is near the tunnel," Tannen announced.

Chase looked at Jeffers. The lead agent nodded, "Let's go. All together!"

Jeffers took the lead with each of his agents keeping close with their assigned paranormal researcher. Weapons drawn, they moved through the heavy doors connecting them with the staircase leading to the steam tunnels.

Wincing at the loud groan made by the aged metal hinges, they made their way into the tunnel system that spanned the breadth of the old hospital. Jeffers' keen sense of direction navigated the dank halls as he swung down the sloped delivery access tunnel. When they reached the end, they were perplexed. The main gate was secure with no way for access.

"Think they are unlocking and locking the doors as they move about?" Sohn asked.

"They might. I don't know how else to explain each time we isolate, we are up against a perceived dead end," Dr. Chase shrugged.

"The attackers seem primitive in their demeanor, at least in frenzy mode," Tannen said. "But as the footage from Wally's attack illustrates, there is a level of calculated intelligence."

"They've avoided us zeroing in on them so far," Agent Dunlap added.

The sheriff's voice came through their radio, "We had a subject under drone surveillance, but it disappeared. The thermal on this thing is a bit fritzy."

Jeffers dropped his head in frustration. "Alright, Sheriff. Where was the last known?"

"We tracked it through the brush towards that far out building," the sheriff responded.

Dr. Chase cocked his head, "The crematorium."

"Let's go," Jeffers urged as Dunlap worked the keys for the big service doors.

Slipping through, they waited for the junior agent to resecure the gate and they made their way through the brush, up the hillside towards the crematorium. Passing several deputies who had been following the trail, each panning their lights searching for clues.

As they had become accustomed to, reaching the crematorium building was a dead end. No one was there and they couldn't detect anyone near the perimeter in the brush.

"There's no one here," Jeffers threw his arms up in frustration. In a fruitless search, the investigators scoured every inch of the small building, including wrenching open the oven doors themselves.

Spinning, the hapless lead agent faced the team, "Any ideas?"

The room was thoughtful for a moment before Dr. Chase spoke. "Based on the last known sighting from the drone, the subject was heading this direction based on our estimation. Does the drone record actual geographical coordinates?"

Jeffers called the question into the Sheriff. Receiving the data, they used Tannen's phone to plot the location. "Let's see where it goes," the FBI agent led the team back out of the building on to the hospital grounds.

It did not take them long to find the coordinates would lead them directly into thick blackberry bushes. With a sigh, Jeffers called to the sheriff, "Your team have machetes by any chance?"

"My deputies down by the tunnel have a couple. They were slashing the underbrush looking for clues. I'll have them run them up to you," Sheriff Watts offered.

As the team waited, they paced the edge of the trail as a group. "It's hard to tell what is natural spacing or not," Tannen offered. "But it looks like there are narrow paths through the thicket."

Agent Dunlap eyed the lanes Tannen observed, "I wouldn't want to run through there."

"Didn't say it would be an enjoyable journey," Tannen grinned.

"Maybe not so bad for a bullet-tolerant individual," Chase murmured.

Jeffers rolled his eyes. They lit up as the deputies jogged up the trail, machetes in hand. The agent thanked the men. He and Dunlap wielded the blades, cutting a swath through the blackberries while Tannen kept them on track with the GPS on his phone.

Deep in the thicket, roughly one hundred yards from the hospital, they reached a miniscule respite in the heavy growth. The trace of a path Tannen thought he saw became a clear patch that appeared to have foot traffic. They spun in all directions, trying to locate what they were missing.

Agent Sohn spread her hands wide and hissed, "Do you hear that?"

The crew froze and fell silent.

All at once, each cocked their head slightly as a sound caught their attention. "What is that?" Dunlap asked.

"Scratching?" Tannen frowned.

"Animal, probably," Jeffers shrugged, dismissing the fervor.

"I don't know. Like shuffling, but where?" Agent Sohn played her light around the clearing.

As she walked forward, Dr. Chase stopped her, his arm across her chest. With his foot, the professor stomped on the ground. Moving his foot over a few feet, he stomped again.

"There's something under here!" Chase exclaimed, kneeling on the ground. Feeling with his hands, he found a ridge in the ground underneath the layers of dirt and leaves.

Jeffers knelt on the other side of him, "There is! Dunlap, get down here. See if you can get your fingers under this edge."

Together, the three men dug around until they identified a rough rectangle. As they tried to grasp an edge, they struggled to gain any leverage.

"Gentlemen," Agent Sohn observed. Brushing leaves away from a root, she found that it formed a U and turned back into the ground.

With a yank, a hinged door flung open. As it did, a wall of stale air blasted at the investigators kneeling on the ground. Along with it, an eruption of arms and legs exploded through the exposed hole, trampling Jeffers, Dunlap and Chase to the ground, knocking Agent Sohn and Tannen to the side.

For a moment, the highly capable team was at a loss. They struggled to fully comprehend what had just happened and their brains refused cogent direction. Shouts from the deputies at the end of the thicket brought them to action, with Jeffers snapping into salience first.

"I think we found our attackers," Jeffers said, unholstering his service weapon. Jumping to his feet, he led the charge out of the blackberries.

Chase and Sohn looked at the hole, confused of whether to leave it exposed or slam it shut. With a nod, slamming it shut seemed like the most prudent action. Chase pointed to Tannen while Dunlap raced after Jeffers, "Hand me that branch."

Tannen reached over and snatched a thick branch from the ground. Jamming it under the loop handle of the subterranean door, Chase gave it a yank. Satisfied it was secure, he gave a nod to Agent Sohn and Tannen for them to follow the others.

Outside of the blackberry thicket, the hospital grounds were chaotic. The FBI team and county deputies spun as figures raced erratically around the grounds. Weapons drawn, but no prescribed imminence to fire, they watched with mouths agape.

"Uhm, Sheriff...do we have that drone back airborne?" Jeffers asked.

"We do. The thermal is out. We have IR on board," Sheriff Watts said.

"Are you seeing this?" the FBI agent continued.

"Who is running around?" the sheriff asked.

"I believe that is our million-dollar question," Jeffers said.

"Can we contain them?"

"Maybe, if the fence holds," the FBI agent replied.

"It looks like they found the gap from the original attack. The patch job seems to be...nope. They're gone. They're all gone," the sheriff announced.

"Sheriff Watts, we've got a problem," Jeffers stressed.

TWENTY ONE

Skagit County deputies stood at their assigned post, blocking the main entrance of the Northern State Mental Hospital. They heard the growing commotion on their radios and heeded Sheriff Watts' calls to be vigilant.

Despite the warning, they were not prepared for what came there way. Sprinting around the fence towards the main road that connected the abandoned hospital to town, a pack of flailing bodies sprinted directly at them. Like a school of fish, they moved in near unison, dancing along the edge of the shadows. They slowed for a moment as the deputies came into view and then veered away to follow the road in the ravine near the tree line.

The deputies shared confused looks followed by immense indecision. With weapons drawn, their orders were to only shoot if there was an imminent threat and try and apprehend if they could. They elected to exercise the out-card provided by the sheriff to merely call their location in.

"Uh, Sheriff, this is Deputy Johnson at the main entrance. The...subjects just passed by headed towards the main road," the deputy spoke into his radio.

"Copy that, Deputy Johnson. Hold your position and continue to watch the main entrance. We're sending a team to track the subjects," Sheriff Watts informed the deputy.

Turning to his partner, all Deputy Johnson could do was shrug.

Sirens wailing, three cruisers sped towards the intersection with the hospital road. Slamming on the brakes, they lined their vehicles to block the path, their searchlights trained on the road ahead.

A series of silhouettes crested into their view. In a rough line, a dozen figures ran towards them. The ravine they traveled emptied directly towards the deputies as the roads intersected.

The deputies readied themselves, one member of the pair stood with a tazer and the other with department issued firearm. Neither sure what to expect or what to do when the swarm of bodies approached.

The frenzy was chaotic as the pack of suspects divided. Some dove headlong into the culvert that ran under the road. Some split left or right diverting through the nearby forest away from the waiting blockade.

One leapt headlong out of the ravine, catching a deputy full on. Sinking its teeth into the deputy's neck as electrodes from the tazer took hold. The figure yelped, jumped off the deputy and on to a patrol car. In a mighty leap, it cleared the deputy's partners. One got off a shot before the figure slipped into the shadows and disappeared with the rest of the pack.

Officer Downs didn't hear them coming. He sat on the end of his cruiser texting his wife that he would be home late as it was an "all-hands" night.

By the time he heard the footfall behind him and the twig snap, the figure had launched from its steady creep towards his position. A pair of powerful hands wrapped around the officer's neck, pulling him backwards and onto the ground.

Officer Downs slid his hand towards his holster as more figures joined the first. Pouncing in a frenzy of limbs, teeth and nails, they consumed the deputy to the point of unconsciousness before they unceremoniously scattered as the headlights of approaching vehicles swept the scene.

Officer Jacobs hopped out of his cruiser, letting the tray of coffees he brought for their shift fall to the ground. As he ran, he called into his shoulder radio, "Officer down! Officer down! Need immediate medical assistance and backup!"

Special Agent Devon Jeffers leapt out of his SUV as he arrived at the scene. The team followed as they joined the Sedro-Woolley police officers who scrambled to assist their injured fellow officer. Sheriff Watts pulled to a stop behind him.

The officers formed a perimeter around their fallen teammate as two provided first aid while they awaited the ambulance wailing in the distance. Tannen pushed his way through and after identifying himself as an EMT, took over primary care on the officer.

Jeffers observed the scene and the condition of the officer. He also tracked the points of travel of the subjects. As the Sheriff stood beside him and Chief Roberts joined, arriving just ahead of the ambulance, they conferred.

"They're heading towards town," Jeffers observed.

"What can we do?" Watts asked as Roberts was consumed with checking on his man.

"Shut down the town," Jeffers said.

"What?" Sheriff Watts choked.

"We need to lock down the town of Sedro-Woolley, the citizens are at risk," Jeffers stated flatly.

"What do we tell them?" the sheriff asked.

"A dangerous animal, a manhunt, a killer is on the loose…whatever will get them to lock their doors and stay inside," Jeffers said. "Tell them to report any activity immediately."

"What do my deputies do?" Sheriff Watts pressed.

"If attacked, they shoot. If they can, they capture or at least corral until help can come, do that. Beyond that, protect the citizens, protect themselves," Jeffers replied.

"Do you have tranquilizers?" Chase asked.

"Why?" Sheriff Watts asked.

"If they aren't specifically attacking, how do we know who they are? Maybe they are victims themselves," the professor explained.

"Well, that's complicating," Jeffers scowled.

"You can't just shoot anything that moves," Chase warned.

"I suppose you're right," Sheriff Watts nodded. "I will see what we can come up with."

The sheriff walked to confer with Chief Roberts on how best to lock down the town.

"What do we have going on here, Chase?" Jeffers asked as the team gathered around, watching the officer get lifted into the back of the ambulance.

"They're people. Feral people," Chase mused, his eyes panning the dense, dark forest around them. "Animal-like, savage people."

Wally was confused by the radio silence, but the flashes of images on the cameras transmitting wirelessly to his monitors told the tell rather succinctly. All hell had broken loose at the abandoned hospital.

He wanted to reach out to the team, but he knew they would communicate when appropriate. For all he knew, he would give away their position by squelching on their radios.

For the time being, he had to rely on whatever glimpses he could catch on screen. The increased Skagit County Sheriff's Deputy presence on the path near where he had been attacked suggested there was more activity there tonight.

Reaching for a bag of chips, he paused as he squeezed either side, ready to pull the seam apart and free the salty goodness it held. The sound of a trashcan toppling over outside followed by what sounded like a scream brought his attention to the hotel room window.

Casting the curtain to a side, Wally watched as figures much like the one that attacked him, streaked by on the sidewalks of Sedro-Woolley. Several figures ran by in an irregular pattern, bouncing from cover to cover without slowing or stopping.

"Well, that can't be good," he muttered.

As Wally stood at the window, he didn't hear his phone buzz on the table by the monitors. Hobbling to answer it likely wouldn't have produced much value as his caller's SUV careened into the hotel parking lot and screeched to a stop outside of his room.

Agent Sohn hopped out of the passenger seat of the SUV, her weapon drawn, making a sweep of the parking lot before urging Chase and Tannen to follow.

"This *really* can't be good," Wally said as he let the curtains fall and moved to unlatch the hotel door.

Opening the door just as his friends reached the threshold, the tech let them in. Agent Sohn placed her back to the door as she addressed the team. "Things went from unusual and dangerous to downright catastrophic," Agent Sohn said.

"What's going on," Wally asked.

"We seem to have unleashed a throng of feral humans that have attacked two officers in the same manner as they attacked you and the teens. By rough count, thirteen of them have made it into town and pose a considerable threat to the population," Dr. Chase informed his teammate.

"Let me go on record stating I was nowhere near the old hospital tonight," Wally said.

"Agent Jeffers is putting the town on lockdown. He is coordinating with Watts and Roberts right now. It's going to be a long night," Agent Sohn said. "I need you to hole up here. Stay away from the windows, do not go outside for *anything*. Keep the door latched. The other agents and I will identify ourselves, otherwise, I don't care if Chief Roberts is smiling on the other side of that peephole, you don't open it."

"What are you going to do?" Wally asked.

"I'm going to work with Jeffers and Dunlap, along with the local L.E.O.s to try and keep the town safe," Agent Sohn said, her visage grim.

"I'm going with you," Chase said.

Agent Sohn began to protest but the look on his face and his reminder, "It's safer to be in pairs, at least," swayed her.

"Fine. You do exactly what I say, exactly when I say it. You stay close to me," Agent Sohn warned.

"Kind of wishing I wasn't injured with commands being doled out like that," Wally sneered.

The look of severity on Agent Sohn's face instantly melted the smile from the paranormal researcher. Bobbing his head in shame, Wally waved Sohn and Chase a safe night.

TWENTY TWO

Agent Sohn directed Ryder Chase through the streets of Sedro-Woolley, her firearm never finding its way back to its holster. Their eyes remained peeled as the powerful lights of the SUV swept the town.

Vigilant, on the look-out for any shadow that moved. Watchful for either a citizen that needed to be remanded home or a feral that needed containment. As they pulled into the Sedro-Woolley police station, the parking lot looked like a S.W.A.T. convention.

A man in a suit was animated in his discussion with Chief Roberts. Sheriff Watts and Jeffers did their best to support the police chief's case.

"You're the police. If there are dangerous people threatening our citizens, just shoot them. I don't want to infringe on the rights of my law-abiding citizens!" the man said, his voice blanketing the parking lot.

Jeffers frowned when he saw Chase with Agent Sohn, but was soon glad to see him as he interjected into the conversation.

"Mister...," Chase began.

"Mayor Hill. This is my town. I'll say whether it gets cast into Marshall Law or not," the man spat.

"Mayor Hill, we can't be sure if the people running around town *are* your citizens or not. We have no idea if all or some pose a dangerous threat. The *last* thing we want, is an officer shooting a citizen. The only way to be sure is for your people to lock down for the night. So, unless someone is running around with a badge, they might be well be fired on tonight," Chase warned.

"What exactly are we dealing with?" the mayor asked.

"We aren't entirely sure. Some group of feral people. Why they are that way, we don't know. Are all or only some dangerous, we don't know. What we do know is several people have died at their hands, two officers and one of my team have been attacked and seriously wounded while being in their path. Do you really want to take chances tonight? Do you think a federal agent, an elected sheriff and *your* police chief are taking this request lightly?" Chase continued.

The mayor cast his head down for a moment before looking Chase in the eyes, "No, I suppose not."

"Then how do we get the word to the town to hunker down for the night for their own safety?" Chase asked.

"We have an alert system. We use it for forest fires, earthquakes and such. I'll get the word out," the mayor said softly.

"Thank you, Mayor," Chief Roberts said.

"I want a full report in the morning," the mayor said.

"Yes sir," Roberts nodded. Spinning to his men awaiting orders, the police chief turned attention to Agent Jeffers.

"We don't know what we are dealing with. We know if they can single you out, they will attack. We know they stick to the shadows to ambush their victims. Be safe. Stick together. Don't confront them. Call in your position and my team will respond. Above all, keep them away from the people in their homes. Let the subjects roam the streets out here, keep them from the residential areas," Jeffers said.

"You heard him, deputies. Hit the residential areas. Chief Roberts' officers, concentrate on those closest to town. My crew will work on the outskirts," Sheriff Watts called out.

The officers began filing towards their vehicles with their assignments, each prepared for a long night patrolling the streets.

"I was going to question your presence here, professor, but you proved quite useful in getting the mayor on board," Jeffers said.

"Politicians fret about losses. The mayor is worried that the shelter-in-place orders will only add to the anxiety that is already cast over the town. Everyone needed to understand the threat is real and what his mayoral seat would suffer if more people got hurt if he didn't place the order," Chase said. "Appeal to his concern versus applying federal authority."

"I've seen it work both ways," Jeffers grunted. "The town can be split east to west or north to south. The main road separates north to south and provides a fast conduit to respond, so let's use that tract. Dunlap and I will hit sightings to the north. Agent Sohn, you and the professor have the south."

For the first few hours, the agents responded to spot calls. Each time they arrived, the ferals had slipped into the shadows and disappeared. Nearing midnight,

Agents Jeffers and Dunlap arrived to assist deputies on the edge of town.

Getting out of their SUV, they met the deputies flanking either side of their vehicle. They shined a light at the corner of a home only to have a face appear on the opposite side. The whack a mole routine lasted for several minutes while the agent observed.

By the time a pattern had emerged, Jeffers motioned for Dunlap to circle one way while he went the other.

Hunching from cover to cover, they approached their targets who seemed intent to keep playing the game with the deputies. When Dunlap stepped on a branch, he elicited the attention of the feral on his side of the residence. Frozen, both Dunlap and the feral studied each other until the deputy swung the light in their direction, prompting the feral to burst out of its position and dart to the next house.

From house to house, the game continued with each agent closing in on a feral until it sprang with surprising agility to the next location. The game drew tremendous ire from Agent Jeffers but he took solace in the fact that the match kept the ferals away from the residents inside their homes.

Agent Sohn received the call just after midnight. Residents reported seeing figures creep by their lawn on the southern edge of town.

Dr. Chase pushed the SUV's V8 engine hard as he accelerated to the neighborhood. Stopping at the end of the street, they slid out of their seats, standing behind their open doors as they listened and observed.

A whisper and a giggle behind the bushes of one of the houses caught their attention. The pair cast a glance to one another and moved towards the noises.

As they approached, their flashlights penetrating the shadows cast by the bushes, they heard a prolonged, "Shh!"

Agent Sohn rolled her eyes at Chase and nodded for him to enter one direction as she moved the other. Closing in they, bookended two teenagers huddled behind the hydrangea they used for concealment.

Agent's Sohn's light played over the pair of wide-eyed faces, "You two are breaking curfew, but I am guessing you are well aware of that."

The girl dropped her head, "It was date night."

"It seemed exciting, like the movies," the boy added.

"You ever notice in the movies its couples like you that get killed early on?" Sohn levied.

The two teens swung their heads in each other's direction. The girl scrunched her nose, "Yeah, that is pretty true, huh?"

"Let's get you home. I can tell you the threat out here is very real. Where do you live?" Agent Sohn asked.

"I live over there," the boy pointed.

"This is my house," the girl admitted.

"Good. Get inside!" Agent Sohn's eyes were fierce, sending the girl scurrying without even a goodbye to her boyfriend. The agent remained just long enough to hear the click of the lock behind the girl. "Now to get you home," Agent Sohn prodded the boy.

As they escorted the boy across the street, Dr. Chase spun. In the deep shadows of a hedge separating the neighboring yards, he heard rustling. As they stopped, it stopped. With a hesitant nod forward, Agent Sohn continued escorting the boy across the road. As they moved, the rustling continued.

"Move!" Chase yelled as he stepped in between the hedge and the agent and the boy.

A figure sprung from the foliage towards Chase.

Agent Sohn placed her hands on the boy's shoulders and looked him dead in the eyes, "Listen to me. I need you to run home and lock the door behind you. Now!"

The boy nodded and sprinted towards his front porch. Jamming his key into the lock and twisting in the same movement, he disappeared quickly inside.

Agent Sohn turned to see Chase in an athletic stance bouncing laterally back and forth dodging the feral's attacks. When the feral lunged with a vicious swipe, Chase rolled to his right and sprang back to his feet, ready to dodge more attacks.

Agent Sohn dashed in front of Chase. Snapping a tactical baton open, she swiped at the legs of the feral, striking upwards, she caught the feral on the chin before bringing the baton down over the base of the feral's skull. To her horror, she saw two more ferals approaching.

"Come on!" she yanked on Chase's shoulder, propelling him forward in a dead run away from the ferals. The footfalls behind them told them the chase was on and the ferals were closing in.

As they sprinted full tilt, Agent Sohn wished she had the instinct to lead them towards their SUV instead of away. Spying an open window of a detached garage adjacent to one of the neighborhood homes, she prodded, "There!"

Chase nodded. Brushing off Sohn's grip on his jacket so they could both run full speed, they raced to the window. Sohn paused for just a moment as the professor dove through the tall window with surprising agility. Leaping through herself, she spun and slammed the window shut. Spying a pile of lumber nearby, she grabbed a piece of plywood and slammed it against the window. Chase followed with a two-by-four, jamming it against the plywood and the body of a parked car just as the first feral slammed into the window, shattering it.

Fists began hammering against the plywood. They could hear feet circling the garage and fists testing various parts of the building. Footfalls on the roof scampered its length as a feral searched for entry.

Hearts racing, Chase and Sohn shone their flashlights around the garage, inspecting for any point of entry. The plywood shrouded window and the bowing garage door loomed to be the greatest weaknesses.

Scanning the space for additional cover, Chase nodded towards a sixty-five Mustang. Chase's glance revealed the front seats and dash were removed for restoration, but the doors and windows were intact.

Agent Sohn nodded and followed the professor into the old Mustang. Slamming both locks into place, they slunk back onto the rear bench seat. Shutting off their lights and sitting perfectly still, they listened and waited. The FBI agent never lifted her finger from the trigger of her firearm.

Minutes ticked by and the commotion seemed to die down. They could hear pacing back and forth, like the ferals were frustrated, trying to find a way in. Unrelenting as they circled the garage.

Agent Sohn used her free hand to call her superior.

"Yeah, Sohn, what is it," Jeffers called into the phone, panting as he played defense against a feral, preventing it from closing in on a house.

Agent Sohn explained their situation.

"Are you safe?" Jeffers asked.

"We seem to be, at least for the moment," Sohn admitted.

"We're dealing with…a bit of a situation here. If you're safe, stay put. If anything changes, I'll come running. You have my official permission to fire away if threatened."

"We're good, for now," Sohn breathed.

"Great! I'll check in once we, uh, have our situation contained," Jeffers panted.

The phone went dead. Sohn put it away, still ready with her firearm. "I guess we wait," she whispered.

"We seem safe in here for the time being," Chase admitted as he watched Sohn in the fading glow of her phone. Despite the imminent danger, he couldn't help himself but to be taken by her beauty illuminated in the bath of blue L.E.D.s.

Sohn leaned back, her side pressing against his. Never relaxing her grip on her Sig Sauer pistol. "I guess we're stuck here for a while."

Just as Chase's heart began to calm to a normal rate, it began racing again. As the agent's head turned and her breath softly fell against his skin, the professor's pulse reached a new peak which only sustained as her lips met his.

TWENTY THREE

Only the buzzing on their phones alerted them that it was morning. The plywood barricaded the only window in the garage, keeping them shrouded in darkness. The Mustang's windows fogged with their breath, further veiled morning's arrival.

Chase woke with his arm around Agent Sohn. Her head pressed into his shoulder as he slept. Watching her breath rise and fall as she pressed against him belied the peril of the night that they had escaped. Here was a beautiful woman in what would otherwise be a beautiful moment marred in the stale stench of danger and death.

Still, he waited, absorbing the moment. Allowing her senses to come to life. He eyed in the turned down glow of his cellphone, as content as Danica Sohn appeared, her finger laid against the slide of her firearm.

Stirring, she looked at him, allowed her weary mind to connect the dots of where she was and why she was there, she smiled.

"Hello," she purred.

"Good morning," Chase said.

"As things go, not the worst sleep I've ever had," Sohn shared.

"I was…surprisingly comfortable," Chase admitted.

Checking her phone, she cursed and giggled at the same time, "Well, this should be fun to explain."

"Agent Jeffers did order you to hunker down," Chase reminded.

"That he did," Agent Sohn pressed into him. Her mouth gliding past his chin, seeking his lips. Finding them, she pressed hard while sucking in her own morning breath, only to pull away abruptly as shafts of light penetrated the garage.

Sliding to their respective sides of the car, Sohn lunged forward for the driver's side door handle and spilled out onto the floor of the garage. As she looked up, she cast a disheveled look towards a grinning Agent Dunlap.

"Good morning, Agent Sohn!" he declared. As the female FBI agent stumbled her way upright, Dunlap watched as Ryder Chase crawled out after her. His eyes went wide with ideas of the evening.

"Let me remind you, Agent Dunlap. You are a subordinate agent. Any loud noises without offering me coffee in the morning or wild, baseless accusations will cost your career dearly," Agent Sohn spat.

"Yes, ma'am!" Dunlap snapped to attention. The warning did not stop him from casting a devious grin towards Professor Chase.

"Nothing happened," Chase snapped, following Sohn's lead.

They refused Dunlap's hand extended to help pull them out. Dr. Chase casually walked to the garage door, flipped the latch mechanism and shot the rolling door open, allowing them their escape from their evening exile.

Agent Jeffers stood in front of the doors, his arms folded in front of his chest. "I'm glad you two are okay. Come on, we have work to do," Jeffers spun without another glance backwards.

"I was a little concerned when you did not return my texts and calls," he muttered as he marched him towards their SUVs.

Agent Sohn winced, "After you commanded us to hole up, I turned my ringer off, so we didn't continue to attract the ferals."

"Frustrating but prudent," Jeffers said, not breaking his gait.

"How did you guys fare last night?" Sohn asked.

"The town seems relatively safe and I'm glad our actions weren't being recorded," Jeffers responded, his voice gruff.

"We played a long night of zombie tag until dawn came and they just kind of...disappeared," Dunlap admitted.

"Instead of an all-nighter of keep away from the residents, it would be a lot easier if we could just shoot them," Agent Jeffers was surly from lacking sleep.

"What's the play?" Chase asked.

"Police Chief Roberts reported lots of activity, few major incidents. Some minor wounds from brief conflicts," Jeffers reported. "We're on our way to confer with the chief and sheriff now."

Sedro-Woolley was largely a ghost town. Schools and businesses were closed. The state police barred entry to the town from the various arteries, including the interstate.

As weary officers and deputies gathered, Police Chief Roberts and Sheriff Watts shared a makeshift podium in the back of a pickup truck.

Chief Roberts started, "We had a long night. We thank you for your dedication and service. We thank your families as well. I'm sure they would have liked to have had you home last night."

Sheriff Watts reported, "We recorded numerous encounters, a few close calls with minor injuries along the way, but by all accounts, no major casualties. We do have a couple of officers wounded during the initial…break out. They are both stable and should recover fine."

"We need to scour the town. Ensure each residence is safe. Then see if there are any subjects hiding in the commercial district and then the nearby woods. We have additional resources coming in from the state police. It's probably going to be another long day," Chief Roberts declared.

As the two law enforcement leaders handed out specific duties, Chase saw two figures ambling towards the police station parking lot. With a wave, Wally grinned as Tannen wrapped an arm around his shoulder for support.

"Had to see what was going on," Wally said.

"He wouldn't take no for an answer," Tannen frowned.

Chase nodded, "It's alright. Things seem calm at the moment. Busy but relatively safe night. Time to poke the bushes and see what we find by daylight."

They were surprised by two eager men who made a beeline towards them. One of them carried a folder while the other, held a box triumphantly in front of them.

"Hi, guys!" Dr. Lazenby called as he sauntered over. "We brought news."

"And bagels!" Dr. Burbee presented the box in his hands. Lifting the lid, he revealed, "With the town locked down, the selection was what was left over. Mostly cranberry and raisin bagels."

Lazenby frowned, "Which in retrospect makes the salmon schmeer an unfortunate choice."

Burbee pursed his lips, "Hmm. I suppose it does."

Wally reached in grabbing a raisin bagel and used the plastic knife to wipe a substantial blob of the salmon cream cheese on it. Taking a big bite, he nodded approvingly, "Kinda hits the spot, really."

Affirmed, Burbee thrust the box out for the others who waved him off.

Lazenby shook off the breakfast disappointment and smacked the file folder in his hands, "From the bite marks in Wally here's leg, we were able to get another dental records match. A missing undergrad in Seattle."

"We matched him up to the Bureau's missing persons list. He's one of the ones listed in this region," Dr. Burbee added.

"What do you make of that, professor?" Agent Jeffers asked.

"It means our ferals aren't some group of undeveloped humans living in the woods. These are functional citizens that have somehow…turned," Dr. Chase said.

Wally's eyes went wide as he opened his mouth to speak.

Agent Jeffers cut him off, "Don't say it."

"They're salient with a reasonably high level of consciousness," Chase added for Wally's benefit. "Certainly not how they're depicted in the movies."

"The question I have, is if I shoot them, will they die?" Jeffers asked.

Chase spun his head, his tone serious, "That is a question our limited experience can't answer. So far, the data leans to no. Limited 'N', however."

On cue, the North Cascades Wildlife Officer pulled up in his large SUV. Opening the hatch, he reavealed half a dozen rifles. Handing one to Chief Roberts, one to Sheriff Watts, he paused before deciding to hand the remaining guns to Special Agent Jeffers.

"Air rifles. I've got limited ammo in the form of tranquilizer darts in the back there. You can take all of it. I have additional resources coming, should be here late this afternoon," the ranger said.

"Thanks, Raines!" Chief Roberts acknowledged.

"I'm wrangling some additional bodies to help in the search. I've got a couple of buddies who are good at this sort of stuff," the Officer Raines said.

"As we make concentric circles emanating out from city center, your experience in the boundary woods would be a big help," Sheriff Watts said.

"No problem," Raines said as he headed back to his vehicle and closed the hatch as the ammo boxes were retrieved. "Be safe out there!"

Official vehicles began pouring into the small town and didn't stop. Among them, a blacked-out SUV followed cloesly by a vehicle that wore an ambulance body labeled in bold letters "FBI Evidence Response Team".

A man hopped out of the lead SUV while others exited their vehicles and stood by. Striding up to the only other man on the scene in a suit, however weathered from the previous evening, "You must be Special Agent."

"I am," Jeffers nodded.

"Agent Hanley, Seattle Field Office, my partner, Agent Foote. Agents Miles and Hawes are our forensics experts. We're here to help any way we can," the agent offered.

"We can use it. This case has been…a challenge,"
Jeffers.

"I read the reports. Whatever I could make of them,
at least. More loose ends than a bouquet of balloons,"
Hanley quipped.

Jeffers raised an eyebrow.

"It's been a peculiar case, to be sure," Chase
interjected.

Hanley eyed the professor, "This must be the
consultant working with you on the case."

"This is Dr. Ryder Chase. He and his team have
been…helpful," Jeffers nodded.

"We don't typically use consultants," Hanley
scoffed.

Agent Sohn began to speak to Chase and his team's
defense, but Jeffers waved her off. "We were just about to
head back to the old hospital. It will be a good time to get
your forensics team set up," the lead agent suggested.

"It's your show," Hanley conceded.

"I don't think he likes us much," Dr. Chase
observed on the way to their vehicles.

"Still on the fence myself," Jeffers muttered, the
slightest grin forming at the corners of his lips.

TWENTY FOUR

"Fill me in on what you have so far," Hanley asked as they marched through the property.

Jeffers shared the state of the investigation, including the previous evening's activities and the revelation of the college student being Wally's attacker.

Agent Foote, Hanley's partner swiveled his head around, in awe over the hospital and grounds. "It *is* creepy," he remarked.

"Creepy is a state of mind. I'm sure we'll find some kids cooking a bad batch of meth or something," Hanley corrected.

"He's like Jeffers 2.0," Wally whispered to Dunlap who grinned.

"Wally, why don't you and Tannen lead Agents Miles and Hawes to the Command Center. You can get off your feet there. Give them the lay of the land. We'll catch up to you there after we open pandoras box in the field and investigate it," Jeffers suggested. "Agent Dunlap, I'll have you escort them."

Reluctantly, Agent Dunlap watched as the paranormal researcher winced with every step and nodded, "Probably a good idea."

As the team broke into two, Jeffers largely ignored Hanley and Foote as he was focused on what he was convinced to be a key to the puzzle. The concern over the safety of the town thwarted their ability to investigate it the previous night.

Fresh deputies guarded the area at each station. Sheriff Watts' staff rotated, maintaining the roadblocks and guarding the entrances. Jeffers acknowledged the men and turned into the blackberries they had hacked with machetes the previous evening.

From the perspective of daylight, its proximity to the hospital and linear track towards the crematorium made sense. "The hospital staff could move bodies from the morgue, move them into the tunnels below, exit the hospital here and head for the crematorium with little visibility from the patient rooms," Chase pointed as he tracked the procession in his head.

Jeffers nodded, "Plausible, Dr. Chase. Let's get in there and find out if the theory holds."

Freeing the branch Chase wedged into the handle, the lead agent nodded. With weapons drawn and flashlights burning, they flung the door open. They revealed a sloping slab that lead to a tunnel below. The tunnel was crude, appearing to be an afterthought dug into the side of the hospital after it had been built.

Following Agent Jeffers, they were halted by a door. Lacking a handle, they found an iron key jammed into a crevice. Giving it a twist, they waited, expecting the facade to open. Jeffers gave the door a shove. It appeared bolted shut.

"Turn the key again, Agent Jeffers," Chase suggested.

With a shrug, Jeffers complied. The team heard a satisfying "click". Still, the door didn't open. Stepping forward, Chase pulled the key itself. With a creak, the door sprung open.

Jeffers and Hanley jumped through, each pointing their weapons and lights down an opposite side of the corridor. "It's the tunnel that heads to the delivery gate," Jeffers announced.

Agent Sohn gave Chase an affirmative smile. Stepping through, they studied the door. It hung six inches off of the floor of the tunnel and appeared to be made of concrete, matching the walls right down to the years of dust, dirt and mossy stains.

Chase pushed the door even further open into the hidden tunnel. Slowly, it ratcheted back into place. The door's seams perfectly matching the grout pattern of the tunnel. "Amazing craftsmanship," Chase admired.

"A regular fun house you got here, Jeffers," Hanley said, playing his light around the door.

"A glimpse of what we've been dealing with," Jeffers said, his voice grim.

Running his fingers over where the door clicked into place, Agent Foote shook his head, "If you didn't know it was here, you'd never find it."

Agent Jeffers and Dr. Chase exchanged glances. The observation provided them a hint of dignity for having missed it during the investigation.

"Let's see what other surprises we've missed," Jeffers said, suddenly compelled to poke and prod each slab of concrete that made up the tunnel system.

Chase continued his hypothesis before entering the tunnel, "The rubble used to link the tunnels to the morgue. That was a ramp. It could connect the hospital to the tunnel to within a relatively short distance of the crematorium."

Jeffers stopped under the door they found. Once more climbing atop the pile of debris, he pushed the trapdoor open. "We nearly didn't find this," he said. "It doesn't explain how they disappeared so fast."

The agents searched the walls carefully, looking for a disturbance in the dust, a crack that may belie another hidden door.

Professor Chase studied the trapdoor leading to the hall outside of the morgue. Pulling himself through, he hung from the first floor in the hospital. With his flashlight clenched tight between his teeth, he lowered several inches until he was between the floors. The flowing utility lines and steam pipes caught his eye. They ran through a subfloor roughly ten inches deep. Following the pipes, they would intersect into a 'T' and run vertical.

In nearly every direction, a century of cobwebs netted across the space. Directly in front of Chase to the first 'T' was clear. With a questioning breath, he squeezed between the floors and snaked his way forward. When he reached the vertical section, he had enough space to sit up. Directly between the studs, he could effectively stand.

Shining his light upwards, he found another section suspiciously clear of spider webs.

"Chase! Professor!" he heard his name called.

"I'm in here!" he returned. "There is a little crawl space between the tunnel system and the first floor of the hospital."

"What the hell are you doing in there?" Jeffers poked his head through. Shining his light, he saw the professor's legs disappearing into the hospital studs.

"There weren't cobwebs here," Chase explained.

"Great…?" Jeffers questioned.

"There are cobwebs everywhere else!" Chase pressed.

"Oh!" Jeffers understood. "Let me go first. Who knows what we'll run into."

Chase pivoted, realizing the path was single file. "Alright."

Squatting back down, Chase reversed his course, crawling back through the space and dropping down into the tunnel. Agent Sohn was waiting for him, a disapproving look washed against her face. "What are you boys up to?"

"There is…there seems to be a passage. Jeffers is going through it now," Chase explained.

"Don't go poking into places on your own. This place is dangerous at every turn," Sohn chastised in a harsh whisper.

"Yeah," a muffled voice called. "He was right. It does seem to lead up."

From the open trap door, they could hear the lead agent scramble within the walls above.

"Agent Sohn! You...you have to see this," Jeffers called.

"In there? You guys want me to go in there? Agent Sohn scrunched her face.

Reluctantly, she complied, hoisting herself through the small opening and wriggled her way to the intersection. Once she stood, Chase crawled in after her. Agents Hanley and Foote stood staring up into the opening. "You guys, uh, watch our flank..." Chase suggested.

The FBI agents looked at one another and shrugged.

Using lateral studs, they climbed to a point where they identify the structural split between the first and the second floor. Agent Jeffers had already crawled through and onto the second floor and poked his head down into the crawlspace, "It looks like it goes all the way to the attic." With a hand, he helped Agent Sohn and then Dr. Chase through where they could once more stand on solid floor.

Agent Sohn guided her flashlight around the room, a shiver instantly creeping along her shoulders and down her spine. Closing her eyes tight, she swallowed hard. "Oh, my!"

Agent Jeffers and Dr. Chase stood by the agent.

"There *was* someone in here. Inches from me. Breathing on my neck!" she squirmed and fumed at the same time. "By the time we searched, it dove back into the hole behind this box."

Agent Sohn shook her head, "Unbelievable."

"The space makes a simple matrix. From the tunnel system and the crawlspace, you could reach every floor of this hospital and move around relatively undetected," Chase said.

Jeffers studied the small door that opened into the room. "Being a paneled room, pretty easy to hide a door in the wall," the lead agent observed.

Agent Sohn moved to a row of shelves that ran along the path from the doorway. A small 'V' between two units allowed her to get within a breath of the walkway. The shiver returned, this time she shook it off with ferocity. "Let's find the rest of what this place is hiding!"

TWENTY FIVE

The day was filled with forensics teams combing the tunnels and the crawl space for evidence under the supervision of the field agents. Using UV lights, they found traces of blood from ferals and presumably their victims. Knowing the pressure points on the hidden doors provided areas to dust for fingerprints. The crawlspace proved a haven for hair samples.

With slides, jars and bags of evidence, the forensics team loaded the van and began working the samples they could run in the van while sending a courier to Seattle for DNA and complex analysis.

Within hours, Agent Hawes was exiting the van with several sheets of paper. Finding Agents Jeffers and Hanley reviewing a map for the impending evening watch, he raced up. "We've been able to identify three more subjects from today's analysis," Hawes panted. "Three more students missing from Seattle area colleges."

Jeffers studied the papers while Dr. Chase peered over his shoulder. "They're all from different schools," Chase observed.

"Students from different schools, especially in a metropolitan market party together all the time," Agent Hanley shrugged.

Jeffers had learned to be more patient with Dr. Chase's thought process, encouraged him to continue.

"See if your field office can get their class schedules, going back to their freshman years," Chase suggested.

"They might party together, they aren't going to study together," Agent Hanley scoffed.

"Just run it," Jeffers said, his voice flat.

Shrugging, Hanley handed the papers to Agent Foote. "Send it in."

Agent Foote followed Agent Hawes to the evidence van.

Chase offered Jeffers a slight nod, appreciating his support.

As darkness threatened to fall on the abandoned hospital, Jeffers bristled.

"We need to be ready," he said as much to himself as anyone else. "The state police are maintaining roadblocks in and out of town from all arteries. The wildlife officer has a team patrolling the woods. The town remains under martial law. Chief Roberts' officers are patrolling Sedro-Woolley proper and Sheriff Watt's deputies everything in between."

"What is our role?" Agent Hanley leaned forward.

"All of the other L.E.O.s are to identify, call in and protect life. It is our job to respond and apprehend," Jeffers announced. He sighed and chewed his lip, "As least some of these are college students. Which means lethal force is an absolute last resort to save a life. Period."

"Bunch of hopped up kids. I don't want to see harm to them either, but a criminal is a criminal. They know the risk, right?" Agent Hanley asked.

"Are they?" Dr. Chase asked. "Are they criminals…I mean inherently, when they are not attacking someone?"

"I don't want to live with shooting some college kid who got into the wrong stash at a party," Jeffers admitted. "To save a life, you may have to take a life."

"We have these," Agent Foote hoisted the air gun delivered by the wildlife officer. "The darts are Ketamine. They work three times faster than injections of haloperidol but that stills leaves you five minutes of avoidance before the sedative kicks in, according to Wildlife Officer Raines."

"Alright," Jeffers hoisted an air-propelled dart gun. "Hanley, Foote, Dunlap, Sohn and I will carry these. Keep them locked and loaded"

Dr. Chase looked hopeful at the last one lying on the hood of the SUV. Jeffers shook his head through furrowed brows, "No. Absolutely not."

Sheriff Watts walked up.

"Perfect timing!" Jeffers called. Tossing the remaining weapon towards the sheriff.

Watts instantly inspected the rifle and ensured a clear chamber. Grabbing the box of darts Jeffers handed him, he assured, "We're all set. We have two rotating shifts, every three hours each location gets fresh eyes. You sure we'll see any tonight?"

"I'm not sure of anything with this case, Sheriff Watts," Agent Jeffers admitted. "Be on your toes."

The team gathered their items. Agent Hanley banged his fist on the side of the forensics van. With his fingers circling in the air, he let the team know to head to the hotel for the night. Tannen and Wally emerged from the van to Agent Hanley's chagrin.

"We were trading notes on surveillance and forensic techniques," Wally grinned. "We're going to order pizzas and review our "best of" footage from the investigation."

Agent Hanley shot Jeffers a concerned look. Jeffers shook his head softly, "Let them be. They're relatively harmless and occasionally useful."

Relenting, Hanley nodded as he and Agent Foote climbed into their SUV.

"Dr. Chase, you're with me tonight. Agent Dunlap and Agent Sohn. You know the drill. Just don't get cut off from your vehicle," Jeffers directed.

"If it's all the same, I have an idea, Special Agent Jeffers," Chase announced.

Jeffers paused, wearing a semi-perturbed look on his face. "What is it?"

"These ferals, they have a pattern of attack. I think we can use that to our advantage," Chase suggested.

As Chase shared his thoughts, Agent Jeffers leaned in and ran his hand over his chin. With a grin, he said, "You know, that just might work. Just one thing, I play your role."

Chase shrugged his head to one side, "Alright. Do I get the gun?"

Jeffers scowled.

"Okay," Chase bobbed his head, dejected.

The call came in just after ten o'clock. Sheriff's deputies arrived on the scene on the edge of town responding to a homeowner's porch security camera picking up a figure darting across their lawn.

The deputies parked in the driveway and knocked on the residence door. Reviewing the uploaded clips from the security system, they realized there were more than one, but at least four different ferals in the area. Calling it in, Jeffers' team picked up the call.

Instructing the deputies to remain with the family and monitor the area from the camera and the homeowner's windows, Jeffers sped towards the scene. Parking on the road alongside the home, Jeffers led the team. Standing in the driveway, a deputy pointed to the house next door. They had seen the ferals circling the house, trying to determine how to access the home most efficiently.

Creeping across the lawn, they saw a figure scamper from one corner of the house, to a brick-encased barbecue grill to a bush, maximizing shadows as it moved from point to point. The gap between the next two houses was shorter, creating deeper shadows.

Jeffers saw an opportunity and encouraged the group to move to the next house. As they did, he lingered behind. He couldn't see them, but he could hear the footfalls of the ferals closing in. With surprising speed, they positioned themselves between Jeffers and the team.

Swallowing hard, the lead agent ran, inciting the ferals to give chase. Careening around a corner, he found himself in a dark corner. A u-shaped fence trapped him. He realized he had run into a spot alongside the house the owners used to stow their trash cans.

A figure leapt towards him. Holding the air gun with two hands, he swung upwards, just able to make out a dark mass amidst the rest of the darkness. Landing a blow to the assailant's chin, Jeffers knocked it backwards. He was surprised with the remarkable speed it shook off the hit and leapt to its feet.

Just as hands wrapped around his throat and he saw other masses leap in his direction, one set of hands around his waist and another at his feet, dragging him down, Agents Sohn and Dunlap with Dr. Chase on their heels, appeared, the tactical lights attached to the muzzles of their air guns illuminating the scene.

Both agents struck the feral on top of Jeffers with darts. Chase, knowing the time delay for the Ketamine to work, jumped on top of the feral. With his arm around the feral's throat, he leaned backwards, allowing his momentum to pull the shadowy figure off of the agent.

The other ferals immediately disengaged, leaping over the fence in different directions, disappearing into the woods.

"Not a terribly loyal bunch," Chase gasped as he still held the struggling feral on top of him. Between his closing the figure's air supply and the double-dose of Ketamine, the fight slowly abated.

Agent Sohn grasped the feral by the shoulders and flung it off Chase while Dunlap loaded his air rifle with another dart.

Jeffers gasped, rubbing his throat, trying to get his lungs to open back up. Hands on his knees, he coughed, "Nice work, Chase."

"Sure you didn't want *me* to be the bait?" Chase asked, getting up from the ground. Swinging his flashlight over, he saw Agent Sohn, her foot on the feral's throat as it slowly faded to listless, barely conscious.

"Nope," Jeffers' voice was hoarse. "Worked according to plan, other than how quick they attacked."

Agent Sohn flipped the feral on to its stomach. With a handheld out, she accepted a set of zip-tie cuffs from Dunlap. In quick order, she bound the hands of the sedated subject.

"Want to get the rest?" she grinned, looking over her shoulder.

"I think we frightened the rest away," Jeffers gasped, slowly regaining his voice. "Let's get this one back and regroup."

As the team pulled into the police station parking lot, they were surprised to see a commotion outside.

Jumping out of the vehicle, Agent Sohn and Agent Dunlap bookended the feral they apprehended. Dragging the sedated subject who stumbled one listless foot after the other, they broke through the crowd.

Ahead of them, the burley Wildlife Officer and a man in civilian clothes toted their own feral into the police station. The crowd cheered as they brought in the first of the ferals.

Jeffers looked crestfallen, "Someone beat us?"

"Wasn't Hanley and the other FBI team," Sohn shrugged, taking solace in that fact.

"No…," Jeffers scowled. "A Wildlife Officer and some guy off the street?"

Wally and Tannen had walked over from the hotel with the forensics team in tow to see what the fuss was. "Hey, you got one," Wally gleamed. "So did they."

The wildlife officer was regaling the crowd with how they tracked, distracted and captured their feral to the delight of the crowd.

"What do we do now?" Agent Sohn asked.

"Treat them like an agitated victim," Tannen suggested. "Strap them, sedate them."

"That would allow us to take a few quick samples before they're shipped off to Seattle," Agent Hawes suggested.

"Sounds good, whatever," Jeffers waved them on.

"You alright, Jeffers?" Chase asked.

"A *wildlife officer* caught the first one?" Jeffers groaned.

Chase leaned against the SUV with the FBI agent, "To be fair, they are a lot more animalistic in their behavior than human."

"Yeah," Jeffers sighed. "Eleven more to go."

TWENTY SIX

The hint of sun painted the peaks of the North Cascades with pink and orange accents, making the majestic range only the more striking. Even in the midst of exhaustion, stress and real danger, a weary Ryder Chase paused as he helped march another feral towards the Sedro-Woolley police station.

"It's amazing," Agent Sohn said, one hand on the collar of a feral, the other on shackled hands leading him towards the waiting gurney to be strapped down. "In my business, there are days where it's good to remember what you're fighting for when you get run down. Like restoring order to a beautiful community. Returning missing people to their families."

"If they get to return," Chase frowned.

"Sometimes the worst-case scenario of closure is better than never knowing, always wondering," Sohn replied. "Though there are times when I've looked into a mother's eyes and wondered, is false hope better than no hope?"

They handed off their subject and leaned against the rail of the police station steps, the sun kissing their faces as they took in the morning view.

"The truth is the truth. It isn't always pleasant. But I think understanding things for how they are is the best for the long run. Healing can't begin when someone is relying on false hope," the professor said.

Danica Sohn just nodded as she watched the sun fully crest the mountains.

A voice broke their brief interlude of chasing feral, zombie-like people, "Well, that's the fifth one caught. The wildlife officer and his friend caught another while Hanley's team was able to subdue one."

Jeffers joined Chase and Sohn against the rail.

"By hitting it with a car," Agent Dunlap scoffed.

"It was an accident!" Foote called from the other side of the police station parking lot. "EMT said they'd be fine, just a concussion!"

The team chuckled at the visceral response from the federal agent.

"It's sunrise," Jeffers stated. "Must mean it's time to get a little shut eye."

"A little backwards, isn't it?" Dunlap asked.

"Just another day for a paranormal investigator," Chase grinned.

"We'll rally here at noon. There are still a lot of questions and at least eight more subjects on the loose that pose a danger to the citizens," Jeffers said.

The weary team didn't argue and walked towards their nearby hotel rooms.

Noon came early, the team, including Wally Smyth and Dan Tannen, assembled in front of the police station for the daily briefing. Once more, Chief Roberts and Sheriff Watts took the stage in the rear of a pickup truck.

"Shouldn't you be up there with them, Agent Jeffers?" Dunlap asked.

Jeffers shook his head, "It's their town. The people need to see that the local authority is in control. They are keeping them safe with their patrols. The feds are just here to deal with the weird stuff."

"Spoken like a true paranormal investigator, Agent Jeffers," Chase grinned.

The lead agent rolled his eyes and turned his attention to the police chief and sheriff.

"Our coordinated effort last night brought in nearly half of the unknown subjects. They've been transported to Seattle for medical and psychiatric reviews. There are several more at large, so we need to remain vigilant," Chief Roberts announced.

"There were a few incidents to report, most on the outskirts. Rural homes along Hansen Creek and Siskiyou Slough had smashed windows and a few nervous moments before the subjects could be chased away or in one case, the quick response of Wildlife Officer Raines and some of you know Sean Kendall, were able to subdue one," Sheriff Watts stated.

"We had two officers wounded protecting homes, they were treated and released, oh, there's Frank, already back on duty," Roberts started. "We don't know what we're dealing with. If you are scratched or bitten in the course of dealing with a subject, seek medical treatment immediately so we can run a blood panel. We want to make sure you…and your family are safe."

"Since the activity seems to heighten at night, we are going to run light shifts throughout the day so we are all fresh for our nighttime duty, which will again be all hands," Sheriff Watts concluded.

Special Agent Jeffers wrangled his team towards their vehicles to continue their investigation of Northern

State Hospital. Agent Hanley flagged his down with Agent Foote on his heels.

"Just came in from Seattle. One of the subjects matched another missing college student…this one from Nebraska," Hanley reported.

Jeffers stopped and frowned, "In town visiting a local college?"

"It's possible, I suppose. There is nothing in the report to indicate that. The missing persons was reported in Lincoln after attending a class. No mention of a trip west," Hanley said.

"Implications could be big. Hard to say until we know more," Jeffers commented.

"You think this could be the start of a widespread phenomenon?" Dan Tannen asked.

"I hope not," Jeffers replied, opening the door of his SUV. Glancing around the town that was in chaos over the past week. "I hope not."

The Seattle based forensics agents Miles and Hawes were already on the scene lugging new equipment towards the old hospital.

As the FBI and paranormal teams arrived, Agent Hanley announced, "I figured we could tap and poke all over this place and still miss some passage that holds who knows what. Had Hawes and Miles bring GPR and HHR to the haunted hospital. Won't be any more secrets after today."

Chase shot Wally a look. Wally replied softly, "Ground penetrating radar and hand-held radar."

"Thanks," Chase said as they followed the agents into the old asylum.

Miles set up outside and began mapping out a grid flowing from the hospital outwards.

"The GPR will create a map of imperfections in the ground. Things like anomalous objects or mysteriously hidden tunnels," Wally explained to the professor. "Their van has a computer that will record the data and make 3-D maps. The device Agent Miles is pushing has a screen that will show him real-time, at least a rough sketch, what's down there."

Agent Foote followed alongside Miles as they made their slow and steady search of the hospital grounds.

Following Agent Hanley and Agent Hawes with the hand-held, they entered the hospital. "Top or bottom?" Hanley asked.

"Bottom!" Jeffers and Chase called out at the same time.

The lead agent glared at the professor, "Let's not make a habit of that."

Chase merely grinned in return.

Eager to tackle the mysteries of the unknown catacombs below the hospital, they quickly descended to the tunnel system that followed the length of the hospital and seemed to be a consistent factor in the events.

Hawes wasted no time firing up his equipment. Recognizing Wally as being tech savvy, he handed the paranormal researcher the monitor. "You mind?"

Wally grinned and readily accepted the tablet-sized screen, "Are you kidding?"

With a nod, Hawes began methodically scanning the tunnel system for any imperfection, gap or other change in basic architecture that might suggest evidence could be buried behind it.

The excitement of the new equipment waned as the appropriately methodical pace made for slow going. Despite marking a couple of modest distinctions, there was little yielded by the time they stopped to enjoy food that Jeffers had delivered for the team.

Dr. Chase chewed his sandwich, but his mind was elsewhere. Once teased with a question, he was relentless to try and find an answer, a trait that both fueled and plagued him in his field of paranormal research.

Pacing, he catalogued the events reported, experienced, and recorded over the course of the investigation. Flipping over his sandwich wrapper, he pulled out a pen and started sketching a rough map of the hospital and grounds. He then circled the areas of highest activity.

When the teams went back to work, following either device the forensics crew brought in, Chase asked, "Do you have fingerprint powder? I mean, like a lot of it?"

Agent Jeffers shot the professor a glance, "Sure, probably. Especially with the forensics van here."

"I know that look, Chase," Agent Sohn looked amused and curious to the paranormal researchers' intentions.

Jeffers relented, "Dunlap, go see what they have in the van."

As the junior agent returned with a gallon tub of ferric oxide and lampblack powder, Chase thanked him and opened the tub. Leading the team to the high-traffic areas according to his notes, he began liberally sprinkling the dust typically used for finding fingerprints and coated the floor of the tunnel.

Stepping back, the professor kneeled, shining his light. The tiny flecks in the dust allowed for separation of tracks as the dust settled into the minute groove of every footprint laid in recent history.

"I see what you're doing," Agent Jeffers frowned. "But we have tainted this entire tunnel over the past week of investigating."

Chase was undaunted, even after not finding what he sought at the first location and repeated the process, wondering far from Agent Hawes and Wally.

"Is your guy okay?" Hanley asked, watching Chase work diligently.

Jeffers shrugged, "He's a scientist...sort of."

Hanley nodded in understanding.

As they wandered to the third location, an area not far from the trap door leading to the morgue and the crawlspace, intersecting with the "death chute" tunnel and the secret route to the crematorium, Chase once more knelt down and played his light across the myriad of footprints collected in the dust.

"It's true, we have trampled all over this tunnel, all over these grounds," Dr. Chase explained. "What I was looking for was an area that was markedly differential to the other areas."

Agent Sohn knelt next to the professor, shining her light in the same manner of Chase, "And you found it."

Curious, Jeffers joined them with Agents Hanley and Dunlap peering over their shoulders.

"Tannen, get Wally and Agent Hawes. Have them mark where they are breaking from the pattern with chalk and have them bring the hand-held tool over here," Chase suggested.

Without receiving an objection from either FBI agent, the EMT jogged down the corridor as requested. For prosperity, Agent Dunlap snapped several photos of the area in an attempt to capture what the professor saw.

Starting where the pattern began and moving to where it dissipated, Jeffers drew vertical lines in white chalk on the tunnel walls. Chase tilted his head slightly as he watched the FBI agent mark his lines.

"What is it?" Agent Sohn asked.

"The area closest to the wall, by Jeffers' feet...something is off," Chase said.

Sohn played her light in the area Chase mentioned. Frowning, she admitted, "I don't see anything."

"That's just it," Chased nodded.

The response only made the agent more confused.

Tannen returned with Wally and Agent Hawes.

"Indulge us if you will," Agent Jeffers requested, pointing at the wall between the lines he drew. "If nothing else other than to break the monotony."

Agent Hawes nodded and guided Wally to follow with the monitor. Starting at the floor nearest Jeffers' left-most mark, he slowly raised the device until he hit the ceiling. Moving the length of the device, he brought it slowly down to the floor and repeated the pattern until they hit the right most mark Jeffers had placed.

Wally and Hawes bristled with a twinge of excitement as they were halfway through their review but waited until they had completed their scan to announce their finding.

"There is something here!" they both turned towards the team and exclaimed.

Agent Hawes frowned, "Or rather, something *not* here. There is a gap here, a rectangle roughly the size of an industrial refrigerator door."

Chase recalled how the crematorium tunnel door worked. With his flashlight, he searched for a crack or seam that could disguise the locking mechanism. As the professor meticulously smoothed his hands over the area, Jeffers frowned and strode forward. With a mighty push, they heard a click, and the wall swung outward.

TWENTY SEVEN

The team watched as the tunnel wall opened up. Studying the door, they had to once again admire the precise detail and artistic touch that went to make the door blend seamlessly into the tunnel wall. A tall threshold required that they step up to enter the interior chamber, reducing tracks and wear at the location.

Chase cocked his head as he shone his light at the bottom of the door. As it moved, a light layer of dust wafted down to the floor. "The door is rigged to cover the signs of traffic leading into it," the professor announced.

Jeffers saw what he was pointing at and shone his own flashlight around the structure of the door. A flexible tube led to a barrel just inside the room. As he played the door, a small pump delivered a soft showery waft of dust carefully mixed to match the natural layer that consumed the tunnel over the past century.

Moving through with caution, each investigator worked their flashlights around the room, amazed with the endless hidden discoveries the old hospital continued to throw at them.

"Someone went through a lot of trouble to conceal this room," Jeffers stated.

"Question is, who?" Agent Sohn said, moving through the room with her firearm drawn, held in front of her clamped to her light.

"And when? I've learned not to discredit old architecture and ingenuity, but doesn't strike me as early 1900s," Chase said, following the agents closely.

The room led to a heavy industrial door. The fixtures looked new, their shine reflecting in the beam of the flashlights. Jeffers ensured his team was ready and flung the door open.

The FBI agents in the lead, the paranormal team trailing, they moved into the adjacent space. Low L.E.D. softly lit the space. Several desks with modern computers seemed to monitor a range of variables. The room opened up to a small hallway. Along the hall were several rooms with door markers such as those of medical facilities.

Jeffers tried the first door, the handle wouldn't budge. The next three opened to reveal empty patient rooms.

"All of this equipment is new," Tannen observed.

As they reached the end of the hallway, their voices echoing throughout the room, Wally froze and held his hand up. "You hear that?" he called in a hoarse whisper.

At the end of a corridor, a heavy door stood in their path. Cocking his head, the paranormal investigator said, "Shuffling of some sort."

The group nodded in unison as they crept forward. The agents readied their weapons as the team closed in. Suddenly the shuffling erupted into enraged banging. The sound of dozens of fists frantically hammering at the door from the other side shattered the halls.

Exchanging glances, the FBI team shrugged.

"Someone might need help," Agent Hanley said, raising his voice over the commotion. His hand reaching out for the handle.

"I think we might have found what we've been looking for," Chase whispered.

"Is this a good idea?" Agent Dunlap asked.

"Probably not…," Wally admitted.

"Be ready," Jeffers warned.

With a nod from Jeffers, Agent Hanley yanked the handle of the door. As the door barely breached the frame, a frenzy of limbs struck out, reaching, clawing, trying to grasp at anything they could come in contact with.

The agents pushed their shoulders into the door to hold the agitated occupants at bay. Unsure of what to do and in threat of losing their hold, the investigators stammered to come with a viable plan. Wally and Chase aided the agents in keeping the door no more than cracked, a pair of arms and a leg pinned in the doorway from the other side.

Agent Hanley was closest to the opening continuously dodging repeated swipes of an opportunistic hand. "We need to do something…quick!"

"We could shoot them!" Jeffers gasped under the constant strain of the door.

"They might be college kids!" Agent Sohn reminded him.

"Nice kids," Hanley scoffed as one swiped at him, scratching him from the forehead to the bridge of his nose.

"I have an idea," Tannen called, running frantically around the lab. "This is either going to be really good or really bad. Either way, you are going to want to cover your mouths!"

With little to do other than comply, the team turned so their backs pushed into the door as opposed to their hands, freeing them to cover up.

Tannen arrived at the door with several vials and a tank of compressed air. Injecting a hose connected to the tank and tossing depleted vials over his head, allowing them to rattle on the floor, he took a deep breath and opened the nozzle on the tank. With a hopeful nod, the team released their hold just enough to allow the door to open the span of the tank. Tannen tossed the container into the room.

To the team's relief, the container gathered momentary interest, allowing the door to slam shut.

As the commotion within the next room started to slowly recede, the team looked to Tannen with curious expressions. Shrugging, the EMT grimaced, "I found bottles of atropine and nitrous oxide."

Agent Jeffers' jaw dropped, "You made a nerve gas."

"Or antidote depending on how you use it. They should be fine...I think," Tannen said. "We'll want to monitor them for tachycardia and they'll not feel great for a bit."

"I'm already thinking they aren't right," Wally shrugged.

Hanley pushed his ear against the door, "I think it worked."

Tannen covered his mouth and Jeffers held his firearm in front of him. Hanley yanked the door open. This time, instead of a frenzy, the team was greeted by a dozen ferals crawling listlessly on the ground.

Tannen rushed in and turned off the valve on the nitrous tank.

As agents pinned the feral subjects down and bound them, the EMT did a quick check of their vitals. "All of them have elevated heart rate, I am only concerned about those two," he pointed. "They are all suffering from minor dehydration."

Hanley radioed in for emergency crews and law enforcement support.

As the room settled, the investigation crew tiptoed through a floor littered with semi-conscious ferals. The smells of rot and urine began to overtake them.

The hidden medical lab was encircled with chairs, each fitted with leg, wrist and chin straps. EEG equipment, syringes and a variety of powders and liquids lined shelves.

Agent Jeffers spun, taking the scene in, "What in the world was going on in here?"

"It's a horror show," Dunlap murmured.

As the mildly induced ferals on the floor began struggling against their bindings, Agent Hanley called, "I've got more doors." The agent began working the lock. An electronic device, it connected to all three door latches that could be worked independently or in tandem.

Chase shone his light in the agent's direction. As he did, he spied a crude, handwritten sign scrawled "Quarantine".

"No!" Chase yelled.

His warning was too late as the mechanism clicked into place and three doors flung open. A fury of bodies expelled from the rooms, one toppling Agent Hanley and tearing at him as they pushed through the room. With speed and ferocity, they made a beeline towards the first person that stood in their way.

There was a different demeanor, a look on their faces and even a smell that screamed warnings in Chase's head. He didn't have time to contemplate as one cued on him. Instinctively, the paranormal researcher sprung into fight or flight mode with flight being the victor. In a sprint, Dr. Chase ran as fast as he could, a hand swiping at him, just missing the back of his head.

The agents were stunned in their frustrating muddle of needing to protect the team and themselves, while trying to not fire their weapons at the subjects. Instead of decisive action, the underground turned into chaos. Ferals chased Dr. Chase and Dan Tannen, while Agent Dunlap grappled with the feral on top of Agent

Hanley. A losing battle, Agent Jeffers stepped into assist his Junior agent.

Together, they pulled the snarling man off of the fallen agent. Pinning him down, they struggled to contain the subject. Through his injuries, Agent Hanley grabbed the impromptu neutralizing device that Tannen created. Jamming the hose in the ferals mouth as it gnashed at the agents, he turned the knob.

Feeling woozy themselves, the agents were grateful the direct injection of gas and chemicals lent the feral unconscious first. Holding their shirts over the mouths, they rolled off of the feral and collected themselves just long enough to bind him and close the nitrous tank valve.

Agent Sohn cast her fellow agents a glance and turned her attention to the civilian investigators and their pursuers. They ran at full tilt through the lab, leapt over the bound ferals still writhing on the floor. Dashing into the main tunnel system, they sprinted for the nearest exit, but the ferals were gaining on them with every step they took.

One closed within a breath of a slashing arm's length of Tannen. The EMT could feel the breeze of the close call, his heart already about to explode out of his chest. "Cardio!" he gasped.

Behind them, Agent Sohn stopped running, instead, she steadied her firearm and fingered the trigger. For the safety of Chase and Tannen, she wouldn't hesitate. Knowing she would be taking the life of some college kid who got caught in some twisted chemical experiment gone wrong, she didn't feel good about it.

"Get down!" a voice screamed through the tunnel in front of Chase and Tannen.

With little choice but to comply with the ferals literally breathing down their necks, a pair of bright beams lit up the tunnel. Diving to the ground, Chase and Tannen could feel projectiles rush over their heads.

"Get away!" Tannen urged Chase.

Scrambling against the floor of the cave, they did the best they could to get away from the ferals that fought through the suppressive chemical working its way through their systems.

The hammering of feet against the hard surface of the tunnel stopped abruptly as a pair of boots slammed down on each of the necks of the ferals. Sohn raced up to them, her firearm still pointed in front of her, her flashlight leading the muzzle.

The light catching the bright smiling face of a man standing on one of the ferals as he said, "Looks like we got here just in time."

"Officer Raines?" Agent Sohn called as Dr. Chase moved to assist subduing the slowly deflating feral.

"At your service," the burly red-haired man beamed.

"Here," Sohn handed Chase a pair of zip-tie handcuffs and tossed a pair to Tannen.

As Tannen laced the feral's writhing hands into the loops, he pulled hard. Sohn handed him a second set as she assisted Chase with binding his feral's feet.

Tannen's subject, hands bound behind him, suddenly arched like a caterpillar. One heady push, the feral used his face against the tunnel floor to push himself upright. In a mad dash, he streaked away, an armless human projectile. The man who arrived with the wildlife officer caught the feral by the side with a pair of strong hands and redirected his momentum towards the wall of the cave.

With bound arms, the feral couldn't defend the imminent collision, ramming headlong into the concrete tunnel wall. In seemingly slow motion, the feral toppled over, falling backwards to the floor in an unconscious heap.

The man wrinkled his nose and offered a sheepish grin, "Stopped him!"

"Attaboy, Sean. Nice work!" Officer Raines nodded approvingly.

"What are you guys doing here?" Sohn asked. "Don't get me wrong, I'm clearly glad you are."

"Got another shipment of darts. Thought your team might need them. One of the agents up top pushing the lawnmower thing said you'd be down here," Officer Raines said.

"And you happened to be carrying your air rifles?" Sohn raised a brow.

The wildlife officer's eyes brightened, "Oh, right. I brought these!"

"*We* brought these," the other man corrected.

"Sorry, *we* brought these," Raines adjusted. "Similar to the other rifles, they have a higher FPS so the darts'll fly straighter for longer."

"It's a good thing, we'd either have two dead paranormal investigators or two dead college students on our hands," Agent Sohn said.

Raines looked down on the ground at the haggard ferals, "Those are college students?"

"Kinda," Dr. Chase shrugged, his face twisted.

"Anymore we need to take care of?" Raines bobbed his head back and forth peering down the hallway.

"I don't think so. I just wouldn't open any doors that are unfamiliar to you," Agent Sohn warned.

"Got it. Good advice. Especially these days. Well, got a few more deliveries to make. Good luck," Raines said and nodded to his friend to head back up the tunnel.

Turning his head, he added, "Be careful out there. It's dangerous.

"Thanks. You too!" Sohn called.

TWENTY EIGHT

The full-force of the FBI descended on the town of
Sedro-Woolley. Countless black vehicles began arriving to
town with an advanced mobile field office to support the
effort to manage the operation and sift through evidence.
Helicopters landed in the open field and hovered overhead,
sweeping the Northern State Hospital grounds and the
town of Sedro-Woolley.

The investigation team was assessed for injuries and
released with the exception of Agent Hanley who was sent
to Seattle for care of his wounds. The ferals captured were
all secured to patient carriers and transported to a
psychiatric hospital for care, observation and analysis.

Before Agent Jeffers was swept away into the
incoming flow of federal agents assembling to take over

parts of the investigation and assist with others, the team took stock of one another and the unfolding mystery they had pulled the string on.

"You guys okay?" Jeffers asked, looking over the paranormal researchers who had literally run for their lives.

"We had a little help," Dr. Chase nodded. "But we're fine."

The lead agent spun around the room, taking it all in, "So, this is what it's all been about. Chemical experiments. What are we looking at, designer drugs?"

Tannen rubbed his chin, "I haven't taken full stock of everything and I'm sure your forensics team will know more than me, but I think this wasn't about recreational drugs. I think it was human enhancement."

"Or human reanimation!" Wally blurted.

Jeffers cast the tech a scowl.

"Most of the chemicals I see out on the shelves serve to stimulate the nervous system, maximize blood flow, and bodily reactions like that. Not anything a pleasure seeker would look to achieve, but rather people looking for a mental or physical edge. Even the atropine I used to subdue the ferals in conjunction with the laughing gas can be used to counter chemicals in the nervous system. The military uses it to counter nerve agent damage. In this case, it may have been as sort of an antidote," the EMT suggested.

Eyeing the remnants of chaos caused by releasing the ferals, Agent Jeffers said, "Doesn't seem to have worked."

"I was…," Tannen started before a noise caught the room's attention.

All eyes swiveled to the door that was locked when they first searched the lab.

Jeffers sighed, "Not again." Ensuring a dart was chambered in the rifle the wildlife officer dropped off, he levelled it at the door.

A light thumping began rhythmically hitting the door from the within the room.

Dr. Chase raised his hand, "Something's different." Placing his ear closer to the door, "It not frenetic like the other ferals."

Agent Dunlap's brows furrowed.

"He means crazy, frantic," Tannen said.

"Oh," Dunlap nodded. "He's right."

"Be ready for anything," Jeffers muttered. "Apparently that's going to be my new motto."

With a nod, Agent Sohn began picking the lock. After a few moments and a held breath, she was rewarded with a satisfying "click".

"Here we go," she called, her hand on the knob.

With a deep breath, she pulled the door open, the entire room ready for an onslaught of ferals. What they were met with was almost of equal surprise. As Agent Sohn flung the door open, three wide-eyed figures, arms outstretched, wriggling through the door, towards the investigation team and out of the room they were locked in.

The three figures seemed to struggle for the strength to carry themselves forward.

Tannen dropped to his knee and quickly assessed the first figure, "I don't think these are ferals, or at least they aren't yet...or now. They have no signs of the excitatory state. I think these three are just dehydrated and hungry."

"And been living amongst their own piss," Wally observed as he poked around the room.

"They used buckets and tried to cover them. Tannen's right, these aren't ferals and I don't think they were intended to be. I think these are scientists," Chase said as he took in the conditions of the space, seeing three lab coats piled on the floor.

"Let's get them medical help," Jeffers said.

As the team ascended to the surface for the first time in hours, they were surprised by what they found. A small city of tents had been erected on the lawn of Northern State Hospital. Several men and women in dark suits shouted orders as scores of similarly attired workers carried out the commands.

A pair of semi-trucks parked alongside the vehicles. One was fitted with a set of stairs leading to doors in the side of the truck, the other with a ramp similarly situated.

The sound of helicopters hovering overhead with the chaos was disorienting. It reminded Dr. Chase of scenes in a war movie.

A woman walked out of the truck with the stairs and leaned against the railing, taking in the scene. Her eyes picked Special Agent Jeffers out of the crowd. With a pair of fingers, she waved the lead agent to meet her. Without waiting for a response, she spun and retreated into the trailer.

The entire team began walking in the direction of the woman. Jeffers spun and for the first time since Chase met the FBI agent, looked genuinely uncomfortable. With a slight wrinkle of his nose, he said, "Just me. You guys, uh, for now...stay out of the way."

Without another word, the agent headed for the truck and the woman who summoned him.

"What was that about?" Dr. Chase asked.

"Mostly about who's in charge of the investigation," Agent Sohn replied.

"And?" Chase pressed.

"And it's no longer Agent Jeffers," Sohn said.

The team roamed the small Bureau city erected on the grounds. Catching up with Agent Foote and his forensics team of Agents Miles and Hawes, they conferred on Agent Hanley's condition.

"Mostly superficial wounds, a cracked rib and humbled spirits. Otherwise he'll be fine," Foote shared.

"Glad to hear," Agent Sohn said. "You guys consolidating with the forensics team?"

Miles and Hawes shot each other looks. "We're handing all of our work over to them, we're heading back to Seattle once we pack up," Hawes admitted.

Wally frowned, "But you'd think they'd want the insight from the people who've been working the case."

"Welcome to working with the feds when things spin out of control. There's always a higher-ranking team to punt you back to your more…standard assignments," Agent Foote remarked.

"What happens to us?" Dr. Chase asked.

"That all depends on how persuasive Special Agent Jeffers is. Maybe a word with Deputy Director Witt, but I bet the new Special Agent-in-Charge taking Jeffers' place has a higher-ranking version of Witt in her pocket," Sohn said.

"But we broke this case!" Wally complained.

"We also let a dozen dangerous crazy people out to terrorize the population," Sohn winced.

Dr. Chase wasn't tracking the conversation, instead, he started walking nonchalantly towards the hospital.

Sohn snapped her head, "Chase?"

"This might be our last chance to gather evidence on our own," he said softly as he continued walking calmly away.

The team cast each other looks and shrugged to follow.

"Good luck!" Agent Foote called.

Slipping into the hospital, they scurried to the tunnel system and made their way to the hidden medical laboratory. Tannen and Agent Sohn, having the most medical background, sat in front of the computer terminals and began sleuthing while Chase and Wally snapped photos and poked around the lab, looking for anything that might hint towards the objective of the operation.

Wally sniffed, the stench of ferals and scientists locked in their cells, especially ferals not trying to contain their bodily excretions forced him to cough, "You know, I'm kind of in favor of the new team taking over this part of the investigation."

"They'll get their turn soon enough," Dr. Chase said, snapping pictures of the various medical bottles arranged on a shelf.

"Might be case closed. We have the scientists," Wally said as he flipped through chart notes, taking a snapshot.

"I don't think so," Agent Sohn called. "We found three scientists, but I am seeing notes from four different names in the registry."

"Maybe the fourth turned feral," Wally shrugged.

"Maybe," Sohn said as she resumed her search.

"Well, I know what the med panels are going to find from the ferals we caught," Tannen called. "I think I was right. Listen to this, the chemical panel shows a marked increase in stress hormones, elevated cortisol, epinephrine, and dopamine with a near complete loss of serotonin and oxytocin affecting the limbic system leading to a heightened state of stress. PET scans show minor brain scarring, each case consistent with the other only trace difference in size of incision. PET scans onsite means lead aprons, by the way."

"What were they cutting out? Did they have cancer or something?" Agent Sohn frowned, glancing over at Tannen's terminal.

"No, they didn't have cancer, at least nothing in the medical records would indicate as such. It looks like the objective was to sever one of the pathways in the prefrontal cortex that would regulate stress, meaning the stress state could be sustained for longer, if not indefinitely," Tannen reported.

"Why would you want to do that?" Wally frowned.

Agent Sohn wriggled in her seat, "Bring me the patient files."

Wally grabbed the stack he was sifting through.

The FBI agent quickly flipped pages until she referenced each subject's profile. "These students, they are all high performers jockeying for careers in high stress roles. We have athletes, several in the ROTC and even a couple in law school," Sohn said.

Chase was quiet in a corner, punching details into his phone.

Agent Sohn was beginning to notice when the professor was on to something, "Chase?"

"I was cross referencing the subject names. The athletes, one was a back-up quarterback. He was vying for starter but was beat out by an underclassman. One of the

ROTC students washed out of Ranger School before returning to his studies," Chase announced from his research.

"The experiments lured kids who were struggling to succeed," Agent Sohn shook her head.

"It looks that way," Chase nodded.

Agent Jeffers strode into the room, "What looks that way?"

The team filled the lead agent in on their findings.

Jeffers sighed and looked away, "We'll share that with Special Agent-in-Charge Adams and her team."

Agent Sohn winced, "Agent *Stacy* Adams?"

"Yes," Jeffers said, his voice short.

"That's not good," Sohn declared. "Adams and Jeffers have a bit of a contentious history."

"Really?" Wally grinned wide. "What kind of history?"

"Not *that* kind," Jeffers snapped.

"So, she's available?" Wally inquired.

"They were rivals in Quantico. Jeffers finished first in his class, but the need for more high-ranking female agents catapulted her up the FBI org chart," Sohn informed. "Sorry, Jeffers, they should know what we've gotten into."

"None of it matters, now. She's in charge of this investigation from here forward. We are allowed to stay in a…consultative role, but we'll be on a short leash," Jeffers warned. Looking specifically at Wally, "No fooling around from this point forward."

"We'll gather everything we have collected so far down here and turn it in to the Evidence Response Team," Sohn agreed.

"Any chance we can get in to talk to the scientists? There is one that seems to be missing," Tannen asked.

"I don't think that will be possible. If you've got a line on something, we'll have to share with Special Agent-in-Charge Adams and her team," Jeffers said. "Now, let's get out of here before that leash becomes a choke collar."

Agent Stacy Adams met the team as they spilled out of the hospital. "Oh good, you're all here. I need you all to debrief the agents in my charge. Any evidence you have needs to be turned over, in detail. When you are finished, you're all dismissed," the agent-in-charge directed.

"We are supposed to remain on in a consultative role," Jeffers argued.

"Yes, you can consult with my agents and then return to…," Adams eyed the motley paranormal crew, "Wherever it is you came from."

"Deputy Director Witt, said we get to stay on," Jeffers pressed.

"The agents can remain, if you must. The civilian consultants are no longer needed. Or wanted," Adams forced a fake smile.

A team of agents joined her, "The lab is down here, right?"

Adams walked past without giving them a second glance.

"She seems nice," Wally's quip met with an angry glare from Jeffers.

"You heard her, debrief and we're out of here," Jeffers said.

"Don't you want to see this through?" Chase pressed.

Jeffers stopped and addressed the professor directly, "I never leave a case. I'm not going anywhere. But I, and apparently Deputy Director Witt, don't have much of a say in keeping you on. I'll have my office furnish flights home for you."

"Something is nagging me still about this case," Chase pleaded. "We have to find that fourth scientist."

"He might be a feral. He might be dead. Who knows?" Jeffers shrugged.

"The other scientists," Tannen said softly. "The other scientists might know."

Jeffers sighed and glanced around for other ears, "I'll see what I can find out. And then, you are guys are on your way to Sea-Tac to catch a flight."

Jeffers grabbed the folder from Tannen and marched towards the medical tent. Leveraging rank over the agents guarding the med tent, he pushed his way through.

Waiting for the attending physician to complete a check, Jeffers asked, "How are they doing?"

"Now that we have fluids and glucose replenishing their starved bodies, much better," the medical doctor acknowledged.

"May I have a moment?" the agent asked.

"That should be fine, don't stay too long, they do need rest."

"Yes, doctor," Jeffers nodded.

Standing at the foot of the middle of the three beds the scientists were receiving treatment, he introduced himself, "I'm FBI Special Agent Jeffers. As you might imagine, I have a few questions for you. Most pressingly, who is the fourth scientist and where can we find him?"

The man to his left rasped, "Holder. Doctor Holder."

"Is he still alive? Turned feral?" Jeffers asked.

"He wasn't here when the…they escaped," the woman to the right of him said. "We worked under Dr. Holder."

"This Dr. Holder, he was the in charge?"

The man directly in front of him nodded. "It was his experiment. It…went wrong."

"Clearly," Jeffers stated. "Where can I find this Dr. Holder?"

"Seattle. At the university," the woman replied. "Stop…"

Jeffers cocked his head.

"Stop him," the woman completed her sentence after she swallowed.

"That's what we're here to do," Jeffers admitted.

"Agent Jeffers!" a voice called from the entrance to the medical tent.

"If you'll excuse me. Thank you for the information," Jeffers said to the scientists. Moving swiftly, he found an irate Special Agent-in-Charge Stacy Adams looking cross at the front of the tent.

"What are you doing, Agent Jeffers?" Adams barked.

"*Special* Agent," Jeffers corrected.

"We'll see," Adams snapped. "This will be reported. You are hereby removed from the case along with the rest of your riffraff."

"Well, hold on now, Adams. We have information and knowledge instrumental to this case. Dismissing us doesn't make sense," Jeffers said.

"I can hold you in a cell and ask your advice when needed or you can return to D.C. and I can call if you I have any questions," Adams said.

"I have identified the fourth scientist. He works at a university in Seattle, he runs their neuro-psychiatric hospital program," Jeffers informed her.

"Thank you for the information, *Special* Agent Jeffers. Now get out of my crime scene," Adams ordered.

Chase's eyes widened, "That's where Sara Whitman was taken."

"And a few of the ferals for assessment," Tannen added.

"They're in danger!" Chase said.

"You need to have a detail dispatched to the hospital," Jeffers agreed.

Adams stared at the paranormal researchers and then at Jeffers, "I don't have time for wild goose chases brought by a couple of what, amateur ghost hunters? What happened to you, Jeffers? You used to be good agent."

"They might be…odd, but they are correct, Adams," Jeffers pressed.

"Agent Jeffers, please escort yourselves and your Scooby-Doo team off the premises while you still have an ounce of dignity, or I'll have you escorted in cuffs," Adams glared.

The team started to protest, but Jeffers corralled them forward.

"What are we going to do?" Agent Sohn asked.

"We have to pass the university to get to the airport," Jeffers grinned. "We're going to Seattle!"

TWENTY NINE

The team hastily packed and headed south on Interstate Five. Getting help from their D.C. team to tap into the university internal internet system, Agent Sohn flipped through data as Agent Jeffers drove.

"It looks like the Professor Holder is returning from a conference today," Agent Sohn said. "He was a speaker on neurological studies for military advancement."

"Using students as guinea pigs," Jeffers said.

Sohn worked into the university surveillance network. "He's not scheduled for classes today, but the good doctor seems to be on campus," she said, matching the university security cameras with the doctor's campus directory photo.

"That's not good, and that's a no *good* doctor," Jeffers said, pushing his foot down on the accelerator.

Looking in the rearview mirror, he saw that Dunlap in the paranormal team's rental was keeping pace.

Dr. Chase sat in the backseat in Jeffers' SUV studying the photo on his phone of the Professor Holder. "I know I've seen this guy before. I think he was in D.C. at a conference. Maybe, even my campus. I can't remember why..."

"Hey guys," Tannen's voice came over their radio. "I've been reviewing the evidence from the photos we took in the lab. The data on the computer notes match code names listed on one of the medical racks. There are several vials missing, but they aren't recorded as administered. Their logs are quite good. I can't see this being a simple oversight."

"Let me get this straight," Jeffers said as he passed traffic. "We have a scientist with horrible secrets on campus where key witnesses are being treated. And he might be wandering around with a mysterious concoction in his possession that turns people crazy?"

"Can't confirm that, but it looks that way," Chase said.

Jeffers kept his foot planted on the accelerator, "Until we know for sure, let's not trouble Agent Adams with this news just yet."

Agent Jeffers wheeled in front of the university hospital doors and slammed on the brakes. Launching himself out of the SUV, he darted for the entrance.

A university security guard raised his hand towards Agent Jeffers, "Hey! You can't park there!"

"Federal Agent!" Jeffers flashed his badge with Agent Sohn and Dr. Chase in tow.

Behind them, Agent Dunlap, Dan Tannen and Wally ran past.

"We're with them," Wally grinned at the bewildered security guard.

Finding the front desk, Jeffers held his badge out, "We need the patient room for Sarah Whitman."

The woman looked up at the federal agent, at his badge and then at her screen. Her affect never deviating. "Let's see…Whitman…Sarah…," the woman looked up from her screen as the computer did its work. She stared blankly at Jeffers before bowing back down to the monitor. "Here it is. Hmm, looks like she is scheduled for emergency surgery. She's in prep now. You won't be able to…"

Agent Jeffers and the team were already sprinting for the elevators before the woman could finish her sentence. She cocked her head and stared after them until they disappeared within the elevator before pivoting her head back in front of her, resuming her flat affect for the next person waiting in line.

The doors opened up and the team ran through swiveling their heads down either hallway, Agent Sohn pointed to a placard on the wall, "Surgery. This way!"

The team ran full sprint down the corridor until they hit a set of electronic doors marked "No Admittance".

A nurse walked by and Jeffers reeled her in, "Federal Agent, I need to make these work."

The nurse studied Agent Jeffers and the motley crew behind him. "I don't have…"

Jeffers looked up and saw a man in surgical scrubs, "You!"

"I can't let you guys in there, it's a sterile…," the man started.

"Are the halls sterile?" Jeffers asked.

"No, I mean not…," the man looked up at the agent and reluctantly nodded.

Waving his key card over the sensor, the doors parted allowing the team to sprint forward. Finding a nurse's station, Agent Sohn hip checked a nurse out of the way, "Sorry, in a hurry."

"It's a federal agent thing," Wally smiled and bobbed his head at the nurse.

"Got her!" Sohn exclaimed.

The herd of investigators continued their frenzied dash until they nearly collided with a nurse carry items into a sterile operating room. Startled, the nurse held her tray tight and looked at the group, confusion washing over her face.

"Sarah Whitman?" Agent Sohn asked.

The nurse nodded nervously.

"Where's the doctor?" Agent Jeffers asked.

"He...he hasn't arrived yet," the nurse stammered.

"Have you seen him?" Agent Sohn pressed.

The nurse shook her head, "We often don't until the procedure is ready to begin."

Instinctively, Agent Jeffers scanned the hallway. "Dr. Chase and I will stay here. Agent Sohn, take Tannen and find Holder's office. Agent Dunlap and Wally, I want you to find the security office and monitor their campus cameras."

"Nurse, what has been done to Ms. Whitman so far?" Jeffers asked.

The nurse looked around wildly, "I can't...patient privacy..."

"I can get a warrant. You may be charged with aiding attempted murder or at lease malicious assault...," Jeffers started.

"She's just sedated. The anesthesiologist just left. That usually happens right before the doctor arrives. You should really be speaking with Dr. Holder," the nurse said.

Chase glanced around, "He's here."

Glancing at the photo in his file, he panned the surgical floor for a man matching the description. In surgical caps and masks, it was nearly impossible to tell them apart.

Jeffers could tell the professor wanted to wander, and nodded, "Go."

"Nurse, bring me a doctor that isn't Dr. Holder and the anesthesiologist. Sarah Whitman isn't having brain surgery today," Agent Jeffers commanded.

Dr. Chase meandered the halls, deeper within the surgical wing. Hitting a bank of elevators marked staff only, he swiveled his head before swiping a badge off of a smock tossed over the nurse's station cubicle wall.

Flashing the ID card in front of the scanner, he waited for the doors to open. Joining a pair of physicians, a woman in scrubs, another man with a head down in his files, Chase offered a nonchalant nod before allowing the elevator to take him wherever these doctors were going.

The woman hopped off one floor down, Chase had an inkling he might find Dr. Holder there in pre-surgical scrub. As he stepped out of the elevator, the man reading files looked up for a split second. In the corner of Chase's eye, he caught a moment of recognition. Spinning to confirm, the doors closed.

Chase's heart raced. He couldn't be sure with the brief glance, the man in the elevator was reasonably reminiscent of Dr. Holder. Scanning the halls wildly, he found a door to the stairwell. The second button illuminated in the elevator was five floors down.

Pushing through the door, he heard it click behind him. Racing down the stairs, using the rails to glide several steps at a time, Chase arrived on the landing for the second floor. Trying the door, he cursed. The stairs were for emergencies only and didn't allow for re-entry on the floors.

Descending all the way to the main floor, he burst through the doors, and impatiently jabbed at the elevator call button. Ignoring the unusual looks he received, he slipped into the elevator. Hitting the "close door" button as wannabe riders hustled towards him, hailing him to hold it for them.

Selecting the button that shone when he had entered with the two physicians off the surgical floor, he jumped out when the doors opened. Pivoting his head back and forth, Chase searched for anyone matching the description of Dr. Holder. Based on the floor layout, he made a guess and jogged down the hall.

As Chase rounded a corner of the corridor, he nearly ran headlong into a man and woman. "Dr. Chase!" the woman gasped.

Hearing his name peeled Chase from his mono-focused manhunt. Calming, his eyes took in the faces of the couple he had almost run over. His brow dropped, "Mr. and Mrs. Whitman."

"We were just on our way to visit Sarah," Mrs. Whitman smiled, a fresh bouquet of flowers clenched to her chest.

"She wasn't in her room, hoping that's a good sign she is re-engaging," Mr. Whitman said.

Chase's heart stopped beating for a sickening pulse. "You didn't know about the scheduled surgery," he announced.

Mrs. Whitman's eyes went wide, her free hand covering her mouth, "What surgery?"

"No one told us about a surgery, what is going on?" Mr. Whitman looked appropriately concerned.

"Who is Sarah's attending physician?" Chase asked.

"Dr. Charles, why?" Mrs. Whitman asked.

"He had that specialist working on her case as well, a Dr. Holder," Mr. Whitman snapped his fingers.

Dr. Chase closed his eyes briefly as he pieced the situation together. Gently taking the Whitmans by the arms, he led them towards the nurse's station. "Why don't you two wait for Sarah in recovery. Have the nurse escort you. Don't speak with anyone outside of the FBI team, including Sarah's doctors. Agent Jeffers is by her side now, she'll be fine."

Despite their deep, muddy bewilderment, the worried mother and father complied as Chase took off on his search, which he was fairly certain was now long over.

Agent Dunlap and Wally rapped on the security office door of the university hospital. A woman in a uniform opened the door, an eyebrow raised at seeing two men at the door.

Dunlap produced his badge, "James Dunlap, Federal Agent. This is Wally Smyth, an authorized consultant on a case involving a patient at this hospital."

The security guard frowned, "These things typically filter through the hospital administrator and down through my boss, the head of security."

"And if this wasn't time critical, this case likely would have as well. A young woman is in danger. We need access to your security monitors," Agent Dunlap declared.

"There are HIPAA forms...," the guard started.

"We're all HIPAA certified as a common course in our investigations. We don't care about anyone's medical history, we care that a madman doesn't try and harm anyone…or worse," Dunlap demanded. Without waiting for an affirmative response, he pushed the door open further to allow he and Wally to step through.

A uniformed man at the monitor control panel swiveled in his seat and looked over his shoulder. His partner shrugged.

"Federal agent…," Dunlap began.

"I heard. You want the controls, or would you like me to do it?" the guard asked in a sigh.

Dunlap took in the complexity of the controls, with his lip out he nodded, "I think I'll have you do it."

"What are we looking for?" the guard asked.

"Surgical floor, operating room Two-twelve, every access point in or out of the hospital and the eleventh-floor physician's offices," Dunlap rattled off.

"Anything else?" the guard asked sarcastically.

"No, I think that's good," the agent assured.

Pulling up a seat, he peered over the guard's shoulder and watched as he pulled up the specific locations Dunlap asked for spread across an array of monitors. The exits cycled through several monitors as there were too many to track at once.

Wally pulled up a seat in between the guards. Smiling, he asked, "Anyone up for a pizza? I'll buy."

Heads swiveled to Wally and then back to their work without a response.

"Gotcha. Work first," Wally acknowledged.

Agent Sohn and Dan Tannen approached Dr. Holder's office with caution. As a nurse strode haughtily towards them to object to their presence, Sohn flashed her badge and quietly shooed her away. Moving her jacket to the side, she instinctively dragged her fingers over the grip of her pistol.

Trying the handle, she found it locked. Gently releasing the handle so it didn't rattle back into place, she knelt down and pulled out her lock pick kit. The nurse down the hall watched and frowned. Dangling her keys out in front of her, she held them out for the agents.

"That might be better," Sohn whispered and nodded for Tannen to retrieve them. Firearm at the ready, she waited as Tannen gingerly slipped the key into the lock and twisted. With an instantaneous pull of the handle and kick to the door, Sohn flashed the muzzle of her gun around the room.

"It's clear," she stated. Nodding Tannen inside, they allowed the door to close. Sohn put her firearm away and latched it.

"Let's get back to work. If you hear that door open, I want you to get behind me," Sohn said, her voice serious.

Tannen nodded and followed her lead, diving into files and searching the room for any clues to the doctor's intentions and possible additional victims. It didn't take long for the first concerning item to sift through their fingers.

Tannen whipped a paper out in front of him and held it up for Agent Sohn, "It looks like he was tracking all the victims along with the ferals and first responders transported to Seattle area hospitals and care facilities."

Tannen handed the paper to the agent.

Agent Sohn studied the list. Notations were scribbled next to each name. Attending physicians and phone numbers, along with the institution's address were lined out on the page.

"Sara Whitman isn't the only one in danger," Agent Sohn responded. Taking a picture of the list with her phone, she texted Agent Jeffers.

Special Agent Jeffers monitored the care of Sarah Whitman carefully. He made it clear to every clinical worker, including the anesthesiologist, that her safety was paramount and each was detained to the hospital until further notice.

As Sarah's anesthesia was reversed and her vitals rebounded, she slowly regained consciousness. The federal agent followed her to recovery where her parents were waiting for her.

The Whitman's rushed to their daughter's bed, relieved to see her and hold her hands.

"What's going on?" Mr. Whitman asked.

"I don't care to speculate, but I will tell you, my team and I were concerned for your daughter's safety. We have detained part of her care team for questioning," Jeffers said.

"You think someone on staff was going to harm our daughter?" Mrs. Whitman gasped.

"I don't know, not yet. What I do know, is she is safe now and we intend to ensure she stays safe," Agent Jeffers said.

His phone alerted him to a communication. Turning away, he let the Whitman's coddle their daughter while he pulled his phone from his pocket. Reviewing the text from Agent Sohn, his heart fell.

Stepping out into the hallway, he dialed his office in D.C.

Deputy Director Witt's voice called over the phone, "It sounds like your team is making an early return."

"No one is leaving Washington just yet, sir," Jeffers explained. "I need you to arrange for local law enforcement to place officers at each of the facilities for the patients on a list I am about to send you."

"If it is conjunction with the Northern State case, it should go through Special Agent Adams, you know that," Witt said.

"I don't have time for a pissing match with Adams. People are in real danger, I need these arrangements made," Jeffers snapped at his superior.

After a bristled pause, Witt's voice acknowledged, "I'll make it happen. What's going on?"

"The scientist responsible for the ferals, he is a physician at a Seattle university hospital. He was targeting one of the victims to cover his tracks," Jeffers informed the deputy director.

"Adams *really* needs to be clued in," Witt stressed.

"In time, if she handcuffs me because of her ego driven decision-making, innocent people will be at risk," Jeffers said.

"Both of our careers will be at risk for ignoring Bureau protocols," Witt warned.

"Rather risk my career than people's lives," Jeffers snapped.

"Understood. I'll get it done," Witt promised.

Jeffers was about to hang up when his gaze caught different care coordinators working with Sarah Whitman. He realized he lacked the knowledge to understand what was proper care or not.

"Hey, is Dr. Burbee still in Washington?" Jeffers asked.

"I think so. He was finishing up some work with that M.E. in Sedro-Woolley," Witt said.

"Have him drop what he is doing and come to Seattle immediately. Arrange for a helicopter to bring him right to the university hospital. He may not be the best choice, but I trust him to oversee the care for Sarah Whitman," Jeffers said.

"I'll have one of the helos on site bring him right away," Witt agreed. "Watch yourself out there Jeffers, there's a lot on the line."

Jeffers hung up the phone and muttered, "You have no idea."

THIRTY

Dr. Chase moved his search from Dr. Holder to Sarah Whitman's attending physician, Dr. Charles. Locating the hospital directory, he followed the labyrinth of elevators, sky bridges and hallways to reach the proper floor of the medical office building attached to the hospital.

Offering friendly nods, he hoped to convey a confidence that he belonged there. He knew his physical appearance had likely taken a toll during the long week of late hours and physical danger.

Approaching Dr. Charles' office, he found the door ajar. Working in institutions, this was often an indicator that the individual was available. With a gentle rap on the door, it swung open as Chase called, "Dr. Charles..."

Chase's heart sank as he saw a figure sprawled on the floor beside the desk. Diving to his knees, Chase checked for a pulse. He couldn't find one.

Poking his head out in the hallway just as a nurse was passing by with a handful of files, he called, "We need medical help, right away. Dr. Charles is unresponsive!"

The nurse bolted to the nearest phone. Dialing, she spoke a few words, glanced down the hallway towards the office and hung up the phone. In moments, the halls were filled with the call for a "Code Blue".

Chase returned to Dr. Charles' side as numerous footsteps thundered down the hall towards the office. Relieved from attempting CPR on his own by hospital staff, the professor stood, watched and waited.

The looks on the faces of the hospital staff told the grim tale. Chase closed his eyes and looked away. Pulling out his phone, he put in the call to Agent Jeffers.

The staff, haggard and heartbroken as they were with any victim they were not able to resuscitate, but even more so with their own colleague, turned in confusion towards the strange man standing out of the way in the corner of the office.

As the staff prepared to move the doctor, Chase halted them. "I am here as part of a federal investigation. I am not sure if this is connected, but I have agents on the way. They are going to want him and this office to remain as is."

The confusion of the attending staff only grew deeper. One woman nodded, "I'll stay and look into this."

The staff seemed to trust the woman and solemnly left the office.

The woman looked at Chase with a wary expression.

"I'm Dr. Ryder Chase, we have been investigating a case involving one of Dr. Charles' patients. I came to ask him a few questions."

The woman's eyebrow raised, "You're a doctor?"

Chase danced a little as he glanced at his shoes before responding, "Well, not your kind of doctor."

"I'm going to need to see your credentials," the woman demanded.

Chase flustered as he reached for his wallet, which he knew would not in any way appease the request.

"That won't be necessary," a voice boomed into the room. Agent Jeffers already had his badge out for display. "Dr. Chase is an expert consultant on a federal investigation."

The agent circled Dr. Charles, deceased on the floor of the office.

Chase could see Jeffers trying to determine the importance of the man to the case aside from his present condition.

"That is Dr. Charles. He was Sarah Whitman's attending physician," Chase explained. "I came to ask him some questions about Holder. When I knocked on the office door, I found him lying there. I called for help and administered CPR until a crash team arrived. It was too late. But it was recent."

"Would either of you like to clue me in on what is happening at my hospital?" the woman asked. "I'm Doctor Workman. I'm the Medical Director for in-patient care. Dr. Charles is…was one of my attendings."

The reality of her co-worker's death only just beginning to hit her.

"Dr. Workman, one of Dr. Charles' patients had a specialist working on her case, Dr. Holder," Agent Jeffers said. "We believe he is involved in dangerous medical experiments."

"Holder," the woman held her hand to her forehead and turned away for a moment. With a slow nod, "I can see that. He is on staff as a neuro-psychiatrist. Gifted in trauma recovery. Always wanted to explore surgical options. We always denied him. It's not part of our charter or medical philosophy. Some of the doctors would allow him to observe medical procedures involving his patients. A little weird, but harmless."

"I don't believe he is all that harmless after all," Chase pointed.

"What does his eccentricities have to do with Dr. Charles?" Dr. Workman asked.

Jeffers shook his head, "We don't know yet. Maybe nothing, maybe everything. I have a team coming to find out."

"Dr. Workman, is Dr. Charles' nurse around? She may help fill in some blanks for us as to how Dr. Holder was involved in the patient's case," Chase asked.

"I'll have her paged," the medical director nodded. Glancing at the body of Dr. Charles on the floor, she winced.

"We'll meet her in the hallway," Chase assured.

Agent Jeffers and the professor locked eyes, their look told of their shared suspicion.

Dr. Burbee's first stop was Dr. Charles' office. The FBI Medical Examiner took the body to the hospital morgue. Usually just used for temporary holding and not for functioning autopsies, the coroner only performed a cursory examination.

The most telling was a chemical panel that Dr. Workman fast tracked through the hospital's lab. Sending the report and initial findings to Jeffers, he went to observe the care provided to Sarah Whitman.

After sealing Dr. Charles' office, Jeffers and Chase joined Agent Sohn and Dan Tannen in Dr. Holder's office. Agent Sohn was behind Holder's desk while Tannen sat on the floor, a semi-circle of papers and stacks of notebooks in front of him.

"How's Sarah?" Agent Sohn asked.

"In recovery, her family is with her. For better or worse, I sent Dr. Burbee to oversee her care for the time being," Jeffers said.

Agent Sohn gasped, "Dr. Burbee?"

"I didn't know who to trust around here. He doesn't need to direct care, just deflect anything questionable," Jeffers said.

"As forensic pathologists go, he seemed fairly medically competent," Tannen shrugged.

"Speaking of Burbee, we found Sarah Whitman's actual attending physician deceased in his office. Cursory analysis indicates a heart attack. Burbee thinks it was induced based on the initial chemical panel, but he needs a forensic lab to be sure," Jeffers shared.

"And you think...Holder killed him?" Sohn asked.

"I'm having Dunlap review the footage from that floor. I'd bet Holder was there not long before Charles died," Jeffers nodded.

"Dr. Charles' nurse told us that Holder called not long after Sarah's admittance and asked to be on the case. Dr. Charles didn't see the immediate need for Holder's help but ultimately relented when because Holder was so persistent," Dr. Chase added.

"It took some work, but we've been pulling some strings ourselves," Agent Sohn said. "His recent trip to attend a conference by all accounts seems to have been a recruiting trip. He had a list of attendees. In his own notes, he listed a setback that he could exploit for each potential candidate. Under achieving student athletes at risk for losing their scholarships, medical students struggling to pass their boards, military hopefuls trying to achieve their physicals..."

With a nod to Tannen, she had the EMT fill them in on what he had found.

"Again, I'm not the most qualified, but by from what I've read, he had done a lot of work on stress and bipolar disorder. Pairing different stress hormones and antipsychotics with known activators of manic symptoms. The positive results he was after wasn't to find a cure, but rather maintain a stress load right to the breaking point," Tannen shared.

"By the looks of the ferals, I'd say they broke," Jeffers said.

"In a big way. The worst thing, he thinks the balance isn't in the chemistry, but in the natural adoption in the human environment. The human brain needs to adapt, evolve. His proposed answer is volume," Tannen declared.

"That's why he is recruiting, he needs more subjects," Agent Sohn suggested.

"It's worse," Tannen continued. "He was working on mass distribution."

Chase snapped his fingers, "Leaning towards a picture of Holder that seemed older than the others displayed in his office. I knew I had seen him before. It wasn't at my campus and it wasn't at my university. It was at the University of Edinburgh. I attended a conference on parapsychology. His name wasn't Holder, it was...it was... Holzenhaus. Franz Holzenhaus. I remember because his lecture created quite the stir. It was on bioterrorism and the use of psychostimulants. He declared it was a fine line to create a super soldier or a synthetic virus that would annihilate an army from within."

"Here he is, Franz Holzenhaus. According to his CV, he bounced from university to university throughout

Europe. He was ultimately exorcised from academia and disappeared about a decade ago," Agent Sohn said, tying into the FBI database from Holder's computer.

"Dig into Holder," Chase suggested.

"His CV looks nothing like Holzenhaus'. Conservative, highly regarded. Most of his career right in Seattle at this university after transferring from the east coast," Sohn said, frowning at the results.

"Have D.C. run his records. See if they can be confirmed, particularly his early work," Jeffers requested.

Sohn nodded.

Chase continued to stare at the photos. Pulling up a photo online of Holzenhaus, he compared the two. "Put a beard on Holzenhaus, age him a few years and you've got Holder," Chase nodded to himself.

Tannen flung a book out in front of the team, a look of panic crossing his face. "I think we are forcing Holder, or whoever he is, to speed up his ultimate experiment. He wants to release the stress compound en masse. He wants to nudge the evolutionary response by infecting a number of people and he has already found a method.

Chase looked at the notes Tannen displayed, "Oh, that is not good."

"What...?" Agent Jeffers started. "Is that...?"

Tannen nodded, "He has aerosolized the chemicals he administered at Northern State. Those vials I saw, they're unique. It took me seeing that page to understand why. They're pressurized. Whatever concoction he created, it can be trapped in the bottles until the glass ruptures, allowing the compounds to release into the air. Once inhaled…"

The team froze considering the implications of the event.

Jeffers' phone buzzed. Snatching it open, he stepped towards the door and called, "Tell me you found him."

Dunlap's voice came through the phone as Jeffers put in on speaker.

"It took us awhile, but we finally found him. A man matching his description left the hospital through the rear staff entrance a little over an hour ago," Dunlap reported.

The team shared a mutual look for horror.

Agent Sohn looked out of Dr. Holder's office window at the Seattle city skyline, "He's out there somewhere."

Jeffers hung up the phone. "This is bad," he cursed. Slumping his shoulders, he dialed the Seattle bureau office, "Get me Agent Adams on the phone."

THIRTY ONE

Agent Dunlap and Wally Smyth arrived at the Seattle Federal Bureau of Investigation office to an air of angst. Special Agent-in-Charge Stacy Adams had clearly fueled the environment for the arrival of Special Agent Jeffers' team.

Their role was to watch a wall of monitors fed by cameras throughout Seattle and the area freeways. Dunlap was quickly ushered to a dark room. Handed a pencil and a pad of paper, they left him to review the videos and note any that might lead to information on Dr. Holder.

Wally was remanded to the staff lunchroom as they refused to allow the paranormal researcher access to an official bureau resource. Once left alone, Wally scanned over each shoulder and moved to the refrigerator, rummaging through the contents, he found a container with "Adams" stenciled across a piece of masking tape.

"She won't be needing this since she's up in Sedro-Woolley," he grinned. Opening the container, he found a substantial helping of leftover spaghetti. Giving the contents a sniff, he nodded and tossed it in the microwave.

Leaning against the wall, as he waited for his newly acquired lunch to heat, he noticed that he could see a junior agent's desk from that vantage. On her screen, a live feed from a helicopter combing Seattle neighborhoods was shown. It seemed to be tracking a black SUV. As the occupants pulled alongside a stately home on Lake Union, he recognized them.

Beyond the junior agent's cubicle was a private office. The placard on the door read "SAIC Stacy Adams".

"She's spying on the team," he muttered as the microwave beeped.

Removing a fork from the dishwasher, Wally ate his lunch while he spied on Agent Adams' junior agent spying on Jeffers' team.

Special Agent Jeffers led the team towards the front door of the home. Slapping a piece of paper to the window alongside the front door, he levied a mighty kick, slamming his heel just above the handle, shattering the wood frame allowing the door to swing wide.

Weapons drawn, Jeffers and Sohn pushed ahead while Tannen and Chase followed cautiously behind. Working room to room, they ensured the entire house was cleared before they relaxed and let the team begin their search.

"There's no car in the garage," Agent Sohn called. "The floor is dry as well."

Jeffers frowned, "Unlikely he came home. Span out. Look for anything that might indicate a location Holder might head. Maps, sport stadiums, anything that suggests he has spent attention to any one area."

Dividing up the house, the team searched. Bedroom drawers and closets, office and even photos lining the walls or stuck to the refrigerator were catalogued. When they were confident they covered everything obvious, they reconvened in the kitchen.

"Nothing specific," Agent Sohn shrugged. "The man was obsessed with his work and DaVinci. He had Vitruvian Man pictures as his primary décor."

"Even his coffee table book was Davinci," Tannen nodded.

Chase tossed a stack of pamphlets on the counter, "Just the usual assortment of tourist attraction stuff. He could attack any one of those sites."

Jeffers sorted through the locations, setting each out on the counter. "Space Needle, aquarium, waterfront, stadiums...nothing stands out," he frowned.

"He'd need somewhere not well controlled for fear of inspection, that rules out the Space Needle and the sports stadiums," Dr. Chase mulled. "The waterfront is too open, the aerosol distillate would dilute quickly into the environment."

Jeffers rubbed his chin, "There has to be something!"

The FBI agent hoped the all-points bulletin issued to all law enforcement personnel would turn up a clue. He feared the scientist had already slipped out of Seattle and had a secondary target in mind in the event he was discovered. He hated to think of what would happen if they did not find Holder in time.

Agent Dunlap hunched over the desk he sat at. The bank of monitors he stared at was almost overwhelming. He looked for anything in a list of details- men fitting Holder's description, his grey Audi. He studied toll booths, stop lights and pedestrian cameras along Seattle's busy city center.

Rubbing his eyes, wishing he could break away and grab a cup of coffee, he stared. Flitting from screen to screen, he scanned the tremendous flow of data streaming before him. His eyes didn't register it at first, his brain had him move back two screens.

A bearded man clutching something close to his chest ambled past one of the cameras. Using the controls, Dunlap was able to freeze the image and zoom in. Pulling out his photograph of Holder, he compared the two.

The man on the screen was dressed in a suit, he was disheveled, as he looked over his shoulder, he appeared to be panicked, the height of stress.

Agent Dunlap's eyes went wide. Scrambling for his phone, he placed the call to Jeffers.

Wally watched the junior agent casually monitor the screen. When another agent hastily brought a document they were waving in their hands over, Wally leaned with intensity, setting his mostly eaten container of spaghetti on the counter.

The junior agent changed her screen. A pair of side by side images were displayed, comparative biometrics clearly showing a match. Nodding, the junior agent switched her monitor back as a pair of Seattle Police squad cars pulled in front of the house Jeffers and the team had entered.

Calling Chase, he asked, "Did Jeffers call for Seattle Police?"

"He just did, why?" Chase asked.

"A pair of Seattle finest just pulled up out front," Wally informed his friend. "And get this, the Seattle Bureau just got a facial recognition match on Dr. Holder. They're scurrying into a frenzy."

"They have no idea what they're up against," Chase warned.

"They aren't going to listen to me. They quarantined me to the staff kitchen. Agent Adams... only a so-so cook," Wally said.

"Where's Dunlap?" Chase asked.

"Reviewing Seattle CCTV footage," Wally replied.

"They're freezing Jeffers' team out," Chase said.

"And judging by how the cops are slinking up to the front door, I don't think they're there because Jeffers called them to control the scene," Wally implored.

"They're here to detain us. Gotta go!" the phone went silent.

Jeffers hung up his call with Dunlap, "Might have a hit on Holder."

"The Seattle office has a positive I.D. He's downtown Seattle. Last seen heading south on First," Chase shared.

Jeffers fumed, "That immature…"

"Worse, she sent Seattle Police to detain us," Chase said.

"Out the back, we need to get downtown!" Jeffers urged.

Chase grabbed a cartoonish map of Seattle as he followed the FBI agent through the house.

Flinging the back door open, Jeffers led the team across the yard. Once they were several houses down, they finally moved back towards the road. Flagging down a taxi that was determined not to stop until Jeffers stepped out into the road with his badge. "You can drive or I can drive!" he scowled.

"Get in, I'll take you!" the cab driver was suddenly agreeable.

Piling in, Jeffers told the man to drive. Not having a destination in mind, he was just happy to put distance between them and Holder's house.

Chase was frantically reviewing the map when he called out excitedly, "The market! Head to Pike Place Market!"

The driver looked over at Jeffers who nodded.

"And step on it," Jeffers growled.

When the taxicab driver stopped, Agent Jeffers tossed a handful of bills at him and jumped out. The team gazed towards the giant, iconic sign welcoming them to the large downtown marketplace.

Covering multiple blocks covering several levels cascading the hill towards Elliott Bay and packed with shoppers and tourists, even tracking Holder here was only a minute step towards locating him.

"Where do we start?" Tannen asked, taking in the enormity of the shopping area.

A scream pierced the late evening sky.

"I guess that way!" Chase said, forgetting that the team members with the badges and guns should likely have taken the lead.

Cutting through the crowd that gathered around the center of the main level, they saw a man staggering against the rail of the stairwell leading to the levels below. Dr. Holder stood with a hand on the rail, the other holding a large vial in his hand.

"He is not looking well," Agent Sohn observed as they made their way closer.

A security guard approached the scientist. His presence made Holder agitated, striking out at them and waving the vial wildly in his hand.

"Don't move! Stay back! I'll do it!" Holder called, his voice pitched and broken.

A pair of Seattle Police Officers closed in.

"No! Stop! Federal Agents! Stop!" Agent Jeffers screamed as they raced forward.

Their warning was too late. Seeing the police officers coordinate to cut off the scientist, a cloud burst into the air as the scientist dropped his arm, releasing the vial.

Above the cloud, Chase saw something that made his heart sink even further, a second viral spiraled through the air towards the gathered crowd.

The team froze in their tracks, slamming to a halt. Chase spread his arms out and drove the team away. Turning, they sprinted away from the crowd that stood, mouths agape at the unusual scene.

When they stopped and turned, they could see the scientist doubled over, convulsing. The police, security guard and much of the crowd dropped to a knee, covering their mouths as they choked and coughed.

As more Seattle Police officers arrived, Jeffers urged them to maintain a perimeter and begin to quarantine the area. Placing an immediate call to Washington, D.C., Jeffers ordered a full bio-terror alert.

Helicopters swooped in and a parade of black SUVs, police and fire responders surrounded the Pike Place Market just as the sun finally dipped beyond the reach of Elliott Bay.

Most of the crowd seemed to be confused and fighting the effects, their confusion and panic turned into despondence and a new form of confusion. Police used barricades to contain them. Jeffers and team tried to find a location that afforded them a superior view of the complex while Dunlap did his best to deliver reports from the numerous cameras placed around the market.

Dr. Holder disappeared into the bowels of the market while the infected officers and crowd milled about. Some slunk to dark corners while others wandered listlessly, as though their brains and bodies were fighting one another.

"What do we have for a clock?" Jeffers asked.

"I have no idea. Holder's experiments typically involved a slow and measured dosing over time. His idea for an aerosol was a super-concentrated dose. I don't know if it will speed up the process, exacerbate the result or flat out kill people," Tannen shrugged.

"That's encouraging," Jeffers muttered, eyeing the chaos below their perch on a rooftop.

A helicopter hovered above, a light switched on, zeroing on the investigation team.

"Oh, good. Agent Adams must be here," Jeffers quipped.

As they watched, an entourage split through the first responders, Special Agent-in-Charge Adams waded through and eyed Jeffers' position in the roof. With a wicked grin and a waggling finger, she beckoned the agent to confer with her.

Rolling his eyes with a sigh, Jeffers crawled down from his position and stood in front of the Seattle-based agent.

"Agent Jeffers, I thought I told you and your ham-fisted ghost chasers to get on a flight out of town," Adams snapped.

"And if we had, the situation here could have been worse," Jeffers glared.

Agent Adams burst into a haughty laugh, "Worse...than this?"

"I'm pretty sure we pre-empted Holder's plan. If the Seattle Police hadn't...," Jeffers began.

"Oh, it's the Seattle Police's fault now," Adams sneered.

"No. It's your fault for holding us back and deterring our investigation. Instead of working together, you are so hell-bent on one-upping me, you let a madman unleash who knows what horror on all of those people down there," Jeffers spat.

"Well, I'm here now. We'll take it from here, Agent Jeffers. For the last time, you and your team are excused," Adams waved her hand.

"Why don't we work together, Adams? We need all the help we can to control this situation," Jeffers suggested.

"The situation seems to be contained, thanks to the quick action of the Seattle first responders. The CDC is on its way, we're good," Adams wrinkled her nose and patted Jeffers on the chest.

As the Seattle agent dismissed Jeffers and turned her attention to the hastily erected barrier, her eyes widened in horror. Several from the infected crowd turned at once to the edge of the temporary fencing that separated them from the quarantine zone and the curious onlookers, in a full sprint, they leapt and in unison, rammed into the barrier, toppling it on top of first responders that monitored the area.

Most ran in a frenzy away from the area, heading for pockets cast in shadow where they could more easily evade. A handful paused where they landed and started viciously attacking anyone within reach.

Two transformed ferals turned their attention to the gap Adams made as she arrived. Seeing that route as an escape, they beelined towards Adams and Jeffers. Adams froze just for a moment as Jeffers grasped her by the shoulders and swung her away from a lunging feral. Pulling her along with him, they raced towards the roof his team used to survey the situation. As they reached the roof, Jeffers paused, allowing Adams to leap off his looped hands and into the outstretched reach of Agent Sohn and Professor Chase. Catching her, they pulled, heaving the agent to the safety of the roof as hands clawed at her legs.

A feral tackled Jeffers full on, gnashing with teeth at his face and throat. With outstretched arms, he held the teeth of his attacker at bay. Rolling to the side, he freed himself and gained a step. His only recourse was to draw his weapon. Knowing this assailant was an innocent bystander only a short time ago, he hesitated.

Dr. Chase dropped from the roof, landing on top of the feral, just before Jeffers' finger tightened on the trigger. With a howl, the feral screamed as Chase cast the stricken subject over the edge of the landing and onto the restaurant patio of the next level down. Almost without reaction to the violent fall, the feral was back on its feet leaping towards the men that were out of its reach.

"Thanks," Jeffers cocked his head to the side and pulled his flashlight out and held it next to his weapon. The agent looked lost.

"Come on, we need to widen the perimeter and come up with a different method of subduing the ferals," Chase suggested.

Jeffers nodded.

They cast their eyes out at the scene. The ferals that began as frightened and confused, then turned defensive, had landed as ferociously aggressive.

THIRTY TWO

A contrite Special Agent-in-Charge Adams stood on top of the roof. Her complexion paled as she panned three-hundred and sixty degrees of chaos.

Every law enforcement officer and FBI agent in the Seattle metro area descended on downtown Seattle. Their efficacy in controlling the situation was nil as the ferals were fast, slick and aggressive when cornered. Their claimed territory grew larger and larger with each passing minute. The standing order was to not shoot unless they were saving an innocent life.

Agent Adams jumped as gunshot after gunshot surrounded her.

"There has to be a better way," she gasped, clearly overwhelmed by the scenario.

"We need whatever non-lethal restraint we can find. In Sedro-Woolley, we used tranquilizer darts," Jeffers suggested.

Agent Adams shot Jeffers a glance, "You have a supply of tranquilizer guns and darts that I'm not aware of?"

"No, I just...," the agent started. A blood-curdling scream captured their attention above the already overwhelming chaotic cacophony surrounding them.

A school bus was being attacked just outside of the market's lowest level. Blocked in by traffic halted during the response, the driver froze and encouraged the passengers to hole up. Something evidently attracted the ferals' attention.

Without hesitation, the team leapt off the roof, plowed over the feral still fruitlessly leaping towards their position and down the hill towards the bus.

Using gravity to their advantage, they slid down the rails and cement slopes alongside the stairs. As they closed in, they still had no idea how to subdue them.

Dr. Chase called as they ran, "Get to the bus and drive it away. The sidewalk is clear!"

Any onlookers gawking on the side of the streets had long since cleared away, giving to panic from the frenzied mob of ferals.

"I'm going with you!" Agent Sohn growled as the team ran breakneck towards the bus.

Chase guessed from his observations that aggression met with aggression from the ferals. He tried desperately to plan a route that would give him the slightest chance of survival, having Agent Sohn with him only heightened his need for a plausible path.

As they reached the street level, Dr. Chase leapt in the air, grasping a pole from a street marketer's tent, slipping it free from the awning it held up, he held it in front of him, running headlong into the ferals pounding on the side of the school bus.

The response was instant and visceral. The complete attention of the half dozen ferals intent on the prospect of the bus inhabitants turned to Chase. He stood for a moment with Agent Sohn at his heels. The moment Agent Sohn's hand grasped his shoulder and yanked him away, the ferals snapped to action. Following the forms through the night, they focused on the movement.

Running as fast as they could, Chase and Sohn were able to pace the ferals, each step leading them further and further from the bus full of school children. In the distance, they heard the diesel engine turn over and slip into gear.

As they ran, Chase calculated the problem with his plan. The constant adrenaline rush of the stress compounds introduced to the ferals' systems would keep them propelled, sustaining them forward. Regardless of their levels of being in shape, at some point, his and Agent Sohn's bodies would give out. The signals to give up, give into exhaustion and pain would subconsciously leak from their brains to their muscles and they would stop running. They would be left to fruitlessly fight or ultimately crawl into a ball and give up.

Spying a stairwell leading up to the next street, he knew it was a risk. Hoping to catch the high ground, they might be able to find a way to safety. Sprinting with a fresh burst of hope, they pulled away ever so slightly. As they approached, Chase noticed a pedestrian elevator followed the stairs. On a whim, he pressed the button.

The elevator doors opened. Yanking Agent Sohn inside, they pushed their backs to the wall. The ferals closed in with every waiting second. The elevator doors began closing but the most fleet of the ferals was almost within reach. Chase and Sohn watched as the doors slowly made progress towards one another and their moment of respite, but a hand spliced inside before the doors could close, the rebound effect sent the doors wide with more ferals closing in.

Agent Sohn delivered a kick to the face of the lead feral knocking him back and out of the elevator as Chase leapt forward, leaning into the close door button. The ferals steadied themselves and leapt for another attack just as the doors began closing again. Agent Sohn pulled back the slide of her firearm, ensuring a bullet was chambered and leveled it in front of her.

Her aim was obstructed by stainless steel as the doors were closed and immediately rammed into, the stainless-steel bowing towards them in an amorphic human-esque shape. To their relief, the elevator pulsed and began pulling them upwards.

Through the glass windows, they could see the ferals ramming the stainless-steel doors below. Ferals in the back of the group looked up, tracking the slow moving elevator. All at once, almost as if they procured group speak, they began racing up the stairs.

Suddenly, Chase and Agent Sohn were painfully aware of just how slow the elevator was. Through their peripheral vision, they could see the first of the ferals had nearly paced with the elevator.

Dropping their heads, Chase and Sohn readied themselves. The moment the doors opened, they were sprinting away. They could hear that the ferals were not far behind them. Their footfalls echoing off the damp Seattle pavement, they were beyond keeping pace, but gaining on them.

Chase calculated their odds of escape. They weren't good. He cast a glance at the agent next to him. There was so much of their burgeoning relationship he wanted to explore with her, but he felt they would never have the chance.

Suddenly, Agent Sohn yanked him off course. A sky bridge connecting to a building below might provide a chance for escape. Putting every ounce of energy into their sprint, they drove themselves onto the sky bridge.

They kept running, not knowing where their pursuers were until they reached the end of the sky bridge. Chase glanced over his shoulder. The ferals slammed to a halt, almost as if they had hit an imaginary wall. Suddenly one looked up and leaped. Then another. And another.

In horror, Chase and Sohn could hear fast moving footsteps over their heads. The ferals were running towards them along the sky bridge roof.

Knowing they had no choice but to push on, Chase and Sohn relaunched their run. The sky bridge dumped into an open balcony that led to the Bell Street Pier. To the right, they had the dimly lit street that ran along the cruise ship terminal. To the left, they had the area they had just run from, knowing there were ferals lurking in those dark corners. Ahead of them, they had a restaurant roof and the chilly waters of Elliott Bay.

They hunted for a way to the roof, but the ferals descended the sky bridge towards them. Cutting them off from either left or right stairwell and no obvious way forward, they were trapped. Agent Sohn moved her gun muzzle from approaching feral to approaching feral.

Their back pushed to the wall, Dan Tannen's voice suddenly came over the radio. "Lights! They shrink from the lights!"

All at once, it made sense to Chase. Why the ferals at Northern State were so adept at evading them had to do with their propensity to move in the shadows. What agitated the ferals in the marketplace, was the lights that came on as night fell. What paused the feral from crossing the well-lit sky bridge was that fact that it was well lit. They instead climbed on to the roof of the structure and continued their chase.

Pulling his tactical light from his pocket, he shone it in full intensity at the ferals. Those within its field, shrunk back immediately.

Agent Sohn placed her tactical light against her firearm grip. The ferals on her side backed away. On the advantage, Chase and Sohn moved forward, commanding the ferals backward, corralling them into the limited dark space between them and the light of the sky bridge.

Hunkering down, the ferals gathered into balls as they tried to avoid the light.

"The chemicals that cause fight or flight symptoms and heighten stress also cause pupil dilation. If Holder's solution doesn't account for that, light would be painfully blinding for them," Chase reasoned.

Two ferals escaped and perched atop the sky bridge eyeing their prey. Chase and Sohn effectively detained the remaining four.

Sohn called the event into Jeffers who had gotten the busload of children to safety and was heading to their location in a Seattle Police cruiser.

With the slightest breath of relief, Agent Sohn and Ryder Chase relaxed.

Sohn glanced at Chase, desperately yearning for a true moment of solace with him.

That solace would not come. As they stood, their lights as their shields holding the ferals at bay, Sohn's light started to flicker. "No, no, no, no!" she cursed, smacking the light against her gun hand.

The moment the light faded, the ferals on her side circled. The ferals atop the sky bridge hopped down, looking for an angle of attack. Chase tried to keep them at bay, but with the narrow focus of his tactical light, the only way it held the intensity required to repel the ferals provided room for them to maneuver. Instinctively, they tried to separate the two.

As one lunged for Agent Sohn, Chase leapt against it. Using the tactical light as a weapon, he cracked the skull of the feral, planting it unconscious at his feet. The blow caused his own light to fail, bathing them in darkness.

The weight of the ferals upon them, they shrunk backwards until they hit the wall of the restaurant. With no light available and no chance to run, they were trapped. Other ferals joined the group, doubling their immediate attackers.

Closing in, Agent Sohn had no choice. She knew these were tourists, shoppers, employees. A little over an hour ago, they were people minding their business before going home to their families, now they were singularly focused zombies, angrily trying to tear anything up in their path.

Danica Sohn shut her eyes with the first shot, a tear streaking down her face, dropping a feral that leapt towards Chase. Firing again, she dropped another. Pivoting her aim, she dropped another. With each shot fired, another tear welled. She was compelled to shoot, though each pull of the trigger was hell.

More ferals swarmed as they seemed to sense weak prey. Ignoring their own fallen, they stepped over them with irreverence intent on Chase and Sohn. Agent Sohn emptied her magazine. Instinctively releasing the expended mag and reaching for her spare, her fingers grasped at empty space. In horror, Agent Sohn realized her magazine must have fallen out during their escape.

Sohn and Chase sat with their sides wedged against the other's. The warmth of the other the only solace in their nightmare as the ferals descended.

Cornered, the ferals lunged, swiping and slashing at them. Agent Sohn turned, a single tear lighting on Ryder Chase's shoulder.

THIRTY THREE

Ryder Chase and Danica Sohn huddled together, waiting for their impending end. Fingernails dug into their skin as teeth snapped at their flesh. They punched and kicked and flailed, but the weight of the immense attack was too much.

As they succumbed to their final moments, numb to the pain of their skin and muscle ripped from their bodies, they lay, their heads together, waiting for the inevitable. Feigned counterattacks only delaying the end result.

As their world was darkened by flickering consciousness and the shadow of the vicious, pummeling mass, light penetrated the darkness. The weight upon them lessened. Suddenly they were alone, bathed in brilliant light. As consciousness faded back into life, they held their arms up to the overwhelming illumination.

Chase had to, for an instance, wonder whether it was the final light beckoning. He was encouraged as the silhouette of Danica Sohn was in the light beside him. Reaching out his hand, he grasped hers.

As the worldly noises began to register in his head, replacing the eerie muffled tunnel he had descended into, he recognized a sound. An immense, thundering, but most welcome sound. The blades of a helicopter slashed at the air above his head. The light pouring down was a massive searchlight.

The blanket of light provided a bubble of safety for the weary Ryder Chase and Agent Sohn. Two figures rappelled off the helicopter and onto the landing. Arms circled around their waists and pulled them towards the awaiting ropes.

Attaching each to a harness, they were hoisted into the air. Outstretched hands pulled them onto the helicopter as their rescuers followed soon after. The smiling faces of Agent Jeffers, Agent Dunlap, Wally and Tannen greeted them. Tannen immediately bathed them in red light and began inspecting their injuries.

While he was being attended to, Chase watched in wonder as Wally played the light shining below. With each movement, he sent the ferals scurrying one direction or the other. Chase chuckled in spite of the horror he had just survived. He knew Wally was enjoying the moment, directing the ferals to his whim.

Sadly, a handful of ferals desperately clawed at the ground to try and evade the light as they battled wounds from Agent Sohn's well-placed, non-lethal shots in their defense.

Chase glanced over and saw the sorrow in Sohn's face. Placing a hand on her thigh, he tried to comfort the agent. She offered a weak smile to return her forlorn gaze to the ferals below.

Wally's exercise with the light wasn't in vain. He learned how to maneuver the ferals to allow agents to appear on the scene and tranquilize them. The story was the same across the city as agents used powerful lights to maneuver the ferals into position for safe and as minimally harmful immobilization as possible.

As the helicopter moved on, they could see the remaining ferals on the ground scatter, desperately seeking the comfort of the shadows.

Arriving at the Seattle FBI office, Dr. Chase was pleased to see the adversarial relationship between Agents Jeffers and Adams had abated, at least for the time being. She welcomed them in from the helicopter pad as she ensured Chase and Sohn received medical attention.

They had as many bruises and scrapes from fighting and striking the ferals as they had actual bites and serious wounds. Taking blood and tissue samples as had become protocol, they were patched up to the best of the medic's ability given what they had to work with at the bureau.

Jeffers and Adams both urged the pair to go to the hospital for more complete care, but Jeffers knew they would refuse. Instead, they ambled into the briefing room as the agents were planning a nighttime round up of recently converted ferals.

Politicians debated letting it play out, that maybe the chemical compound would wear out over time. Clinical experts were split on how long the effects would last, whether they would dissipate at all or if they made systemic change that might not ever go away.

From the team's experience, they determined the effect lasted for weeks without additional dosing and the danger to the public and to themselves was too great to "wait and see". Jeffers and Adams decided to act quickly before their hands were tied in bureaucracy.

Standing in front of a room full of federal agents, with more arriving from nearby cities in support, Adams and Jeffers shared the plan for the night.

"Aerial and security camera footage suggests there were approximately seventy-five affected, including the scientist, security guard and two policemen who tried to subdue the subject. Initial response either captured or wounded, brings the remaining number at large to roughly fifty-eight subjects. We estimate that number to have plus or minus three variance," Special Agent-in-Charge Adams shared.

"We know these…ferals as Professor Chase dubbed them, like to stick to the shadows. It's how they move and how they attack. Team medic Dan Tannen identified they have sensitivity to bright light, enough so it can halt an attack and can be used to drive them in a direction. We can use that to our advantage," Special Agent Jeffers stated. "We'll work in two-man teams, one will work a powerful light, the other a tranquilizer gun. Note, a bit of added difficulty for the shooter is that they will need to target outside of the light range as the subjects won't enter it. The light will be used to move the target into a zone for the shooter. Good news is, these darts have a higher dosage and faster acting sedative, drastically reducing the time to effect."

"The…uh…Jeffers' tech consultant, Wally Smyth, correctly noted the subjects exhibit a slightly higher temperature reading on the thermal," Adams said. "When scanning you can delineate a possible subject versus a victim. Ideally, we want positive identification, so be sure, though lifesaving events may require some quick decision making on your part. Remember, feral people are still that, people. We'd like to give them the opportunity to return to their former selves, if possible. That's it. Good luck out there. Be safe!"

Adams dismisses the room. Jeffers and Adams thanked one another and moved to meet with their respective teams.

"Did you…did you two just give us credit," Wally was incredulous.

Jeffers facial expression remained flat, "I had to create some layer of credibility for you three or they would have kicked you out."

Wally cocked his head, "Come on, you know it's more than that. You really like us!"

"You guys *occasionally* come up with a good…theory or two," Jeffers reluctantly admitted.

Wally's eyes went wide, "So, do I get a gun?"

Jeffers scowled.

"Right, I'm on light duty," Wally conceded.

Jeffers doled out roles, "Tannen, I'll have you with me. Smyth, you're with Dunlap. We'll be air support, you two on the ground in a tactical vehicle."

The lead agent turned his attention to Agent Sohn and Dr. Chase, "You two stand down. You're injured. You nearly lost your lives tonight. You deserve to rest."

Sohn and Chase shared glances ensuring their mutual resolve. Sohn asserted, her eyes locking with her immediate superior, "We started this as a team, we're going to end this as a team."

"I thought you'd say that. You can be in a second ground vehicle," Jeffers agreed through pursed lips. He gave a lasting look to the investigation team. "Be safe out there."

The helicopter lifted off the bureau roof, as one by one, the night sky filled with black airborne sentinels, each hovering over a designated portion of Seattle. Fitted with powerful searchlights and thermal cameras, the agents on board swept the alleys and backstreets, searching for movement.

The city under immediate curfew, it was to be assumed people on the streets were ferals. Use of lethal force was more than ever, an absolute last resort.

The copilot scanned with the mounted thermal camera while Dan Tannen swept with the searchlight. Agent Jeffers ensured a dart was within its chamber and the IR scope was pacing just outside of Tannen's sweep or he would render his aim useless.

"Possible subject, helo's two-o'clock," the copilot announced over the radio.

The pilot pitched the helicopter and swung to the area noted. Tannen pushed the potent light even lines. As the beam cut through the shadows afforded by the deep alley and aided by the series of dumpsters lining it, two figures burst out. Tannen ensured he kept the beam right at the heels of the figures.

Jeffers readied the powerful air rifle. Leading muzzle ahead of the alley, he waited, his finger rested on the trigger, his breath even. With a slight exhale, he squeezed, hitting the first feral in the back of the neck.

The impact caused the feral to stumble headlong at the end of the alley. The second, running furiously away from the beam tripped over the first. By the time the feral collected itself and rose, Jeffers was ready with a second shot into that subject's shoulder.

The copilot called in the coordinates and the helicopter hovered as the ground teams moved in. Continuing to track the ferals with thermal, Tannen used the searchlight to push the ferals down the next alley.

A medi-van followed a pair of tactical vehicles to the area as they raced to the location. Separating as they neared the zone, the tactical vehicles bookended the alley. Each vehicle switched on their beams containing the ferals to the middle of the alley as a pair of high-powered air rifles remained trained on them.

As the tranquilizer doses began to take effect, the ferals stumbled in their dark confines of the alley. The ferals weakened and dropping to their knees, the medical team rushed in with hand carried gurneys. A pair of agents accompanied the team and assured the subjects were safely in restraints before they were carried to the back of the medi-van.

Subjects secure, the helicopter swung away from the alley and began searching for the next targets.

Agent Sohn and Ryder Chase rode in tandem turret posts atop the armored tactical vehicle. Riding with just their torsos exposed, Chase manned the light while Sohn stood at the ready with her air rifle.

Their primary task was to support the air assault and provide cover for the medical transport teams once the ferals had fallen. For much of the night, the plan followed the format well.

When the call came in, Agent Sohn could hear the terrified voices behind the call, including those of children. Without hesitation, Sohn deviated from their route and moved away from the helicopter.

"No, Agent Sohn, stand down!" Jeffers called.

"Can't do that," Sohn replied. "An apartment complex is under attack, we're the closest."

"I get that. There is nowhere close for us to land, you need support," Jeffers said.

"Then support us from the air!" Agent Sohn commanded. "Dunlap, hit the street on the south side of the building. We'll flush from the north."

"Copy that, having the driver proceed to north side of the apartment complex," Dunlap said through the radio, tapping the driver on the shoulder.

The tactical vehicle screeched to a halt. Chase aimed the powerful beam of the searchlight on the northern facade. They could see the building had lost power, a burning transformer with the vague shape of a human silhouette hinging in its midst.

"What the hell? Poor guy," Chase turned from the gruesome sight.

"Front door has been smashed in," Sohn said, her tranquilizer gun at the ready.

Screams from within the building beckoned them. Chase turned on the hand-held tactical light. It was the most powerful flashlight he had ever seen, though he was warned the battery life was limited.

"Come on," Sohn raced ahead. Kicking jagged glass pieces from the exposed door out of the way to aid their entry, she slipped inside.

Chase was close on her heels, ensuring the light was cast in her direction. Ferals scattered down the hallway, banging, scratching and lunging towards apartment doors as they ran.

Dunlap's tactical vehicle arrived on the opposite end, the light from his vehicle forcing the ferals in a fervor. Some found the darkened stairs as respite while three successfully made entry into an apartment.

"Wally, kill your light!" Chase called into the radio. The south side of the complex went dark.

Sohn burst into the apartment, using light streamed in from their vehicle to locate the first feral. Taking a shot, she hit it in the chest. A second took flight towards her, ducking, she avoided the outstretched arms of her attacker and delivered a blow with the butt of her gun to its chin, scattering it to the floor on the opposite side of the apartment.

The third maneuvered for an attack while Chase held it at bay with his light. The feral shrunk with its hands in front of its face, trying to avoid the light. Sohn chambered a round and shot it into the feral. The first feral, still writhing as the sedative worked its way into its system, tried to navigate around the beam while the one Sohn hit was recovering behind her.

Chase used the light to move and corral the ferals on the far side of the room. Running behind Sohn, he placed his heel on the recovering feral's throat. Ignoring the fingernails trying to dig into his legs, Agent Sohn chambered another dart and fired point blank into the feral.

Taking a step away from the writhing figure on the floor, Chase was able to force it in the corner towards the other two.

Agent Sohn leaned her head against the closed door. From behind, she could hear sobs of a young child and parents trying to console, having no idea what was taking place in their living room.

"Federal Agent. You should be safe, at least for the moment. Keep your door locked and cover yourselves with whatever is available. A mattress would work well," Sohn called. "Do you have flashlights, candles, cellphones, anything to transmit light? If you do, train it at the door. More help is on the way. My partner and I are moving on to assist with other neighbors. Sit tight!"

With a nod, she encouraged Chase to leave the apartment. A quick glance showed the ferals on the ground were nearly convalescent.

Looking at the ceiling above them, they could follow the rampaging footsteps. "There must be a dozen of them," Sohn said chambering another dart.

The sound of splintering wood followed by multiple screams told them the ferals upstairs were having more success penetrating residences.

"We need to push them with the light," Chase said. "Get them to one side of the building and the residents on the other. It will be chaos in the exchange, but it's our best shot."

Agent Sohn radioed Chase's plan to Jeffers in the helicopter as they ascended the stairs. As they entered the upstairs hallway, it was pandemonium. Flailing bodies sped down the hallway, as Chase approached with his beam, they scattered, some leaping headlong into closed doors, a few having success. As the wood splintered, they streamed into the exposed apartments.

Chase and Sohn ducked into the first apartment, a man covered his wife as a feral pummeled and slashed at his back. Chase moved his beam towards the scene, moving the feral off the man. Before Sohn could react, a figure leapt from the side, wrapping its arms and legs around her, pulling her aim off her target.

With his beam aimed at the first feral, Chase pulled tranquilizer dart from Sohn's bandolier and punched the dart into the feral's back. Slowly, the feral peeled off the agent as she choked to regain her breath.

"I guess that works," she tilted her head towards the sedated attacker. With a resolved glare, she took careful aim at the feral in the corner and fired a shot into its chest. "We're going to need medical attention standing by for room…221."

The agent wanted to stop and assist the man with his wounds, but the sounds of terror from down the hall told her they had to move.

From outside, a voice called over a loudspeaker for the residents to move as quickly to the west windows as possible. "The ferals will move away from you if you move towards the light, you'll be safe, you *must* get to the west windows!"

A brilliant beam of light filled the westside of the apartments. Unfortunately, the beam only hit a fraction of the windows at any time. Dan Tannen moved the light as he saw shadows present in the windows.

What he saw made his heart skip. As terrified apartment dwellers clung to the windows, Tannen swung the light in their direction. Panning to one section of the apartments, he could see silhouettes of residents, behind them, he could see the lurking shadows of ferals ready to attack.

Using the light, he could halt attacks, knowing that left another set of apartments vulnerable. Like a live game of whack-a-mole, the EMT moved the light from section to section, trying to keep the ferals at bay.

Agent Jeffers steadied his rifle. Over the shoulder of a vulnerable resident, he fired, hitting a feral in the neck. Without taking his eyes off of the facade of the apartments, he loaded another dart and located another target.

Tannen wiped sweat off his brow. In all of his years of helping to save lives, he never felt so responsible for the mortality of others. Behind the light that he wielded; he had the power to prevent death. Each time, he repelled an attack, he feared that he might allow another.

"This is an absolute horror show," Tannen gasped in desperation.

"Keep at it, we have to trust Sohn and Chase!" Jeffers encouraged.

Moving through the halls, as the light from the outside shifted, beings would leap from apartments on one side of the hallway to the other.

Chase used his flashlight to aid the push Tannen levied from west to east, by maneuvering ferals towards the end of the building on the south side. Agent Sohn moved from apartment to apartment with her tactical light as they moved, clearing each one, delivering tranquilizer darts to figures in the east while ensuring families to the west were safe.

Nearing the middle of the hallway, Chase's light started to flicker, "No, no, no, no!" he cursed. The FBI tech who handed him the light warned him that the powerful beam limited its battery life.

"Uhm, Sohn...we have a problem!" Chase called. As the light went completely dead, he pulled out his personal tactical light, which had a limited close-range impact, affecting only the few ferals that were in direct eye contact.

Using the strobe effect, he found it had more impact on those it hit in the eyes, but no impact on the ones it didn't.

Sohn joined with her own light. As ferals began to swarm, dancing around their limited light, they jockeyed for position. Slashing and lunging, they tried to separate the two.

Understanding their tactic, Sohn and Chase pressed their backs to one another. Circling, they held the ferals at bay. Shining their lights directly into their assailants' eyes, they could deter an attack.

Closing in and surrounding them, they could feel them close. Their breath could reach their faces as they lunged. They were so close the vibrations they made on the floor would alert them to their movement. Chase grabbed a dart from Sohn's bandolier. The agent did the same.

Moving in a sinewy dance, they launched a counterattack. As a feral moved to attack from the shadows, the agent and professor would strike with the dart. When they felt the needle tip penetrate flesh, they'd release and grab another, ready to strike again.

One moved at Sohn, ducking, she avoided the attack, slammed a dart into its neck and delivered a kick to its midsection, expelling it from the swarm.

The pulsing of Chase's light had an undesired side effect, the strobing light belied the speed at which the attackers moved. Bobbing late, he felt a hand on his neck. Spinning, he tried to duck and pull himself free. He was able to deliver a dart to his assailant's midsection. In the process, his flashlight was knocked loose, spinning on the floor of the hallway.

The ferals responded quickly, overwhelming the professor, leaping on him. Agent Sohn used the rifle as a club to try and free him, but the ferals were oblivious to the pain.

Suddenly, the hall was filled with light from behind them as a second helicopter dropped level with the second floor and blasted its beam throughout the second floor as an assault team burst into the apartment complex and moved room to room to clear it out.

The ferals atop Chase suddenly lifted their heads. Shielding their faces, they kicked away, trying to avoid the light. As they got to their feet, they turned and ran blindly towards the southern end of the apartment building. With a horrific crash, the ferals leapt one after another through the window to the dark space on the opposite side where Dunlap and Wally were waiting.

The two-story drop was enough to shatter limbs, but all were still alive. As they writhed on the ground, the FBI team was able to systematically inject them with a sedative.

Agent Sohn lifted Chase to his feet, "Are you okay?"

Chase stepped over a sedated feral as they huddled to the end of the hall. The scene of bright lights, advancing agents, fallen ferals and frightened residents was otherworldly, surreal.

Chase nodded, "Yeah. I'm okay. Mostly reopening existing injuries. I appreciate the armored vest the FBI gave us. It protected most of the important stuff."

Agent Sohn swept a smear of blood off his forehead, moving her fingers gently across his skin. Looking into his eyes, she sighed, "I was afraid I was going to lose you...again."

Chase grinned, "I wasn't worried. We make a good team!"

Sohn nodded, "That, we do."

Agent Dunlap and Wally Smyth were on their way back to the Seattle headquarters when their driver received a distress call. "You fellas got enough in the tank for one more stop?"

Wally nodded to Dunlap, "We're in!"

"Copy that, hang tight!" the driver called and wheeled the tactical vehicle in the direction of the requested scene.

Chase and Sohn were recalled to headquarters after they concluded the apartment sweep, while Jeffers and Tannen in the helicopter had to bug out to refuel. Wally and Tannen toured with a S.W.A.T. team as they worked through the remainder of the night.

Reaching the scene, they found a chaos of tents, spot fires and a circus of silhouettes chasing other silhouettes. "Homeless camp came under attack, not much light under the bridges where the encampment is, these poor people are nearly defenseless," the driver announced.

Wally swung the light around, targeting ferals in one direction, but losing them in the other. As ferals and unaffected people alike scampered wildly, the tactical team couldn't differentiate targets.

With the rest of the city collapsing in the evening's operation, the site seemed to be the ferals' last stand as they overwhelmed the camp. The other two tactical vehicles of the S.W.A.T. team tried to work in concert with Wally, but the area was too vast, diffusing the light.

Dunlap swung his rifle from subject to subject. "I don't know who to fire on."

"All of them?" Wally scrunched his nose.

Dunlap looked away from his scope, "That doesn't seem right."

"I suppose you're right," Wally nodded and looked thoughtful. "S.W.A.T. have battlefield illumination flares?"

The driver called on his radio. "They have a few M127's."

"Light up the area above the overpass. The unaffected run out from under while the ferals remain," Wally said.

"That might work," Dunlap nodded. "Each flare only lasts about half a minute; we'll have to work quickly to deliver sedative rounds."

"Like, maybe, you could use another shooter," Wally suggested.

"I don't know…yeah," Dunlap sighed. "Let's do it." The agent handed the paranormal researcher an air rifle and a box of darts.

The first flare flew in the air and the sky erupted over the night sky. With the clock on for the flare's luminescence, the teams went to work and locating their targets.

Wally sighted his first, squeezing the trigger, he let out a "whoop!" as he placed a dart in a subject's leg.

As the flare started to subside and S.W.A.T. readied to launch a second, Dunlap sighted Wally's shot and frowned. "Wally, I think that wasn't a feral."

Wally stared through his scope as the night turned to day for another round. The man he hit fell to the ground. His wild hair, ragged beard and especially the shopping cart he was madly trying to extricate from the overpass lent well to Dunlap's theory. "Yeah, I think that guy lived there," Wally admitted.

"My training says if you aren't a hundred percent sure...," Dunlap started as he sighted his next target and delivered a clean shot. "...don't shoot."

"Roger that," Wally said. Taking time with his next target, he waited a little too long as he watched the figure leap and grab the leg of a fleeing man. "Well, that's *gotta* be one." With a squeeze of the trigger, he fired. His aim low, the dart hit the concrete. Skipping across the ground, it hopped, sailing by the victim, inches from his head and into the shoulder of his attacker.

"Did you see that?" Wally exclaimed in glee.

"Yeah, you missed," Dunlap said as he adjusted his aim, waiting for the next flare.

"Yeah, but *then* I hit!" Wally grinned.

"Let's not tell Jeffers about this," Dunlap suggested.

Wally offered a sideways shrug as he hastily jammed another dart into the rifle.

THIRTY FOUR

The team gathered at the Seattle FBI headquarters. A few hours of sleep, fresh clothes and for some, fresh bandages, they were ready for a final assault to put the horrors of the feral campaign to rest.

Once again, Special Agent-in-Charge Stacy Adams shared the podium with Jeffers. "Starting with the good news. Thanks to the research from the lab at Northern State and Dr. Holder's office at the university uncovered by Agent Sohn and Dan Tannen, the neurologists at the university hospital have been able to piece together a possible solution. Dr. Albers…," Adams introduced.

"Thank you. Thank you all for the effort you have extended to save lives and bring as many of the affected in as safe as possible so that they could receive the care they so badly need," Dr. Albers shared. "Understanding Dr.

Holder...or Dr. Holzenhaus' intent with his research was pivotal to coming up with a game plan to neutralize the compound in the aerosol he released yesterday and the subjects he affected in Sedro-Woolley. The agents who found that hidden data, should be commended."

The doctor panned the crowd of agents who responded to plans of action better than academic findings, continued, "A negative of Holzenhaus' work, it restructures the body's own process to create and release neuropathic chemicals which would ultimately result in non-repairable neurological damage. Long story short, there would be no cure for those who languished in that state for too long. It was otherwise brilliant. If he could have stricken the right balance and tamped the fight or flight..."

"That's the trouble, though. He couldn't strike the right balance. Human neurology is too unique to one another. The millions of minute changes for each subject would make it near impossible. Holzenhaus should have known that. The arrogance of science, humans think they can master all domains, but, they just can't."

The audience nodded at the last sentence, understanding what the neurologist was driving at. "Through a cocktail of non-stimulant ADHD and mood disorder medications along with a healthy dose of oxytocin, we have been able to bring most of the affected subjects to a state closer to normalcy. The agitation has all but been abated. They suffer as greatly despondent, but it is early. Overall, the prognosis is quite good."

"What happens to the patients now?" Tannen asked.

"We'll continue to monitor their neurological, biochemical and brain physiology. Continued effort to home in on the ideal medication is still underway, but I feel...rather good about their outlook," Dr. Albers stated.

"Thank you, doctor," Agent Adams acknowledged.

"That brings us to our mission for the agents in this room. There are still roughly eight or so feral people still missing, most notoriously, Dr. Holder himself. Our experience in Sedro-Woolley is that due to the pain exhibited on their eyes by lights, they will remain hidden until nightfall. City of Seattle Police, King County Sheriffs and Washington State Police will continue to have heightened patrol. They will call us in as they encounter a possible subject," Agent Jeffers announced.

"Stay fresh, stay ready. The university where Dr. Holder worked has supplied us with catering which will be refreshed throughout the day. They know the stress the long nights put on you," Adams said.

Wally's eyes lit as he wandered towards where Adams pointed when she spoke of the catering. His hopes for perusing the smorgasbord were dashed as Jeffers pulled the team together, "A word."

"I just wanted to personally say nice work last night. Really over the course of the entire investigation. I had my doubts, in particular with some of the early setbacks, but…," Jeffers began. He paused as he noticed Dr. Chase pulling his lip, his eyes in a far-off gaze. "Oh, no. I know that look. Trouble always follows."

"I know where Holder is," Chase suddenly snapped and returned his gaze to the team. "Not far from Pike Place Market is the Seattle Underground. It is famous among paranormal researchers as being allegedly haunted. It was among Holder's tourist information. If I was feral person afflicted by the light, that's where I'd go."

"I'd rather hunt the ghost of the prostitutes that are supposed to wander down there," Wally blurted. Looking at the appalled reaction of his team, his eyes grew wide, "No, not like *that*! Just had enough of zombies, I mean."

"They're not really zombies," Tannen corrected.

"I know, but when else are we going to be able to say 'zombies' and have any real world relevance," Wally argued.

Dunlap and Tannen glanced at one another and shrugged as they nodded at the tech's reasoning.

Jeffers crossed his arms and stared at the three. "Can we focus? We still have a madman to catch."

Using his credentials, Jeffers gained the team access to the tunnels that once were the surface of the city of Seattle. Constant flooding forced the people of the frontier city to build up, on top of the existing infrastructure.

Some of the tunnels were maintained as a tourist attraction where stories of shanghai' d soldiers and thieves attracted to the gold miners that frequented the markets and prostitution rings. Ghost stories were a mainstay of the attraction, especially for night tours.

Evidence of an overnight break-in heightened their expectations as they entered the old tunnels. It didn't take them long before the first of the ferals was flushed out by their lights. Running through the maze of tunnels, it led them to a swarm of ferals hunkered down, waiting for the sun to fade when they could make their escape.

"There's a lot of them," Agent Dunlap whispered.

"By our estimated count, that might be the rest of them," Agent Jeffers nodded.

Keeping their lights at the ferals feet, they tried not to scatter them. The pack of ferals shuffled nervously as they backed as far as they could in their somewhat confined space.

Mostly, they squatted, their heads turned away from the light, their peripheral vision never diverting from the investigation team. Ryder Chase couldn't shake the feeling that they were staring at a nervous animal, coiled to strike at any moment.

Jeffers doled out air rifles to his team and spare darts for worst case scenario planning to the paranormal investigators. The team readied as they maneuvered for the concerted approach.

Wally played with the dart in his hand and stared at it. He had the luxury of never being very close to a feral since he was assaulted in Sedro-Woolley. He didn't relish the idea of being close enough to stab one with a dart.

Glancing around, he found a lose baluster on the wooden walkway railing. With a kick, he removed it completely. From his pocket, he pulled a pair of zipties and fastened the one of his darts to the baluster. He held his weapon in the air admiringly, with a grin, he panned the group, "Tranq on a stick!"

Even Jeffers struggled to stifle a laugh towards the childlike paranormal researcher.

The three agents aimed their air rifles at the three closest ferals. On Jeffers' count, they fired. The howling of the ferals hit and their pained response sent the rest in a frenzy. They scurried trying to find a clean exit, when that proposition seemed empty, they turned toward the investigation team.

Jeffers was quick to reload and locate a target. Dunlap had to backpedal and maneuver away from one lunging at him while Tannen aided him in steering the feral with his light.

Agent Sohn's gun jammed as a faulty dart shattered in the barrel, rendering her rifle useless. Ryder Chase saw the feral she targeted headed straight for her. Diving to separate the two, he jammed his dart into the midsection of the feral as he flew through the air.

Rolling out of the path of the now even angrier feral, something in the back of the pack caught his eye. A white-haired, bearded feral reacted differently from the rest. Instead of entering reactively into fight mode, it spent more than a cursory review of the possibility of flight. Slinking to the back of the tunnel, he slipped through the gaps in the exposed timbers that held up the original structure of the tunnel. It was Holder.

Chase stood up and took after the affected scientist. Agent Sohn grateful he was able to prevent her assault, she rolled her head disapprovingly that he took off. Tossing her defective weapon aside, she raced after the professor.

As Sohn climbed through the wooden beams propping up the location of Seattle above them, she saw

Chase cornering Holder with the beam of his tactical light. The two stood in a stand-off, each contemplating their next action. Each knowing their lives very well depended on it. Chase with the light as his only weapon. Holder with his chemically enhanced self.

Holder leaned away from the light as Chase kept the aim carefully placed on the scientist's eyes. Holder suddenly dipped, swiping something off the ground. Glistening in Chase's tactical light, he recognized it as a shard of green glass, likely dropped from a grate on the sidewalks above.

To their horror, Holder gripped the shard tightly in his hand and began plunging it in the back of his head, stabbing mercilessly at his occipital lobe. Blood streamed, coating his hand and his head in thick, red liquid.

As Sohn and Chase positioned themselves around Holder, he struck without warning. No longer impacted by the bright tactical light, he spun and leapt in the air directly towards Chase, the glass shard held high, ready to strike.

Agent Sohn drew her firearm and fired three quick shots, each imbedding into Holder. The scientist fell hard to the ground, the glass shard rattling at Chase's feet.

The team raced around the corner. The smoke from Sohn's firearm still hanging in the air.

Sohn's head hung towards the ground, Chase knew she didn't want to shoot. There were mysteries in the doctor's head, that when treated, might have been instrumental in helping the people affected by his experiments. Whatever he had in his head, was now spilled in blood on the floor of the Seattle Underground.

THIRTY FIVE

The Seattle FBI office continued to ensure the final ferals had been found and brought in for medical treatment. A portion of their forensics team continued to work the grounds of Northern State Hospital.

Special Agent Jeffers and his team decided to return to Sedro-Woolley prior to catching flights back to D.C. Connecting with Sheriff Watts and Chief Roberts, they were happy to hear that the town was slowly returning to normal. Houses that had never locked their doors began embracing new habits after the trauma they experienced.

New security at Northern State Hospital was installed and a new effort to find a proper suitor for the magnificent estate, despite its infamous history and more storied recent events, were underway. The county was considering purchasing the land so that they may have more control over its usage.

The team was excited to meet with the Whitman family as Sarah was allowed to come home. She would have months of trips to Seattle for check-ups and treatment, but she rounded the corner towards being herself once again.

The team walked the grounds of Northern State Hospital once more. They absorbed its beauty, marred by such tragedy. A century of tragedy that, at Dr. Holder's hands, continued.

"Well, that was weird," Jeffers commented as they walked along.

"Not paranormal," Dunlap said.

"Not exactly 'normal', either," Jeffers conceded.

Wally wrinkled his nose, "That, is the very definition of paranormal."

"Whatever. I call it 'case closed,'" Jeffers scoffed.

"Things good between you and Adams?" Dunlap asked.

Jeffers cocked his head and laughed, "More like back to normal. By the time we left, she was tallying her team's captures versus ours. She didn't even include the ones in the apartment complex that they rounded up thanks to our team's efforts."

"She included the ones that leapt out of the window," Dunlap pointed out.

"Sure, there's a whole lot more paperwork with those," Jeffers noted.

"She realizes we're a team of six, right?" Dunlap asked.

Jeffers laughed, "She only counts us as a team of three. So do I, for the record."

"Aw c'mon, we're starting to grow on you," Wally said.

Jeffers winced, "You guys growing on people is something that people go to a doctor to have cut off."

"Speaking of growing on each other," Dunlap motioned towards Agent Sohn and Dr. Chase who walked apart from the group.

"That? That's just what people who've been in life or death circumstances together do, it's a bit of a bond," Jeffers said. As he looked on, he paused. He, himself had to wonder.

Agent Danica Sohn and Dr. Ryder Chase walked along one of the many trails streaking through the grounds of Northern State Hospital. With the conclusion of the investigation, the estate seemed starkly different.

It was peaceful. It was beautiful. It was pleasant.

"I'm glad that's over," Chase said, his head bowed slightly, watching his feet move along the trail as it wound through the meadow.

"No kidding. Those poor kids," Sohn nodded. "Chasing their dreams and given a magic vial to help reach them."

"And those people in Seattle, minding their own lives. Wrong place, wrong time," Chase shook his head.

"I mean, who can plan for a throng of zombies," Sohn grinned playfully.

"I'm a parapsychologist and I can't say the reality of it ever entered my mind," Chase admitted.

"Why didn't Dr. Holder react like the others?" Sohn asked.

Chase shrugged, "Different neurological make up. Instead of following suit in the panic of fight or flight, his higher sense of reasoning helped him find a more viable escape."

"I wonder how I'd react," Sohn pondered.

"You? You're a fighter, all the way," Chase grinned.

"What? No higher state of reasoning?" the agent scowled.

Chase stammered, "I…I didn't mean…"

Danica Sohn giggled, "I know what you meant, and you're not wrong anyway."

Sohn slipped her arm into Chase's.

His own brain was hijacked as his amygdala didn't know how to properly respond to the new stimuli. He just kept walking, trying to appear calm though on the inside he was anything but.

As the sun began to set, painting the hills with its colorful evening display, Sohn shivered. Instinctively, Chase paused and pulled his jacket off to place around her shoulders.

Sohn looked up at him. She didn't shiver because she was cold, the thought of the last week when the sunset, sent the sensation of impending threat down her spine. Instead of correcting his action, she let him straighten the jacket as she faced him. Pressing towards him, his arms naturally fell around her.

Pushing up on her toes, she brought her lips to his. Suddenly, together, the horrific events of Northern State melted away. The pink and orange hues painted them in with the backdrop of the Cascades draped behind them.

THIRTY SIX

Deputy Director Witt leaned oppressively close to the camera on his computer as the group assembled. "Can you guys see me?"

"We can see you, Chief," Agent Jeffers nodded. "You can relax in your seat, we'll still be able to see you."

"Oh," Witt looked confused, "Like this?"

"Yes, sir. That's perfect," Jeffers assured.

"Great. And you have Dr. Chase's team there?"

The team crowded around Jeffers to his chagrin.

"Ah, there they are," Witt acknowledged. "Thanks for jumping on a call. I know you were supposed to be heading to the airport. First, I wanted to congratulate you on closing the case. Another great job! Zombies…really!"

"Not zombies, sir. They weren't dead...just not themselves," Chase explained.

"Still, quite a case. You all pulled it together quite nicely after a particularly challenging start. Most importantly, you saved a lot of people from serious danger," Witt continued. "All the zombies...err...feral people captured and brought in for medical care?"

"We think so, sir. The exact number of affected is a bit murky, but we were able to match the Northern State subjects with Dr. Holder's logs and analytics team has the count via camera footage from Pikes Place Market to a variable of less than three," Jeffers reported.

"And they aren't in any way contagious, they can't spread their condition. You would need to be inoculated with the serum or inhale the aerosolized version," Agent Sohn.

"Agent Sohn, I understand you had some tough choices to make," Witt said.

"Yes, sir."

"Firing on the ferals when you and Dr. Chase were trapped and again bringing Dr. Holder to a fatal end," Witt said.

"Shooting any of them was unfortunate. Fortunately, none of the ferals outside of Dr. Holder were fatal," Sohn swallowed.

"It seems you did what you had to. You did well, Agent Sohn," Witt assured. "Agent Jeffers, you and Agent Adams had some exemplary things to say about Dr. Chase's team in your reports."

"Well, yes. They proved to provide some sound theories and when called upon, they handled themselves well overall," Jeffers struggled to articulate his admission.

"You've worked well together," Witt pressed.

"I suppose so," Jeffers offered a weak, non-committal reply.

"We may just continue to find a use for you guys," Deputy Director Witt chuckled.

The lead agent bristled and sighed, "I was kind of hoping my next case might be a nice interstate theft ring or murder spree, sir."

"Well, there was another reason why I wanted to debrief before you flew home," the FBI deputy director said. "There is something else I wanted you to check out while you were in Washington state."

"For the FBI team…," Jeffers stressed.

"For the *entire* team. Dr. Chase and his crew could prove quite useful on this case. How familiar are you with cryptids?" Witt asked.

"It's an offshoot but relatable arm to what we do," Chase replied.

Jeffers looked confused, "Cryptids? What's a cryptid?"

Wally patted him on the shoulder, "Don't worry, this will be fun!"

THIRTY SEVEN

Senator Nathaniel Cruz held his breath in the late evening hour. The setting sun cast a soft glow through the trees. He had waited for half an hour for his target to set in his cross hairs. Rarely seen in this corner of Washington State, the senator couldn't resist being patient to try and capture the moment.

To his delight, the Northern Flying Squirrel leapt from its branch, gliding right passed the camera lens. With a grin, he played back his photos. Delighted, he flipped through the shots. Passing the rapid-fire photos of the flying squirrel, the final photo he had taken from their trip to the summit of Hamilton Mountain caught his eye.

To the northeast of the summit, something gleamed in the photo. Zooming in he could see something almost hidden in the trees. He had hiked that area many times and didn't recall any structures that far into the wilderness. Shrugging, he put his camera equipment away and began heading down the winding staircase set into the face of the giant monolith.

The sun had nearly disappeared further down the Columbia Gorge on its way beyond the Pacific Ocean. Glancing at his watch, he knew his family was going to be angry with him for disappearing on his own again.

Reaching the bottom of the trail, he had the eerie feeling he was being watched. Scanning the trailhead and nearby parking lot, it appeared that he was alone. Shrugging, he began walking towards the family campsite scarcely a quarter of a mile away. The smell of their campfire and the dinner he was late for wafted through the trees.

The sound of a twig snapping made him freeze. An avid hiker, he didn't understand why his senses were on such a high alert. In his peripheral vision, he saw a black mass where the sound had come from. Walking cautiously, making a wide loop around the mass, Cruz assumed it was a black bear. He had encountered many on his nature hikes.

Suddenly, the black mass rose as he passed. It was larger than any black bear he had seen. It was taller than him, a solid six-feet himself. Suddenly the hair on the back of his neck rose. Terrified, the senator was stricken with the realization of what he faced. In a panic, he turned and ran.

The sound of footsteps behind him was unmistakable. They were thundering. Long strides and an easy gait easily kept up with the senator as though his pursuer wasn't even trying. Ditching the trail, Cruz hoped the varied terrain might provide him an advantage. The moment he did, he realized what a miscalculation he had made.

The beast on his heels, closed even faster in the rough undulations of the raw forest. He could hear breathing behind him. It was guttural, almost a growl.

The senator darted in between the trees, trying to shake his pursuer. Coming to a ravine, he leapt, landing his leg extended, he slid to the creek below. Hopping to his feet, he splashed through the creek and ran headlong into a stand of blackberries, ignoring the thorns slicing his face and arms as he pressed through.

His assailant navigated around the bushes, giving Cruz a small window. Dashing into the forest, his lungs on fire, he ducked behind a tree. Pressing his body against the wood, he tried to catch is breath.

The footfalls persisted, darting through the stand of trees. The snarling, heavy breathing sounded angrier as his pursuer searched. Slow and steady, it was only a matter of time before the senator was found.

The pounding footsteps, heavy on the earth approached ever nearer. Each rustle of leaves brought his predator closer, dropping the senator's heart into the pit of his stomach. His heart raced so hard against his chest, he was afraid his pursuer could hear it.

A knowing grunt told Cruz his hiding spot was a secret no more. Collecting himself, he sprang from his brief respite and ran wildly away only to be met with the crescendo once more of footsteps behind him.

Crashing through branches ripping at his clothes and his flesh, the senator raced. In a wild moment of inspiration knowing escape was futile, he popped the lens on his camera and spun, snapping the shutter just as a massive, hairy fist came slamming down on him, knocking him to the ground.

Bleeding and out of breath, Cruz pushed furiously with his feet against the ground, trying to put whatever distance he could between himself and the monster. Directly over him it stood. Raising his head into a bellow, he lifted a boulder high over his shoulders and brought it crashing down on the senator, casting his world into inky blackness.

Made in the USA
Columbia, SC
09 November 2021